a little neighborhood murder

DOUBLEDAY

NEW YORK   LONDON   TORONTO   SYDNEY   AUCKLAND

a little neighborhood murder

by
A. J. Orde

PUBLISHED BY DOUBLEDAY

a division of
Bantam Doubleday Dell Publishing Group, Inc.,
666 Fifth Avenue, New York, New York 10103

DOUBLEDAY and the portrayal of an anchor with a
dolphin are trademarks of Doubleday, a division of
Bantam Doubleday Dell Publishing Group, Inc.

Library of Congress Cataloging-in-Publication Data
applied for

ISBN 0-385-26037-7

Printed in the United States of America
August 1989
First Edition
BG

Designed by Bonni Leon.

a little neighborhood murder

one

No matter how the rest of the week goes, I reserve Sunday afternoons for sloth. Sloth may be preceded by a trip to the deli and turn into sloth-*cum*-gluttony. A stack of new auction catalogues can make it sloth-*cum*-avarice. On occasion the afternoon has even become sloth-*cum*-lust. Most often, however, Sunday P.M. is simple sloth, which means soft music and a long nap interrupted only by the *ker-blump* of the dog door downstairs as Bela comes in or goes out. Once a week, I feel I owe it to myself.

Sometimes, sloth gets thwarted. As it did on this particular Sunday. A battering of fists on the front door shattered my dreams. Something I'd wanted for a long time got snatched away. I struggled to the edge of the bed feeling robbed, madder than hell, my feet fumbling for shoes I couldn't find. I scowled at the clock, grit-eyed, wondering if it was four in the afternoon or four in the morning and whether I could get away with killing whoever was outside.

As I stalked stocking-footed across the hall and down the curving stairs, the noise at the door continued, actually increasing in volume. Over the hammering I could hear muffled shouts in a familiar voice. It was George Whitney, my neighbor. Identifying George did not make me feel better. "All right, all right," I snarled, running fingers through my hair and stuffing my shirt back inside my trousers.

The hall is like the inside of an ornamental bass drum. Every time George hit the door the thud bounced off the marble and filigree bronze of the stairs, ricocheted from the beveled glass partitions at either side of the vestibule door, and caromed around the coved plaster ceiling like a panicky chunk of thunder, trying to get out. As I got to the foot of the stairs, the crystal chandelier chimed in warning and I looked up, half expecting to see the monster plummeting toward me. Sometimes I have daydreams about this chandelier, or some subsequent chandelier, falling and skewering a client. Preferably a dislikable client, of whom I have my fair share. Not this particular afternoon. The thing just hung there and twinkled, tightly held by the slanting, gold-covered cable I'd hauled it up with.

The noise outside got louder.

"All right already!" I yelled, opening the inner door into the vestibule and disconnecting the chain on the outer one. "George, for God's sake. What is it?"

My neighbor had been leaning against the discreet bronze plate beside the front door which says JASON LYNX. INTERIORS, but as I opened the door he looked up in pout-lipped surprise, his pudgy right hand aborting yet another assault upon the panels. "Jason?"

"Yes, that's who I am. At least I was when I tried to take a nap. Who did you think I was?" George was not one of my favorite people—there are only a few—though I think George would have been surprised to know that. He was the kind of man I could meet for the first time at a party who ten minutes later would introduce me as his old friend Jase. I hate being called Jase by people I hardly know.

His pouty lips sank at the corners. "Don't be mad, Jase. Listen, Betty just called me from Southglen Mall. She's had some kind of accident in her van. They're taking her to the hospital. I'm on my way out there, and I wondered if you'd go over and feed the dogs for me if I'm not back in time? I left the back door open."

I was still angry, but now I felt slightly guilty. George was George, but Betty wasn't all that bad. "Of course I'll feed them. I hope she's not badly hurt?"

"She called, I mean it was her on the phone, so it couldn't be too bad. I don't know. She was crying, you know. Listen, Jase, thanks. I'll call you when I get back." He scuttled in a half run, half waddle down the sidewalk to his car, which stood facing the wrong way, engine running, door open. It pulled away with a shriek of tires, and I stepped outside onto the portico to watch it go.

The sun was down behind the house, throwing a long shadow into the street. Christmas in two weeks, the days shrinking down to almost nothing, the long nights sneaking up on the late afternoons and turning them glum and cold. There was snow on the ground and in the air. Down Hyde Street to the south, toward the park, the big old houses that were still homes glittered with Christmas lights. The houses that had been converted into businesses, like mine, stood Sunday-dark and dour, like family members dragged unwillingly to the reunion, glaring silently at other people's fun. I knew how they felt. In the other direction, traffic hiccuped past the light on the avenue, some of it dribbling into the parking lot of the new restaurant on the corner. The Painted Cow, despite its name, seemed to be doing good business. It wasn't a steak house, and I had no idea why it was called the Painted Cow. Maybe the owner got a special price on a sign somebody had ordered and not paid for. A fluorescent Holstein on a Victorian building offends my interest in historic preservation, but what can you do?

I shivered and went inside, closing both the outer and inner doors behind me. I'd let in a lot of cold air. There was a thick Irish knit cardigan in the hall closet that my assistant, Mark McMillan, had given me for my birthday. I had one arm into it when an icy nose pushed into my right hand. One of my favorite people. Dog people, that is. "What's the problem, Bela? Ha? All that noise bother you?" Bela hadn't barked, so he must have known it was George. The big white dog made a noise in his throat, tail wagging slowly. "It's all right, boy. Yes. Just your Uncle George, making his usual racket."

Though that probably wasn't fair. Betty Whitney was the loud one. Talk talk talk or giggle giggle giggle, or, if the mood wasn't right, yell yell yell. George usually contented himself with a few "Oh, shut up, Betty"s or "What the hell are you talking about?"s and an occasional alcohol-fueled explosion of pointless rage. Not that either of them was blatantly public about it, but I could hear the sound if not the content, particularly in the summer when windows were open. Betty's prattle and George's bellowing had become as much a part of the urban soundscape as lawn mowers and dogs barking and fender benders at the corner. It hadn't made me like them better.

"If George isn't back by dark, I'm going over and feed your family," I said as I buttoned the sweater and checked the thermostat. Before Bela, I'd never thought of myself as the kind of person who'd talk to dogs. I'd never had a dog as a kid. None of us at the home had. Dogs were messy. Dogs were expensive. The first few times I'd caught myself talking to Bela I'd been embarrassed. Then I got used to talking to a dog and having the dog almost talk back, and I quit worrying about it. If a man can't talk to his dog, who can he talk to? Ghosts, maybe. One ghost. God knows there had been enough of that.

"Come on," I told the dog. "Let's take the comb to you."

Bela wagged after me as we went up the stairs under the curving line of ancestral portraits, not my ancestors, thank God. They were a stiff-necked, self-righteous-looking bunch and were possibly no living person's ancestors, though probably whoever bought them would claim them after the pictures were hung somewhere else. The portraits were for sale. So was the French tapestry on the opposite wall and the crystal chandelier, and the Bokhara carpets down in the sunken living room and the eighteenth-century harpsichord and the little ivory Venus—remarkable because she was carved with a bushy pudenda rather than the usual baby-naked one. The Chippendale secretary with the ruby glow in its varnish was for sale, and the pair of Rococo Revival couches, lavish with carved leaves and fruit. Everything down there was for sale including the stark Shaker furniture in the unused ground-floor kitchen and all the stock in the cavernous, echoey basement with its rows of floor-to-ceiling cabinets and the dim roaring room where the ancient furnace thrusts tentacles out and upward into the fabric of the place, breathing ominous sighs. I can wax poetic about 1465 Hyde Street. It's a great old house with umpteen cubic feet of salable stuff in it.

On the second floor, however, nothing was for sale. "Not thee, dog," I told Bela as I combed. "Not thee and not me, nor thy bed nor mine." My bed was an early American walnut sled bed, with painted decoration; Bela's was a huge willow and osier basket, ca. 1820 or so, with a sheepskin mattress in it. The rest of the bedroom was in keeping. The large bathroom across the hall, however, with its sybaritic double tub, was as close as I could get to the year 2000, and so was the adjacent kitchen, though the offices and living room were good examples of period rooms made comfortable enough for present-day living. The nameplate out front might say simply INTERIORS, but I wanted the people who came through that door to learn that Jason Lynx's name meant a good deal more than mere decoration. I wanted it to mean space that people enjoyed living in, not just rooms that were magazine-illustration slick. "Any charlatan can be slick." My foster father, Jacob Buchnam, had said that more than once.

Bela rolled over and the steel comb followed in the once-a-week going over, which was actually more than he needed to keep him looking kempt, sheveled, even neat. Though Bela is sometimes a little off-white, he seldom looks dirty. I finished him off with a few strokes, then stood up to look at the clock. Getting on toward five. I found my shoes in the bathroom when I went in to run the electric razor over my face. This Sunday's sloth had been complete. The man in the mirror had stubble.

As usual, the man in the mirror was not me. The mirror man had thick, pale skin—like white chamois, according to Chip Harris, a recent and temporary female friend whose given name was Letitia. My reflection had red-brown hair springing up at the forehead and worn a little long to hide a badly scarred left ear and the scars on the back of my head. Wide-set amber eyes with level brows. A straight, almost classic nose. A vertical cleft in the chin so deep that the mirror man's chin looked split in two below a too-wide mouth. Only that mouth saved the man in the mirror from being pretty.

The person I knew from inside was a different guy. He was bonier, meaner, with a calculating expression and a tighter mouth. He had a broken nose and lumpy ears, like an old club fighter. He drank and told ethnic jokes in bad accents. The inside man, who had been around ever since I was a kid and who might be, a psychiatrist had once told me, someone I remembered, this inside guy was who I sometimes thought I was, but he didn't show. What showed was this other face, like some advance man for a dog and pony show, out to put on a spiel and impress the natives. It never ceased to amaze me, finding him in the mirror every time I looked.

I nodded to him as I put the razor away, accepting him as much as I ever had. All I needed to put on was shoes. The sweater was heavy enough that I didn't need a coat to go to George's.

Outside the back door, taking up the south half of what was once a back yard, is a black-topped parking lot opening on the alley. Across the alley is a board fence with graffiti all over it and a back yard and a tall gray house. One lighted window looked down at me from the narrow facing gable as I raised my hand and waved. I knew Nellie Arpels was up there, peering at me from her upstairs window. Even though I hadn't been over to see her in . . . well, in a long time, I knew she was there. My wave acknowledged that she was watching and invited her to go on doing so—not that I could have stopped her. I crunched across the snowy driveway that runs along the south side of the house, through a gap in the hedge, and then along the side of the Whitneys' dog run to the Whitney back door. From inside the run George and Betty's three dogs looked at me with trustful eyes and slowly waving tails. This wouldn't be the first time I'd fed them when the Whitneys didn't get home or ended up someplace they hadn't planned to be. I'd gone over with food and water several times in response to some emergency phone call, though this was the first time George had left his door open for me.

"Ladislav." I greeted the big dog. Ladislav barked, a husky bark with a distinctive squeak at the end of it. He'd been barking more than usual for the past couple of weeks, moved, perhaps, by some unfathomable need to let the world know he was there. "Eva, Snowball," I said, leaning over the fence to pull their ears. Eva was Bela's mama, and Snowball's as well. Snowball had an unpronounceable Hungarian name in addition to her informal one, but I didn't attempt it. She wagged as she stretched, front legs out, bottom high. I went up the back steps and into the enclosed sunroom George had converted from the original back porch. The room was freezing. An icy wind slithered around my ankles. I unlatched the dog door to let the animals in and then shut the sunroom door behind me to keep them out of the front of the house. I went through the kitchen into the hall, looking for the source of the cold air. The front door stood half open, wind gusting through it to deposit snow and a few dead leaves on the worn and sodden carpet.

A small brown package leaned against the frame of the door. I picked it up, turning it over curiously. A brown paper parcel, tied with heavy string, addressed to George. A plain brown wrapper, the inner me said to himself, making a snigger out of it. What was George ordering these days, dirty movies? He could get those at any video center. No telling what it was. There was no postage or delivery tag on it and no return. Someone had just dropped it by. A Christmas gift, perhaps. Maybe the door hadn't been quite shut, and the person had put a hand on it, pushing it open. Or, the way he had gone rushing off, George might well have forgotten to shut the door firmly when he went out.

I put my shoulder against the door, pushing against the wind until the door latched tight. The package was too damp to risk marring the glossy finish of the hall table, so I took it back to the enclosed back porch and dropped it on a Formica-covered table there. The matter at hand was feeding dogs, but where might the food and dog dishes be? They hadn't been in the run. They weren't in the deep cupboard by the back door, though the big sacks of kibble were there. They weren't in the kitchen or in the dishwasher. Finally, I located them in the adjacent laundry, on a shelf over the drier, a sizable bowl for Ladislav and two smaller ones for Eva and Snowball.

In the sunroom, things were suspiciously quiet. All three dogs had their noses together, interested in something on the floor. One of them, Snowball probably, since the others were too well trained to pull such a trick, had dragged the paper-wrapped parcel off the table and chewed a hole in the wrappings.

I chased them outside, carried out their bowls of kibble, and then came back to pick up the scraps. I tucked the bits of cardboard and newspaper in my sweater pocket before I picked up the mutilated package itself. That's when I saw the battery through the hole, the battery and the foil and the unmistakable amorphous gray of the explosive. I'd seen the stuff too often not to recognize it.

When the bomb squad arrived I was sitting on the front steps of my own place, feeling paler than usual and shivering, probably from the cold. I pointed the way. The men in their helmets and thick Kevlar aprons went in and came out again. It wasn't until they lowered the package into the double compartmented blast truck that it went off, all by itself, a muffled *whump!* that shook the doors and rattled the windows in the Whitney house and mine. The squad leader, who was also shaking and looked as pale as I felt, came to ask me who lived where and to tell me to stay put because the proper investigative authorities were on their way.

I was still feeling a trifle shook as I went back to my apartment over what Jacob had always called "the shop" and made a pot of coffee—preground coffee, which says something about my state of mind. I'm a coffee nut. I almost always grind my own.

I heard a familiar voice asking, "Are you all right, love?"

and I replied, "I'm all right, I'm all right," just as though I'd really heard her. Just as though she were still there.

I felt cold and told myself it was just from sitting outside making sure no one went near the Whitney house while I waited for the bomb squad. Trying not to admit I'd been scared out of my skin. Watching the coffee drip, I put my hands in my pockets. The scraps I'd picked up from the Whitney sunroom floor were in there. Spread on the counter they looked innocent enough. A bit of brown cardboard. Torn pieces of brown paper and bits of newspaper. The newspaper scraps were from a want-ad section. One piece was from the bottom of the page with the page number on it. I stared at the scraps until the coffee was done, then put them back in my pocket, telling myself I'd put them in an envelope and give them to the police. The way that bomb had gone off, these were probably the only pieces left.

I poured a cup and drank it, wondering whether I had any answers for whoever was going to ask the questions.

"That's all right, love," said the ghost. "You'll do fine."

"Who was it addressed to?" the sergeant demanded. He had accepted my invitation to come in by the fire because it was warmer there than outside. He'd shown no other evidence of wanting to be pleasant or cooperative.

I put my cup on the table between us and prepared to give him the whole thing for the second time. "To Mr. George R. Whitney. Block letters. His address, 1451 Hyde Street, the house next door. No zip code. I noticed that at the time. No return."

"Black ink?"

"Black, yes. Ballpoint, probably. Or a fine felt-tip." I leaned forward to fill the sergeant's cup. Not sharing my coffee would have seemed unnecessarily surly, though the overcoated man across from me hadn't done anything to make me feel otherwise. The cop taking notes in the corner had seemed appreciative, however.

"And what were you doing there?" His tone was sneeringly suspicious. He already knew what I was doing there, but I took a deep breath and told him again about George's request, after which he asked me once again to surmise as to George's current whereabouts. Evidently the police had not been able to locate George or Betty Whitney at any hospital near the Southglen Mall. I'd already told them I didn't know where George was; I couldn't help them: not with that, not with George's license number, and not with the name of his family doctor.

"You've lived next door for nine years?"

I nodded. The detective's name was Renard, Clayton Renard. He was not foxy, however. He was a pit bull, narrow faced and single-minded, naturally combative and either trained to be mean or just unpleasant by inclination. His brown eyes were too small and too close together, and he had no upper lip at all. His hair was cropped so close he might have been recently clipped by a boot-camp barber. He had ugly ears, with long, pendulous, curiously wrinkled lobes. I caught myself staring and looked down at my cup.

"How well do you really know them?" he asked.

"I don't know them very well. I'm acquainted with them. They're both about forty-five. Betty shows dogs. She takes trips. She shops. We say hello over the fence. George also shows dogs. He takes trips. He makes the money for her to shop with. Sometimes they call me and ask me to feed the dogs."

"What does he do?" Clayton picked at his teeth with a dirty fingernail.

"He manages some kind of religious broadcasting system. His office is in the urban renewal area, lower downtown."

"How would you manage something like that? What does he do? Hire people? Raise money? What?"

"He's never really talked about it, but I gather he's responsible for programming and for accounting for the money that comes in. The money comes here, but the transmitter's down in the south somewhere. Texas, I think."

"You don't really know that much about him, do you?" The tone accused me of lying.

I took another deep breath. "I've known them since . . . since I moved into this house about nine years ago, but they're certainly not close friends."

Agatha had known Betty Whitney better than I had. Agatha had spent many a morning over at Betty's, when we first moved in, having coffee, but I didn't want to talk about Agatha.

I tried to make the guy understand. "They're just neighbors. About the closest I ever got to them was when I bought my dog Bela from them three years ago."

"What kind of dog is that?"

"A Kuvasz." I spelled it for the cop. "It's a Hungarian breed. They were developed as guard dogs. In Hungary they pull carts, too."

"American dog isn't good enough for you?"

I was getting pretty tired of the sergeant's antagonism, which, so far as I knew, I'd done nothing to stir up. "I don't know of many American breeds, sergeant. The wolf, maybe. Or the Chihuahua. Most of our dog and cat breeds were brought here from other countries. I got Bela because Kuvasz are good guard dogs without being fierce or temperamental. There are a lot of valuable things in the place."

"I noticed the security system."

"It's a good one. Then there's Bela. Plus a handgun upstairs."

The sergeant's nose lifted a fraction of an inch at one nostril. "Having is one thing," he said. "Using it is something else."

"I know," I admitted. "But I did some competitive shooting for a couple of years. I was on a navy pistol team for a while."

"I didn't know they let your kind in the navy." This time the tone was unmistakably offensive.

"What kind is that?"

"You . . . you interior decorators." His sneer and gesture were an indictment.

I laughed, not with humor, more like a bark. I couldn't help it. I hadn't run into that one for a while. Well, fuck him. "I didn't know they let your kind in the police," I said, copying his sneer. "I thought policemen had to be able to read."

Sergeant Renard turned white. The cop who was taking notes sniggered silently, shoulders heaving.

"It's none of your goddamned business what I am," I went on. "But if you read anything at all besides the sports page and the comics, you'd know there are just as many gay cops and athletes and accountants as there are gays in my profession."

I was ashamed of myself almost immediately. I'd outgrown that kind of stuff. I didn't start fights in alleys anymore. He didn't reply, unless a barely audible snarl could be considered a reply. He got up and stalked out, knocking over his coffee cup in the process.

"Let me clean that up," said the cop. She was a slender, towheaded girl with a pretty, heart-shaped face. The strap of her shoulder holster showed at the front of her jacket. That and the grin made her look like a kid dressed up for trick or treat.

"It's all right. I can get it." I mopped at the mess with a wad of tissues, feeling annoyed at myself. Jacob had told me a thousand times that losing my temper meant losing control of a situation. He'd always said smart people didn't do that. So, I hadn't been smart. Chalk up one more time.

"I'm sorry," I told her. "I shouldn't have rubbed his nose in it that way, but he pissed me off. There may be plenty of gay decorators, but there are lots of straight ones too. I sure didn't make a pass at him, so what made him think I was gay?"

She laughed. "Who knows why Clayton thinks anything? Two or three times a day he makes me want to kill him! He hates blacks and Jews and gays and anybody who doesn't go to his church, which he doesn't bother to attend. He hates women, especially policewomen. He hates most people on general principles. Now he'll hate your dog because it's Hungarian."

"Why does he hate Hungarians?"

"Because they're foreign. Because they're commie. That's the worst thing you can be—foreign or a commie."

"Bela has very little ideology," I remarked, trying to retrieve my dignity. "If somebody comes through a window at night, I don't think Bela will care what the intruder's political views might be. Does your sergeant think the bomb next door is a commie plot?"

"He's not *my* sergeant, but he probably does. I've got to go. Thanks for the coffee." She held out her hand.

"Thank you, Ms. . . . ?"

"Detective Willis. Grace Willis." She turned, then stopped. "Listen, those things I said? I'm not supposed to tell people stuff like that. He just makes me so—"

"I won't quote you," I said.

She grinned at me, nose wrinkling under very blue eyes, and left. Bela looked after her and made a small noise in his throat, the kind he makes when friends come to visit.

When the truck and all the police cars but one had gone, I went out through the yard again, through the gate, along the dog run to the back door, where I left a note for George to call me as soon as he got home.

"Ladislav," I instructed the big white dog, feeling badly put upon, "you and Eva, let me know when your people come home, won't you?" On the way back to the house, I waved at the cop watching the place. He looked bored.

The Whitneys called shortly after ten o'clock. Even though I'd gone to bed, I was still sufficiently agitated by the afternoon's events to get out of bed, put on my overcoat and my boots, and go over there. I got very little satisfaction out of either of them.

"Jason, I can't think of any reason at all," George said, sweat standing in little beads at the roots of his hair. He turned to the cupboard behind him and rummaged among the bottles. "The policeman asked me if I could explain it. I couldn't enlighten him at all."

"You'll probably be getting another visit from the police tomorrow," I told him. "I thought you should know what happened."

"I think it must be a mistake," George said, pouring himself several ounces of Canadian Club. It was obviously not George's first drink of the last few hours. He didn't offer me or his wife a glass. "The thing was meant for somebody else. Or maybe it's one of those random violence things; you know, they just bomb anybody. Like terrorists. They don't care who."

"The package had your name on it, George. Your address."

"I just don't know." The lie stood bare in his eyes, exposing itself. He drank half the undiluted whiskey in the glass and refilled it. The bottle neck made a shivering sound against the rim of the glass.

Betty was sitting at the blue plastic kitchen table, looking wan and vacant. Ordinarily she was a skinny blonde in her mid-forties, trying to look like a slender blonde in her mid-thirties. Tonight she looked eighty. The only color in her face was in the bruises on her left cheek and jaw. Her left arm was in a sling.

"I don't suppose you have any ideas?" I asked her.

"Why no, Jason," she said in a frail, emotionless voice. "I'm as surprised as anybody."

"What caused your car accident?"

"I was leaving the Mall, you know, and just where the driveway comes out onto the street I tried to put on the brakes, and the van wouldn't stop. This other car ran into me. It really messed up the van." Her voice, which should have been tired and petulant, was almost without emphasis, as though she had memorized the words or said them too many times.

"We had to have it towed," George complained, pro forma. "Acme Towing charged me seventy-five bucks! That's plain robbery!"

I was irritated enough to let my anger show. They didn't seem to care that I could damn well have been killed by their bomb. I had a strong urge to hit one or both of them. "Don't get in an uproar, George," I said sarcastically. "A towing fee won't break you, and you can be thankful Betty's not permanently damaged. Well. A real swell guy of a police sergeant will be here early in the morning. I think you can bank on it. Both of you probably need some sleep, so I'll get out of your hair. You may be right. This could be one of those senseless things."

As I went out, George said, "This is all just something dumb." His voice was cracking. "Not one of your puzzles, Jason. Not worth your time."

Now that surprised me. Few people know of my obsession with puzzles, and I'd never talked puzzles with George. Why would he mention it? Up until that moment I hadn't thought George's particular mess, whatever it was, was one of my puzzles either.

I seldom remember dreams. Oh, I know I dream. Everyone does. Once in a while, when I'm wakened during the night or early in the morning, I have these fragmentary visions of something that has just happened, visions that dissolve almost immediately, leaving me feeling as though I've lost something. It's the kind of feeling I get when I try to remember the name of an old acquaintance I've seen on the street. It never lasts. That night, however, I dreamed and woke, dreamed and woke, wakened not from the dream but by it.

Each time I was in Washington, D.C. I was on my way to meet Agatha. We were going to have dinner together when she got off work. There was a little Indonesian restaurant we wanted to try, just four or five blocks off the Mall on Tenth. In the dream I explained the location to her, describing the way the place looked. I told her I'd meet her in front of the Museum of Natural History, and then, abruptly, I was trying to find the museum myself. I knew it was east of the Washington Monument, on the other side of the History and Technology Museum, but the monument kept moving. Each time I looked it was somewhere else. Streets twisted back on themselves. Some of them rippled and swayed under me. I couldn't get there, couldn't find the right place.

I was afraid I'd miss her. I walked and walked, up and down Constitution Avenue, hunting for the building, but it wasn't there.

"I can't wait," she said from some vast distance in the dream. "Jason, I can't wait."

I woke up terrified, my heart pounding, saying her name, as though I expected her to be there when I turned on the light. I looked around, putting a hand up to feel that my face was wet, remembering the dream, remembering Washington. I got up and had a glass of water, remembering it all, very vividly, and then I went back to sleep.

In a new dream I went to her office to meet her, but I wasn't sure which floor she worked on. I couldn't go in and find her, because I didn't have security clearance. Agatha had security clearance. "I'm only a file clerk," she had said, laughing. "I'm only a clerk, but I'm secure." I waited in front of the building, hoping it was the right building. Then I saw her. She had come out some other door and was walking away from me, faster and faster. I began to run, but I couldn't catch her, and she disappeared into the crowds. There was a halo around her, an aura, and I could see the light for a time after I lost sight of her. Then it, too, dwindled and vanished. I looked for her for a long time, in the dream, but I never found her.

Monday morning I got up early, turned on the coffee grinder before I showered, then put the coffee to drip while I got dressed. I was at my desk in the office off the living room by seven thirty, mug in hand—straight Colombian coffee, no fancy blends. I figured Monday morning was a good time to call my East Coast commission agent, taking advantage of the two-hour time difference. In New York, no one begins work until nine thirty or ten. That means I can call at seven thirty, Mountain Time, while the day is scarcely touched, still fresh with possibility, and catch Myron Burstein at the other end before he gets lost in the work-week jungle.

"Myron!" I said enthusiastically. "Tell me things."

"Jason, why is it you always want to be told things on Mondays?" he complained, sounding more than a little hung over. "After a few more aspirin, maybe I can tell you something."

"What about the armoire?" I asked him.

"What armoire?"

"The Italian provincial armoire with the sunburst and rooster carving on it you thought you could get me for under five thousand."

"Oh, God," he said. "That was Friday."

"So?"

"So, I got it. For under five thousand."

That was a good sign. Considering the rooster, an auspice, as it were.

"How about the majolica jars?"

"You don't want them," he told me. "Not unless you want something made yesterday."

"The catalogue said fifteenth century."

"The catalogue lied."

"Ouch," I said. "Myron, I needed those."

"I'll find you something else, Jason. Not those. Put your clients off. Tell them you're sending your representative personally to Italy to find something nice. Majorca for majolica. It'll take several weeks, but I can guarantee I'll find something."

"Sure, Myron. With the margin on this job I could maybe send you to Staten Island on the ferry."

He sighed. "I got the gaming table. It's good. Eighteenth century, no question."

"Very nice. What about my dining chairs from that woman on Long Island?"

"Cheap for cash if you still want them."

"Why wouldn't I want them?"

"They're around 1680 OK. The seaweed marquetry's right, but I think some of the legs have been restored."

"They're Restoration chairs," I quipped, nodding at my assistant, Mark, who had come up, bringing the mail. Mark made a Monday morning face and filled my coffee cup before retreating through the connecting door to his own office.

Myron laughed, unamused. "It's up to you, Jase, but there's sixteen of them, and that's sixty-four legs, some of which I'd be willing to bet are not original."

"Myron, I honestly don't think it matters to this client. Kitty Van Doorn likes the look, but she doesn't care that much about authenticity. All Peter Van Doorn cares about is whether Kitty is happy. The man seems to have money to burn. I'll put a disclosure in the invoice, so they can't claim I put one over on them, and you do the same on your invoice to me. That way everybody knows, right? If, by some chance, the Van Doorns don't want them—which would make things very difficult, since I need those chairs shipped *now*—we'll break them up into sets of eight. Surely eight of them are all right."

"Twelve and four," Myron said thoughtfully. "Or six, six, and four. I only spotted four I think were maybe fooled with."

"Twelve and four," I agreed.

Myron asked about my business and my dog. I asked about Myron's wife and son. I too had a wife and son once, but few people know about them, and those who know don't mention them. When we stopped talking, I drank the coffee Mark had poured for me and went downstairs to make my morning inspection of the shop. Even though we don't open until noon on Monday, I like to be sure everything looks right.

Eugenia Lowe was sorting her mail at the desk in the hall, her back as stiff and her expression as dignified as ever. She had stopped to pick up flowers. Today they were in a narrow cut-glass vase, blue Dutch iris and white freesias. I stopped to sniff them.

"Nice, aren't they," she said, not smiling. Eugenia very seldom smiles. Her best is a kind of Mona Lisa simper.

"I see you bought them to match," I commented, noting her white sweater and soft blue woolen suit with approval. Smiling or not, Eugenia always looks like an advertisement for some small but prestigious woman's college. The president or dean, of course, not a student. "What have you got on your plate for today?" I cast a quick look around the room. Pale sunlight fell through the big bay window in the south wall, but it didn't do much to brighten the winter gloom. The Whitney house is too close to let much light in.

"Not much," she admitted. "The Hoopers are coming back to look at that lowboy in the front room sometime around one." She sniffed. "For the fifth time. There's a decorator coming in at three to see the Shaker stuff. I'm pretty sure we have what she needs, but she will argue discount interminably. I have to pack about five boxes to be shipped this morning, and that's it."

Eugenia is old enough to be my mother. Occasionally she acts as though she is. Actually, she is the widow of an impecunious "antique dealer" from whom she learned the lingo and the manner to awe prospective customers into an appropriate state of mind. Add to these qualities her own good critical judgment, and one has an elegant juggernaught of a saleswoman. I'd hired her five years earlier and only regret it when she does things for my own good.

"Anything I need to look at?" I asked her.

"Just those brass candlesticks I unpacked Friday. Two of them are dented, and you didn't say anything about buying them damaged."

"For the simple reason that they weren't supposed to be damaged." I scowled. "We got those from that place in Philadelphia. Send the guy a note. Tell him which ones were damaged and find out what he wants to do about it. Does it look like shipping damage?"

"I don't think so," she said. "They were packed quite well, wrapped individually in a small box and the small box packed inside a big one full of packing worms."

"Packing worms?"

"You know. Those wriggly plastic things."

Her phrase was a lot more descriptive than "those foam squiggles we pack stuff in," which is what I usually call them. I suggested she turn on some lamps in the showrooms before she opened the shop at noon, sniffed the freesias again, and went back upstairs to work.

I had two expensive jobs running currently plus half a dozen small ones. None of them were putting me under much pressure, and the Van Doorn Cherry Hills house had produced an unexpected pup. Some of the furniture and ornaments already in the house when they had purchased it were—beneath forty-odd years of neglect—worth almost as much as the pieces the Van Doorns were replacing them with. I'd made them a modestly fair offer, which they had accepted. If I hadn't offered to buy the stuff, I could probably have carted it away for nothing without the Van Doorns noticing. Well, without Kitty noticing. Peter would have known. Peter's easy affability was broken by a very percipient look occasionally, when he didn't know he was being observed. A hard, knowing look. I'd classified Peter Van Doorn as a self-made man.

After about an hour of doing correspondence, jotting responses in the margins for Mark to turn into properly typed replies, I fetched myself another cup of coffee. It was a little after nine as I stood at the office window drinking it.

"Is this a mutual admiration society," Mark asked from behind me, "you and Bela?"

Bela was lying on the rug, staring at me with his usual alertly adoring expression. "We like each other," I admitted.

"With good reason," Mark said. "God, I hope when I'm that age I'm half as good-looking."

"Bela's a handsome dog," I admitted. "But I think you're nice-looking too, Mark."

"I meant you!" He flushed.

"Oh? It was *my* age you were referring to?"

"You must be thirty-five if you're a day."

We'd celebrated my thirty-eighth birthday the previous

month, if you could call it a celebration, so Mark knew exactly how old I was. "Watch it, youngster," I said. "And let's not talk about good-looking! All my old ladies get rubbery-legged over you, not to mention what happens to most of the younger ones. If I had any sense, I'd put you down in the showrooms to boost sales."

Mark flushed. He'd been with me for only two years, his first job after the university. He had a wealthy family, a private income, and no need to be employed, but he worked hard nonetheless. However, Mark embarrassed me from time to time, as he was about to do. "I'd rather be here with you than play up to your old ladies," he said with a melting look.

I raised a cautionary eyebrow at him, suddenly glad that Mark had not been here yesterday to meet Sergeant Renard. Mark was well built, blond, and extremely athletic, but his sexual preferences would have made him anathema to the sergeant. He knew perfectly well that I was not interested, but sometimes—as now, because his friend Rudy had been away for a few weeks—he tried to be seductive, more as self-reassurance than anything else. I kept telling myself it was no different from having a female assistant gently leching after me. I would have discouraged that too. Sex and business don't mix happily. Another of Jacob's axioms.

I put on my impersonal-boss voice. "You're doing your job well, Mark. I don't say that often enough, and you should hear it."

Mark got my point, flushed again, and went to answer the phone. Bela whined uncertainly, and I realized he was expecting to go somewhere. I bent down to rumple the dog, calling through the open door, "Mark, you want me to drop you downtown?" His car was in the shop, and he had mentioned a necessary trip to the fabric house.

Mark nodded with the phone at his ear, mouthing "five minutes." Bela and I went on downstairs.

I put on the sweater I'd worn yesterday. Talking to painters didn't require anything more formal, and it would please

Mark to see me wearing it. I stopped in the laundry mudroom to get my boots. The pile of daily papers in the corner reminded me of the newspaper scraps that were still in the sweater pocket. Sergeant Renard had made me so angry I'd forgotten to give them to him. I fished the scraps out and smoothed them on the top of the washer. A corner. Page 153. If the paper was local, that probably meant the Sunday edition. Weekday papers weren't that thick, though seasonal ads did tend to increase their girth. Sunday's paper was on top of the pile where I'd dropped it yesterday on my way to feed the dogs. Page 153 in the want-ad section. The corner matched. Farm implements and supplies. Tractors. Horses and tack. I turned the page over. Cats. Fish, Aquariums. Dogs.

Dogs. Interesting. Maybe a coincidence, wrapping a bomb in the dog section of the want ads and then sending the bomb to a dog fancier.

In my far from expert opinion, coincidence often isn't. I pulled the want-ad section out of the paper, folded it once, and pushed it into the cupboard by the laundry soap. It could wait.

Bela and I dropped Mark off at the fabric house, where he would search for a particular color and type of cotton chintz to suit the contentious Mrs. Smedley. This was his third try. I figured, along about the fifth he'd realize what was happening and start using his head. Lillian Smedley had no idea what she wanted; he'd have to pick. This was something he'd learn for himself, not something I could tell him. If clients have strong likes and dislikes, one should take great care to give them what they want. Clients who have great difficulty choosing between pink or white after-dinner mints do not need to be catered to. They need to be sold.

When Bela and I arrived at the Van Doorn place, the painter wanted to argue matters of taste. He went on about how the Renners had done their walls, how the Strohs had done theirs. I tried listening for a while, hoping he'd talk himself out. Then I offered an opinion or two, but that only warmed him to the subject. When it seemed clear he wasn't going to shut up, I suggested he pick up his brush and do it the way I'd specified or he could find another job to talk about. Paint with it or shove it, I think I said.

At that point—he'd wasted an hour of my time—he changed the subject and began talking about the Broncos. Some days it seemed I spent most of my time going through these rituals with either contractors or clients.

Think of the devil. As I was about to leave, Mr. and Mrs. Van Doorn dropped by to see how their money was being spent, and the discussion of taste began again.

"It doesn't look right to me," Van Doorn boomed, waving a hard, square hand at the half-painted dining room wall. "I think there's too much color." He turned his massive body around, staring at it, chewing at the corners of his full mustache. "When I was at your place last week, I didn't see colors like these."

Kitty put her hand on his arm. "Peter, he showed me the pictures. Historic ones." She looked up into his glowering face with her glowing smile—shining skin, shining eyes, a wealth of curly yellow hair, forty if she was a day and looking about twenty-five, everyone's dream girl. Certainly she was Van Doorn's dream girl. His expression softened immediately.

I prepared for diplomacy. The Van Doorns had come in the previous Wednesday to approve the upholstery fabric for the dining room chairs, and I'd thought then that Peter seemed a bit uncomfortable with anything but beige. When Kitty had grabbed a bunch of samples I had ready for someone else, spread them on a convenient table, and started bubbling, wanting them all as usual, Peter had promptly gotten up and walked to the bay window, where he stood staring out, finding the neighborhood with its noisy dogs and slamming doors more interesting than the materials.

"Your dogs?" Van Doorn had asked, obviously wanting to talk about anything except fabric. Ladislav and his lady friends were barking and chasing one another.

"The Whitneys' dogs," I'd told him cheerfully, waving him back to the table. "My dog is over under that harpsichord, asleep. Peter, you should be included in this consultation, don't you think?"

"Oh, I suppose," he'd said with a distracted air as he returned to the table, putting on his glasses. "What about that one?"—pointing to a soft brown. "Or this?"—another brown.

The walls of the dining room were to be three shades of deep, glowing green. A lot of color, but not too much if I could soothe Peter into accepting it. Certainly brown wouldn't do for the chairs. I'd already selected a peacock velour that I was leading Kitty toward. So, no help for it, I did the little-professional-lecture bit. "Period rooms were often so colorful that today we might consider them garish. I'd love to use those colors in the showrooms, but I can't. What would look right with one setup of furniture would look dreadful with something else. But in your new house, Peter, everything has been selected to go together. I want to retain the brightness, the jollity, if you will, but without any carnival aspects. If I make your walls bland or pastel, they certainly won't look authentic. Our ancestors weren't afraid of color."

"My ancestors—" began Peter Van Doorn, only to stop abruptly, rubbing a hand through his thick graying hair. "Well, I'm no expert. I guess I can get used to it. You're sure it's the way it should be?"

"I'm sure." I gave him a confident grin and a slap on the shoulder. Up until that point, I'd worked almost entirely with Kitty. I'd met Van Doorn himself on only a few occasions, the first when he'd come into the shop a year ago last spring to buy a gift for his wife's birthday. Mrs. Van Doorn, he said, was a little crazy over American antiques. I'd sold him a Queen Anne fret-carved mirror for $11,000. Both of them had come in the following fall to pick out an anniversary gift for Kitty, and this spring they had asked me to refurnish and redecorate the living room, dining room, and study—three really enormous rooms—of the twenty-room furnished house they had just bought.

Counting the visit last week and this encounter today, I'd seen Van Doorn only five times, which was obviously not enough for him to trust me.

"Seems to me you'd be interested in pleasing the man that's signing the checks," Van Doorn said, rather plaintively.

I gave him my standard answer. "Peter, this is how I make my living. If you don't like the way I'm doing the job, the contract provides for severance. You're free to get someone else or free to do it yourself, but I don't do committee work because with a committee no one is responsible for the result. If we do the job as a committee and you hate it, it isn't my fault. If you love it, I can't take credit for it. I get business because other people admire what I've done, so you either have to let me do it or get someone else." I smiled, taking the sting out. "If you'd rather do it yourself and just have me get the furnishings for you, that's fine. You pick what you want and sign a purchase order for each piece. I charge my cost plus shop overhead plus twenty."

"Oh, Peter, no. He's doing it so beautifully!" Kitty protested, patting her husband's arm. "After you were so sweet to move here and get the bigger house, let's not spoil it. I *like* it bright. This house is going to be beautiful, not like that terrible place where we are now."

Peter Van Doorn softened, muttered a little, and then suggested I join them for lunch. I refused as gracefully as possible.

I already had a lunch date. Every Monday noon I visited the home where my son was a resident. I never wanted to go, but I always went.

Sometimes I thought I might be going as penance. The day Jerry had been hurt, I hadn't been there. I'd been in New York on a buying trip. I was new at the business then and didn't feel I could afford to use an agent. The first I'd known of the accident was when I'd come from the airport to find the house empty, the car gone. A note had been pushed through the mail slot. Mr. Lynx was to call the police. Nightmare time. The car had been found wrecked in the mountains. The baby had been in the back seat and was now in the hospital. There had been no other person in or near the car. Where had Mr. Lynx been? Did Mr. Lynx know where his wife was?

It was easy to prove to them where I'd been. Even though the husband is always the logical suspect, I couldn't have been in two cities at once. They didn't suspect me. No one who had known us, the two of us together, could have suspected me, but that didn't answer the questions about Agatha.

Where had she been going? It could have been anywhere. She was fiercely independent, though just as fiercely determined to give Jerry first place in her life for a few years before she went back to her painting.

"I have time," she had said. "When Jerry goes to nursery school, I'll start again. I'm not even thirty. I've got time."

She hadn't had time. Unless she'd started again, somewhere else, under some other name, a victim of amnesia. A strange thought, but one I'd considered. Her body had never been found.

The highway patrolman who found the car took me to the place. We turned off the highway and drove along a gravel road, stopping at a precipitous curve. I got out and stood on the shoulder, peering down at the wreckage. Finally, I climbed down into the canyon myself, finding footholds on the rocks, lowering myself with my arms. Twenty yards from the crumpled foil of the car, deep black forest masked the canyon walls. Farther down, the canyon was a wilderness, deadly and rock littered, yards deep in snow in the winter, according to the patrolman. "She could have wandered in there, dazed," he told me. "Maybe bleeding in the brain from a head injury. She could have gone quite a way, then passed out somewhere: behind a rock, under an overhang. People get lost in these mountains all the time. Sometimes we don't find them."

We had never found Agatha. The rescue teams had come from miles around to look. They wouldn't take payment. The most they'd let me do was contribute for equipment. They spent days up and down that canyon, and up the mountains on either side. I closed the shop and spent days searching with them, thinking my presence was somehow magical. If eyes couldn't find her, love could. I was wrong. Eyes couldn't. Love couldn't, either. If she was there, she was dead by the time they called off the search. I wasn't ready to give up, but they told me she couldn't have lived that long. Not with the nights as cold as they had been.

And if she'd been dazed and wandered onto the highway, if she'd been picked up and carried away? If someone still lived in her body, it wasn't my Agatha. The Agatha I knew would never have left Jerry in that car on the side of that mountain. If she'd been able only to crawl, she would still have taken Jerry with her.

The police had already asked their questions, but as soon as the search was ended I made the rounds myself. I asked everyone who knew her; I asked all the neighbors, everyone up and down the street: had they seen her that day? No one had except Nellie. Agatha had visited Nellie that morning, bringing Jerry with her.

"She brought the baby up here to see me. She said they were on their way to the baby doctor. When she left here, she went straight down into your garage, and a little while later I saw the car leave," Nellie told me.

Agatha had never arrived at the pediatrician's office. She had never, so far as we knew, arrived anywhere. After eight years, I still had no idea where she'd been going. After eight years, I still had no answers. Going over and over it changed nothing, helped nothing. She was gone, and Jerry was where Jerry was.

I kept my Monday lunch date.

When I got back to the shop that afternoon there were people gathered around the Whitney house, and I assumed it was an aftermath of yesterday's bombing. A grim-faced Sergeant Renard was waiting for me in my office, along with Detective Grace Willis.

"We'd like to know where you've been today," the sergeant asked with a dreadful crocodile smile. "Since about eight."

Mark shook his head warningly at me over the sergeant's shoulder. Warning me of what? Maybe just to keep my temper.

I took off my sweater and sat down at my desk, not hurrying. "I was here at eight. As a matter of fact, at seven thirty I called a commission buyer of mine in New York City and talked to him on the phone for over half an hour. I can give you his name and number. I was still on the phone to him when Mark came in a little after eight." I nodded in Mark's direction. "Mark picks up the mail when the post office opens and then comes here."

"And then?" Renard grinned again. It seemed to be almost a reflex, a wolfish baring of the teeth.

"And then I went downstairs to see what Mrs. Lowe was doing. I was there about five minutes. Then I came back upstairs and did some phoning and paperwork until—oh, about nine fifteen or nine twenty. Then I drove Mark down to the fabric wholesaler and myself out to Cherry Hills to the Peter Van Doorn house, where I met with the painter. It took me about half an hour to get out there. I was with the painter for about an hour, until almost eleven. Then the Van Doorns arrived and I spoke with them for fifteen or twenty minutes. I checked my watch when I got into the car and it was eleven thirty, which gave me time to get to my standing Monday lunch date."

"A standing lunch date."

It wasn't anything I particularly wanted to talk about. I said, "With my son, Jerry. He's a patient at McInery." Patient. Inmate. What could one say? "Emilia Montoya, the director at McInery, will know when I arrived and when I left, which was just about twenty minutes ago."

No longer the crocodile grin. Twitches, instead. Small, irritable tweaks of the skin around his mouth. What I'd said had not pleased the sergeant.

"Give Detective Willis the names," he snarled. "We'll

check them." And he was out again, thumping down the stairs as though he wanted to break the marble treads.

"All right, what is it?" I asked.

She looked at me closely. "He hoped you did it."

"Did what? He didn't say, and I was very careful—did you notice how careful I was?—not to ask."

"Your neighbors next door?"

I nodded, already half knowing what she was going to say.

"They've been murdered."

Detective Willis said she wasn't supposed to tell me anything, but since she knew hardly anything, she guessed it wouldn't hurt. She was right. She didn't know very much. When Grace had interviewed the neighbors, she'd found one who'd seen Betty and George come out onto the front steps to fish the morning paper off their porch roof at about eight o'clock. The Whitneys weren't seen again until the meter reader arrived around eleven and found the back door open and George and Betty's bodies lying on the kitchen floor with bullet holes in them. Detective Willis had seen that much for herself before Sergeant Renard had sent her out to interview people in the neighborhood.

"Where are the dogs?" I asked her.

The dogs had been, and still were, out in the run.

"I'd better check them," I said, heaving myself to my feet. "They may need water."

"I'll do it," she said. "Renard's still over there. No reason to set him off again. He doesn't like you."

"I gathered that. Since I'm not gay, not foreign, not a commie, not black, why doesn't he?"

"He checked your navy record, for starters. He has you down as the bomber and the shooter."

"Because I was trained in demolition."

"Partly, and partly because you earn your living doing one of the things he doesn't approve of."

"Like what?"

"Oh, like lawyers or doctors or social workers. He'd like you all right if you were a cop or a fireman or a housepainter or a ballplayer."

"How about car salesmen?"

"Car salesmen, maybe. Not artists, though. Or teachers."

"Not anybody who takes care of anybody else."

"That's about it. I don't think anybody ever took much care of Clayton Renard."

"Is he married?"

"From what I hear, he was. Back in Chicago or Detroit or wherever he came from ten or eleven years ago. The way I hear the story, his wife tried to leave him and he beat her half to death. She wouldn't press charges. It got hushed up. She died, later. Suicide, her folks said. Accident, to hear the sergeant talk about it. He says, and I'm quoting, 'The stupid slut was such a lousy driver, if she'd *tried* to drive off that bridge, she'd have missed.'" Grace delivered all this in rapid half whispers, one eye on the door, as though concerned that Renard might come back. "Anyhow, the story is it made his life difficult, so he moved here. He's been here ever since. And for God's sake, don't let him know I told you."

"You have to work with him all the time?"

"No. Just for six months and that's about over. I can handle it." She wrinkled her nose as though she smelled something bad. "Nasty, but I can handle it. Now, I can't take your gun without a warrant, but would you mind letting me see it?"

I unlocked the bottom drawer of the desk with a key on my key ring, burrowed down to the bottom, and took out the box. The only handgun I'd kept available was the Smith and Wesson model 41 automatic target pistol. I handed it to her.

"It's a twenty-two," she said, hefting it, surprised at how heavy it was.

"It's a target pistol," I told her. "I don't need anything larger than that to shoot targets."

"This is the only one you've got? From the way you talked yesterday, I thought you had the gun for protection."

I flushed. "Renard got my back up. I had five guns originally: two forty-fives, automatic and revolver; two thirty-
eights, the same; and this one. When Jerry was born, I got rid of
all of them but this one. Kids grow up and get into things. I
didn't want a lot of guns lying around." The other four were in
an ancient iron safe Jacob had installed in the basement, but
no matter. They'd been there, undisturbed, for years.

She handed it back to me. "I don't think I'd bother getting a
warrant. Renard may, but the people next door weren't shot
with a twenty-two. Now, what should I do for the dogs?"

"Give them some water if their water dish is empty.
They've got a doghouse out in the run, so they don't have to get
into the house. I've got plenty of dog food here. I'll feed them
until somebody figures out what to do with them."

"Nobody's been notified. Did the Whitneys have kids?
Family?"

I shrugged. "I never heard them talk about any family. Isn't
there an address book or something in the house?"

"We're just getting started." She stood up and brushed dog
hair off her trousers. "You know we'll have to check what you
told us."

"I know." Of course they would. Grace would. Renard
would check alibis only if he thought he could break them. The
sergeant was a very angry man.

"Something I'd like to know, though," she said.

"Whatever."

"Somebody went in there and shot those two. You might
have still been here. You didn't hear anything? Or see anybody?"

I walked with her to the door of Mark's office and pointed
down the hall. "Jacob Buchnam, the man who started this business, originally intended to use the whole house as a shop, so
he built an elevator shaft on the back corner of the house. I
don't use the elevator much, except to take down the trash.
When I do, I usually hit the wrong button by mistake. The guys
who put it in wired it wrong, and the button for the ground floor

is on the top instead of in the middle. I keep meaning to get it fixed, but—"

"That's on the south side," she interrupted, making a note.

"Right. Next to the elevator is the stairwell, with stairs connecting all three floors and the attic. Next to the stairwell is the bathroom and then the kitchen. I was in both rooms between seven and seven thirty, mostly in the shower. I went into the kitchen just long enough to make coffee. There was no reason to look out of the windows. All you can see from up there are the upstairs windows of the Whitney house. The only other room on that side is a little storeroom off the hall and the front guest room with its own bath." It had been our room, Agatha's and mine, but I didn't mention that.

"The rooms we actually use a lot are all on the north side. At the back is my bedroom, then my living room, then Mark's office and mine. Mark's office opens on the hall and into mine, as you can see, and mine has a door into my living room, which you can also see."

"So you were on the wrong side of the house to see or hear anything." She wrote this down.

"Yes. And since we don't open the shop until noon on Mondays, Mrs. Lowe was either in the front hall or in the north back room where we do the packing and crating, and she couldn't see the Whitney house from either place."

She wrote that down too. "Do you suppose the murderer knew that? That you wouldn't be open until noon?"

"It's printed on my card," I told her. "It's on a schedule in the vestibule. I don't make a secret of it."

"Interesting," she said to herself, making notes. "This is my first murder, you know." She seemed more gleeful than was entirely appropriate, but I found myself wanting to encourage her, pat her on the head, tell her she was doing great. Silly, but she made me feel good, the way Bela did.

I went downstairs with her and watched as Renard came out of the house next door and sealed the doors behind him.

"Damn," Grace said. "I'd like to have looked around in there."

"Maybe he already has."

"He hasn't had time to do a good job," she growled. "Clayton is such a goof-off. Damn him, anyhow."

I didn't tell her, but I was rather glad the sergeant hadn't thoroughly searched the house yet. Despite George's attempt to convince me to the contrary, I thought this might be turning into one fascinating puzzle after all.

two

I had some free time late in the afternoon, so on impulse I drove out to Acme Towing. The yard was a desolation of wrecks and half wrecks surrounded by a wall made of old billboards. Betty Whitney's brown van stood in front of a Smirnoff spread, the proximity of sign and wreck making an eloquent argument for abstention. It was pretty well bashed in on the left side. A stout, red-nosed, bushy-browed man made even bulkier by three layers of half-buttoned sweaters came out of the small building and stumped across the yard to where I was standing.

"Somethin' I can do for you?"

"Maybe you can." I got out my wallet. "Have you got a mechanic here?"

"Me. Used to be. Before I got this size."

I waved the wallet suggestively, grinning. "Were you a good mechanic?"

"Well, shit, whaddam I gonna say, I was a lousy mechanic? I was purdy good. Not this new electronic stuff, but I was purdy good."

I pulled out two twenties and offered them. "What's your name?"

"Jake Hensen."

"Jake, I know the woman who owns that van." I pointed it out. "She says the brakes went. I'd like somebody to examine them and tell me what happened. Depending on what's the matter, I might ask somebody to sign a written report about it."

"You her lawyer?"

"No."

"You a cop?"

I shook my head, laughing. "No."

"You an insurance guy?"

"Does it matter?"

"Not to me, fella. Not as long as you're not takin' the car anywhere or doin' anything to it. Maybe it might matter to somebody, but not to me. Not as long as you're payin' for my time."

"When do you think you'll have a chance to get to it?"

"Oh, hell, when my brother's kid gets back from the tow he's on, I'll have him haul this over to the garage across the street and put it up where I can look at it. Say tonight? Call me around six. The number's in the book."

I had no business following up on Betty's wreck. Maybe I wouldn't have if I'd thought the police were going to do anything about it. Grace Willis would have, given half a chance, but from the looks of her partner, I didn't think she'd get it.

What with one thing and another, it was almost six when I got back to the house. Bela was hungry. The dogs next door were hungry. The back door of the Whitney house had a seal on it which I regarded cynically. Seal or no seal, there was something I wanted to look at in that house, something that had been teasing at me ever since the previous day.

When I got around to calling the Acme yard, Jake was all excited about what he'd found out.

"Reason those brakes went, there was one of the hydraulic lines cut. All the fluid ran out."

"Cut. Not torn?"

"I thought it might be worth a little more to you to have another witness, so I had the garage mechanic give it a look. He says cut partway through. I say cut. Clean, like with a sharp pair of dikes."

I thought about that. "How did she get where she was going? She drove all the way from Capitol Hill out to the South-glen Mall. What is that, eight or ten miles?"

"Well, I think it would take a while for all the fluid to leak out. The other guy, the mechanic at the garage, he says it might take a few miles."

"Can you get the line out of there?"

"Sure. I can get it out if you want it."

"It's no good with the hole in it, right?"

"Right."

I thought for a moment. The man wasn't neat, but he'd done what he said he'd do and he'd shown good sense about it. "I'd like you to take it out. Carefully. Wrap it up and mark the package with your name and the date. If the other guy is willing to help, have him sign it too. Then put it away where it won't get lost, just in case we need it. If you catch any heat about the car, I'll pay to replace the line. Maybe I'll bring out a statement for you and the other mechanic to sign, but whether I do or not, I'll send you some extra for your trouble and his."

"No trouble." Hensen chuckled happily. "I'll bet somebody was trying to scare the pants off the woman driving!"

I told him she'd been scared. I didn't mention she'd been killed. If he didn't make the connection, I wasn't going to. It seemed likely that memories might dry up if people knew murder was involved.

I wondered whether someone had sabotaged the van to kill one of the Whitneys or whether someone had done it to decoy the other Whitney away from the house. The latter. It hadn't been meant to kill her, necessarily. Just strand her some distance from home so George would have to come after her. So much for George's dissembling. No matter what he had said about the bomb being intended for someone else, there had been no mistaken identity.

George had talked about my puzzles. Over supper, I thought about that, wondering how he'd known, finally coming to the conclusion that Agatha had probably said something to Betty about them. I'd never made any big public thing out of my fascination with puzzles, criminal ones mostly, since that's what the papers are usually full of. Since Agatha had gone, I'd had lots of time to devote to things like that.

Of course, in my business, solving puzzles is a necessity. Where did a certain piece of furniture come from? Who made it? Who sold it? Where has it been? What color was this wall when the house was built? How did it look originally, before they ruined it? Why did that client give her companion that very strange look in the showroom? How much did this man really intend to spend on this woman's birthday gift? Every day brought that kind of puzzles.

Some of my puzzles had been with me forever. Why did my mother abandon me when I was three, if it was my mother? Who were my parents, or who had they been?

Some were more recent. Where was Agatha? Why did she leave? Why had our car been found wrecked on a mountainside? Why had Jerry been in it?

And now, this new one. Why had the Whitneys died? Why had someone wanted them out of the house? Had someone wanted to search it? Had someone searched it, perhaps leaving only minutes before I came in the back door?

This interesting line of inquiry was interrupted by a chorus of unhappy whines from next door. The dogs had been fed, but they were lonesome. I went out and brought them across into my fenced back yard, where they explored Bela's dog door, one identical to the door they were used to. They came in, went out, came in again. They sniffed the mudroom and the downstairs kitchen. Some dunnage blankets out of the packing room made a bed for them in the mudroom. Bela looked at this arrangement anxiously. Ladislav made tight dog circles on it, then settled, Eva at his side. Snowball watched them from across the room, head cocked. I put down another folded blanket, and she settled as well.

Bela stared at me, his eyes mournful, tail barely moving. "Upstairs," I said firmly. Bela licked my hand, tail wagging vigorously. Things were all right. There were visitors, but Bela still had his own bed upstairs. He was like a kid, worrying about where he'd sleep when Grandma came.

With the dogs settled, I went back to thinking about puzzles. People were the toughest ones. They played games. They pretended to want things they actually didn't. They pretended to be things they weren't. They were two people, or more, one on the outside and others within. They wore masks. They lied.

Betty and George had lied. George had been sweating when I'd told him about the bomb. Betty had been unaccountably silent. Betty was seldom silent, and never when under stress. A lot of the time she didn't say anything relevant, but she never let that stop her from talking. Until last night. Last night she and George had been almost speechless. If it had been a senseless attack, a meaningless attack, they would have been angry, outraged. George would have protested high taxes and how the police didn't protect the public. He'd have zoomed through his angers and annoyances as though on an emotional motorcycle, threatening to sue somebody, anybody, and Betty would have swished along beside him like a little sidecar with its own deafening siren. But there'd been none of that. Instead, there had been a bare-faced denial from both of them without any of the normal outrage and speculation. Terror could paralyze people like that. And if they had been terrified, they had probably had a fairly good idea of why, and of who was responsible.

I couldn't quite figure purposeful murder directed at random dog fanciers. Had it been George's role as religious broadcaster that had attracted lethal attention?

Add to that question the one I had about what I thought I'd seen over at the Whitney house.

The sky through the window was dark.

In my dressing room I changed into jeans and a dark turtleneck and parka I'd picked up at Eddie Bauer's and hadn't had a chance to wear yet. Not that anyone was watching the house particularly, but it made sense not to attract attention. Nellie Arpels might see me from across the alley, but there was nothing I could do about that. Nine years before, when we'd first moved into the house, it had been a warm fall, with windows open much of the time. Agatha had seen the old woman sitting in the window across the alley and had befriended her. I'd gone with Agatha to visit her a few times, but most of what I knew about Nellie, I knew from Agatha. Nellie had lived in the same house for fifty years. For the last twenty years she'd been confined to a wheelchair on the second floor, cared for by her daughter, Janice. Nellie never went anywhere. She spent eighteen to twenty hours a day at her window, sleeping little and watching much. She could have seen who went into Betty and George's house yesterday.

The back door of the Whitney place was still locked and sealed, but no one had sealed the dog door. Though neither Eva nor Snowball were huge dogs, Ladislav weighed about a hundred and five. The dog door was big enough for him. Normally held shut by a magnetic catch, it could be fastened from the inside with a simple latch which would yield to a narrow screwdriver. Since losing things, particularly keys, is one of the things I'm best at, I've performed this little manipulation at my own house. I slithered through the door and onto the Whitney's sunroom floor, where I lay listening to be sure no one else was in there with me.

Silence.

I stood up slowly and switched on the narrow beamed flashlight I'd brought with me. In the kitchen there were chalked outlines on the floor. Blood, brownish and dry. Gray fingerprint powder everywhere. George's tie over the back of a chair. Coffee cups still on the table, along with an almost full jar of marmalade. Coffeepot still on the coffee maker, boiled dry and reeking. I turned it off. Breakfast dishes on the table with bits of egg and crumbs on them. Dishwasher full of clean dishes, probably washed the night before. Oven on low with two dessicated English muffin halves inside. I turned that off, too. This carelessness told me there wasn't likely to be an effective police investigation. Somebody didn't care. Somebody was just going through the motions.

I tried extrapolating what had happened from the leftover bits of food, the unwashed dishes. Betty had fixed breakfast and put the food in the oven to keep warm while she and George fetched the morning paper off the porch roof. They had eaten their breakfast, except for two muffin halves. The plates and cups still on the table said they'd meant to eat the extra muffins along with a second cup of coffee, but George and Betty hadn't made it to the second cup. Someone had come in while the oven was still on, the coffee was still hot. Whoever had looked over the crime scene hadn't seen what was in front of him. Had Grace Willis even been in the kitchen? Probably not. Women tend to see things like ovens left on. If Grace had been in this kitchen, she'd have noticed.

George usually left for work a little before nine. Banker's hours, he had always called it. If the murderer had come after that, George would have been gone. So the killer hit the house between eight and nine. And since the first muffins had been eaten but the second muffins hadn't, it had probably been around eight thirty, eight forty, maybe eight forty-five, though George would have needed a few minutes to put on his tie and coat before he left.

I went out into the hall, looking for the piece of furniture I was almost sure I'd seen. It was there. I *had* seen it. I shook my head at it in amazement. On Sunday I'd stood next to that table to shut the door without taking in what it was—an eighteenth-century Queen Anne drop leaf in mahogany and pine. I knelt beside it, running my hands over it, looking under it. It looked completely authentic. The last auction catalogue that had shown a piece of similar quality had had a fifty thousand reserve price on it! What the hell was it doing here?

When I'd stroked every inch of the table, I got up and went across the hall to the dining room. George's sports coat hung on a chair at one end of the table on which a dozen books were piled, some of them open, all of them dog-eared and stained as though in constant use. As soon as I saw them, I knew what they were. I even remembered Betty asking for them.

"I'd like to redecorate my bedroom, Jason. I know you'd do it beautifully, but I've so much time on my hands I'd like to do it myself. Could you recommend a book?"

"A book on interior decoration, Betty?"

"On antiques. On really nice antiques."

I'd given her a list of a dozen reference works on American antiques, which is what I know the most about. They were all here on the table, even the two or three that had been out of print. When had she asked me, five years ago? Six? Two of the books were open to the same illustration, a little William and Mary inlaid desk box with an estimated value of around thirty thousand dollars. I was halfway out of the room when I saw the desk box itself, the same or a very similar one, sitting on the buffet—a slant-topped box in walnut, with a fruitwood inlay of sweetly curved vines and leaves set into the top and the front. The box had ball feet and a patinaed brass surround for the keyhole. I was stopped again, unable to move. First the table, now this. God, what a little beauty, and where in the hell had Betty Whitney found it? I reached for it, fondled it. Only twenty inches across, ten deep, meant to hold family documents and perhaps the family Bible. This one was locked, and I fretted, eager to see the inside, feeling myself warm with something very much akin to lust. I wanted it! I couldn't believe it was here, in this room. This was almost a museum piece! Regretfully, I put it back where I'd found it.

There were other items of similar quality. In the living room was a Chippendale lowboy that was probably worth sixty or seventy thousand and two Windsor comb-back armchairs that might bring ten to twelve thousand each, among other pieces.

I went up the stairs two at a time. I'd never been upstairs in the Whitney house before. At one time, when we'd first moved in next door, the Whitneys had entertained occasionally, and Agatha and I had come to a couple of small parties, but there had been no reason to see the bedrooms upstairs. I poked my head into each one. Two large bedrooms in use, his and hers, with a shared bath between. Another bedroom, unused, packed with pieces of very expensive furniture. A guest bath opening into the hall. A fourth bedroom, a small one, furnished as an office with a desk and filing cabinets and a word processor. The floor plan wasn't very different from that of my house, except that mine had had an extra bedroom to start with. Jacob had made a kitchen out of one bedroom and the two offices out of another, and my house had the extravagant entry hall, but otherwise they were almost twins.

I went into the office and stood to one side of the window, peering out. No cars parked up or down the block. No loitering pedestrians. Still, no point in letting anyone see the light. I closed the curtains slowly before turning on the penlight to examine the room.

Ribbons and dog pictures freckled the walls. Betty with Ladislav. Betty with Eva. George with Ladislav. George with Eva. Betty holding Ladislav—was it Ladislav?—with one hand and a blue ribbon in the other, under a banner printed in a very foreign language. George holding two blue ribbons under the same banner with a fatuous expression on his pudgy face. Betty with Snowball at a puppy show. Blue ribbons, red ones, gold ones, each with its date and place, a few of them from the United States and Canada, a few from other places.

Over the desk were certificates of merit from the Association of Christian Broadcasters dated each of the past five years. On the opposite wall was a similar set from the New Evangelical World Society, George's outfit. To one side was a world map. Over half of the U.S. was shaded in red, showing where contributions came from. Radiating from the site of the transmitter near Galveston, ribbons were pinned to Central America, across the Caribbean, into parts of South America.

"Not that I believe all that crap," George had once said to us, years ago, in an unguarded and rather drunken moment. "It's just a way to keep starving people from making revolutions. No hope in this life, we tell 'em, but there's hope in heaven. A good revolution would do 'em more good."

"If you feel that way, George, why do you go on working for them?" Agatha had asked.

He had flushed, looked around guiltily as though afraid

someone had overheard him. "Sorry. Shouldn't say things like that. It's a job, you know, Aggie. It's a job."

From the looks of the place it had been an exceptionally profitable job. On the second floor the furniture quality was, if anything, even finer than on the ground floor. The chair outside the office door was a collector's piece. So was the étagère at the top of the stairs. Betty's room held a small fortune in Chippendale: a canopy bed, a highboy, and other pieces from the same period and, possibly, the same maker. I looked in Betty's closet and in the drawers of the highboy, just out of curiosity, expecting to find something elegant. Nothing. No furs, no designer clothing, and no real jewelry. There was one small bottle of expensive perfume and that was it.

Throughout the house the value stopped with the furniture. No valuable rugs or lamps. No paintings. No expensive bibelots, only junk souvenirs of Budapest, of Vienna, of London. I went back to the office. There was no safe, no stash of stocks or bonds or cash, and nothing of particular value except a huge tape recorder with the biggest reels of tape I'd ever seen. Nothing in the desk but junk. No correspondence. No files. Old appointment books, mostly empty except for the dates and locations of dog shows. Old calendars. A library card. A little cassette recorder, much like one I owned. I flicked it on and heard the hiss of the tape running. Then it started screaming at me, and I turned it off. Nothing else in that drawer except chains of paper clips and wads of miscellaneous rubber bands. In the bottom left-hand drawer was the only paydirt: the drawer was completely full of bank statements.

I lifted a few to the top of the desk and began sorting them into piles. Four piles. Four accounts in three different banks. Two checking, one in George's name, one joint with Betty. One savings. Another account with a fancy name that indicated it was part of an investment plan. I chose a statement at random, one dated three years before, and exhaled breathily into the silent room. The balance shown was slightly over three hundred thousand. I put it back into the proper envelope and began arranging the envelopes in order, whistling thoughtfully between my teeth.

Puzzle, puzzle. George drove a cheap car. Well, a medium-priced car. Betty had the three- or four-year-old van she used to transport the dogs to shows. George had never worn expensive clothing. His suits were off the rack. Betty had liked jewelry and wore too much of it, but it was all cheap stuff. And yet the dusty chair by the door was a corner chair made around 1760 and worth upward of twenty-five thou. And there were twenty or thirty pieces in the house of similar or greater value. Quite an estate for the manager of a religious broadcasting company!

I had a sudden spasm of uneasiness, as though someone were staring at the back of my head. No one could see in through the drapes, but I still felt someone was watching me and decided to get out while the getting was available. The plastic liner in the wastebasket looked big enough, and I dumped the bank statements into it before replacing the drawer in the desk. I started downstairs with the sack over my shoulder and got halfway before meaning struck me.

All the expensive stuff was where no one would see it! George had driven a cheap car and had worn cheap clothes. The house was a nice big old house, but it was in this transitional neighborhood where some big old houses were offices and some were businesses, and though it might have been expensive to buy, it could equally well have been a home that had been in the family for years. It certainly didn't scream money.

Another interesting fact was that each piece of furniture was fairly light in weight. The highboy was made in two sections. The bottom part had sturdy brass handles to carry it with. The big bed came apart into at least six pieces. All of it was stuff George and Betty could have handled by themselves. And though they had been quite gregarious when we first moved next door, they hadn't entertained for years, so here was this astonishing collection of furniture which no one ever saw—a kind of secret world! I stood in the kitchen, marveling.

Outside in the real world, Ladislav's family began barking tentatively from my back yard. A car had stopped in the street, and someone was coming toward the house. One set of footsteps. A man.

I went through the sunporch and out the dog door, dragging the plastic sack with me. Someone was coming down the side of the house. The only refuge that offered was the doghouse, and I scrabbled into it, curling up in the back like a thief. Well, I *was* a thief. The bank statements bulked beside me like an indictment.

Across the fence in my own back yard the dogs were still barking, curious "Who's there?" barks. The man paid them no attention. He came to the back door, broke the seal, and went into the house. No lights. After a moment, a dim glow. He must have had a flash in his pocket. The dogs quieted down. I heard the dog door thump several times as they went into the house. In the Whitney house the glow went here and there, then approached the back door. He came out, carrying something.

He fiddled with the back door, the light in his hand shining momentarily upward on his face. Renard. He mumbled to himself as he fiddled with the door, evidently restoring the seal. I couldn't hear what he was saying, but he sounded a little drunk or angry or both.

When he went down the sidewalk, the glow from the streetlight lit what he was carrying. The desk box. The one worth at least thirty thousand. The sergeant must have spotted it earlier, it and the open book on the dining room table with a picture of the box on the open page.

I slithered around the corner of the house and watched him go out to the curb. The desk went into the back seat of his car, wrapped in something dark. His radio crackled, and I heard him clearly as he answered the call.

"No, I'm coming in."

More static from the other end.

"Tell him to wait for me. I'll be there in a minute."

Renard shut the car door and drove slowly away.

I was breathing as though I'd been running for a few miles and so angry I could hardly see. This damned bigot was stealing something I wanted. It was like witnessing a rape! I couldn't anymore stay out of it than I could fly. I dashed across the parking lot to the garage, threw the plastic sack in the car, backed it out, and drove to the police station, telling myself every inch of the way that I'd better not get stopped. With no driver's license, dressed like a burglar, and carrying a sack of someone else's property, being stopped would not be a fortunate occurrence.

When I got to the station I parked outside, on the street. In about two minutes, Renard's car came down the driveway to the lot behind the building. I gulped; I must have driven faster than I'd thought. I cut my lights and slowly followed his car around into the alley.

He parked in the lot behind the station. I waited to see what he'd do. If the box went into the station with him, then he'd taken it for a legitimate reason. If it stayed in his car, wrapped up that way, then he hadn't. He got out, locked the car, and went in empty-handed.

I pulled my car up next to his, opened the door on the passenger side, and tried his door. Naturally, it was locked. As well as forgetting house keys, I also have a bad habit of forgetting car keys, so I'm a world-class expert at unlocking car doors. I had a coat hanger in my trunk.

Three minutes later, the desk box was in my car. I left Renard's car unlocked. Let him think somebody just saw the box there and stole it, the way he had. Half an hour later the desk box was hidden in the Hyde Street basement where no one was likely to find it. In another hour the books on antiques had been removed from the Whitney house and were scattered among the reference works I kept in the office, each furnished with a new but slightly soiled bookplate identifying it as belonging to Jason Lynx. Damned if I was going to have manuals for prospective thieves lying open in the Whitney dining room. The stuff over there was too beautiful.

I thought about blowing the whistle on Renard, but not for very long. All it would do right then was stir things up and make my own life difficult. It might be possible later. Not yet. Now there was something else to think about—a little neighborhood murder.

three

Tuesday mornings I play handball with, or rather against, Joe Piers. Joe is a lawyer acquaintance who plays maniacal handball and has driven all his former competitors into the ground. He's having a little more trouble with me because I refuse to let him know what it costs me to keep up with him. What it costs is a tad more than I've got on any given morning, though the tads are getting smaller. Joe always gets dressed and leaves while I'm still in the shower. Maybe he thinks I sweat more than he does. What I'm actually doing in there is leaning on the wall with the water running down my back, swearing I'll never do it again. I stay there until I can consider doing it again without trembling or until I drown, whichever comes first. Though I am not given to what some people call macho behavior, Joe wants to beat everyone so badly that he's not going to beat me no matter what.

After handball I went to call on Nellie Arpels. Calling on old ladies was about all that Joe had left me fit for. Besides, I'd committed myself earlier that morning by calling Nellie's fifty-ish daughter Janice Fetterling and telling her I'd be by. Janice accepted the prospect of a visitor for her mama without noticeable enthusiasm.

"You haven't been here in a while," she said in an indistinct voice as she answered the bell. She didn't sound as though she cared. She was a shapeless woman with no definable edges. Her hair was pulled back and tied with a bit of faded ribbon and her colorless face was like a pale pudding, bare of any evidence that she had ever done anything to it. Her dress had been made for someone larger. "A long while," she repeated.

She was understating. By my count, it had been at least

seven years. "I'm sorry about that," I said. "I should have come over to visit, but time passes." It was a lame excuse.

"Oh, I know that," she said. "Lord, I know that." She led the way upstairs and through the half-open door. "Mama, here's Mr. Lynx to see you." It was said without particular emphasis, and she did not offer to stay with us. I imagined her melting into a shred of fog downstairs somewhere. Perhaps she only took shape when Mama needed her or someone came to the door.

Nellie Arpels, in contrast, had edges that were as sharp as broken glass. She looked me over with lively interest and a tiny bit of a pout.

"I see you waving at me, but you haven't come to see me for years and years. Agatha, now, she used to come see me all the time."

I fought the urge to run away. I didn't want to talk about Agatha. "I know she did, Nellie. She often spoke of you as a good friend."

"Oh, yes. When you and she first moved in—what was that, eight years? nine?—she saw me sitting up here and came right over to get acquainted. She'd bring the baby, and she'd bring coffee cake or sweet rolls, and we'd sit here and talk." She push-pulled at the wheels of her chair, rocking herself with a brisk forward-back movement. "Baby would lie there on my bed and sleep. Lord, how that baby could sleep! Never stirred, sometimes for hours. She was a nice girl, Agatha. You never found her, did you?"

I ignored the question. I had to ignore it. No, I had never found Agatha. No one had ever found Agatha. "I should have come to see you before now," I said, trying to sound contrite. "There's no excuse for not—"

"No need." She waved her hands. "People do what they like to do, duty or not. Your Agatha liked to talk to me, so she came over. You don't want to be reminded, so you don't. My Janice doesn't particular like to talk to me, so you can't get her up here with a smile on her face for love nor money. I miss Agatha."

I didn't say anything at all. There was nothing I could say. Nellie didn't seem to mind. She waited a moment, as though to let that subject finish itself off, then started a new line of thought. "I bet you want to know what I saw. I thought the police would be coming to see me before this, but they didn't. Made myself a bet if they didn't get to me within two days, I'd get myself another cat, Janice or no Janice. My cat died two years ago, and I'm lonesome. I'd like to have a dog like those dogs you and the murdered people have, but it wouldn't be right to coop one up and Janice wouldn't stand for walking a dog. Janice barely stands for taking care of her mother."

"Well, it's tough on both of you," I replied, trying to avoid the usual self-serving clichés. "She feels responsible for you, and that keeps her tied down."

The old lady flushed, reproved. "I know. I shouldn't go on about her. She's a good girl. Her husband is a good boy. And I've got two nice grown-up grandkids and nothing to complain about. *Did* you come to ask me what I saw?"

"I did," I told her, only slightly surprised that she'd anticipated me. "What did you see?"

"When, Sunday or Monday?" She snickered at me. "Last night I saw you crawling in through the doggie door. All dressed up like one of those men on TV, sneaking around."

"I didn't think you'd see me at night," I admitted, only slightly embarrassed. "There wasn't any light back there."

"The streetlight on the corner shines between your house and your garage and falls right on the Whitney back porch. Not much, but some. I can see everywhere over there except right up at the back door. It's got that kind of wall around it, and the little roof over it, and I can't see in there. Everywhere else, though, I've got eyes like an eagle, I swear I do. Can't read, can't thread a needle, but if you want to know what's happening clear over on Eighth Avenue, I can tell you."

"Nope. I just want to know what happened at the

Whitneys." I got up and stared through her window at the garages across the alley, at the back yards behind their tall board fences, and at the enigmatic backs of the houses, the Whitneys and mine.

"Well," she said, snuggling herself down into her wheelchair as though for a long chat, "first thing was Sunday. Mrs. Whitney went out in her brown van about noon. Then, along about four o'clock, Mr. Whitney took his car out. A few minutes later a man came down the side of the Whitney house and looked in the dog yard and the dogs got up and barked at him, so he went back around the front. He had a package in his hands."

"What did he—"

"Let me tell it. Then you went over later, and you came out and went around front, and then after a while all those space monsters came."

"The bomb squad."

"That's them. They went in and came out, and then something went off—*whoom!*—like thunder. Then a whole bunch of people came and went, back and forth, and finally you came and said something to the dogs."

"I put a note on the door to tell George to call me as soon as he got in."

"Well, then, there wasn't anything until about ten. I guess they came home, but I didn't see them, so they must have come in the front, and then the lights went on and you went over and came back again. And then all the lights went out except the corner window upstairs in the murdered people's house. That never did go out that I saw."

"I hope you felt you could get a little sleep sometime in there."

"Don't be funny with me, young man. It's hard for me to breathe when I lie down, so I don't lie down any more than I have to. Well, next morning . . ."

"Yes?"

"Next morning, the same man that had the package came

back. He came at eight thirty. I was listening to the news, and the commercial was on when he came. He went up to the back door, and I guess they let him in. Then later he came out and went away."

"Mrs. Arpels—"

"Nellie."

"Nellie, what did he look like?"

"He was shorter than you, because his head didn't come up to the bottom of the windowsill of the house like yours does. And he was thin-looking. Not fat or big. And he had a beard, I think gray. I couldn't really tell if it was gray, but it seemed like the same color as the sills over there, and they're gray. Before those people came, the people had that house painted white, you know that? But when those people came, they sandblasted it and it looked just the way it did when I was married and moved in here. This used to be the nicest neighborhood. And now look at it. Used to have neighborhood parties. Now we've got neighborhood murders."

"Anything else about the man?"

"He wore dark glasses. First time he was bare-headed. I don't know why people don't catch pneumonia and die more than they do these days. Everybody goes around without anything on their heads, even bald people. You noticed that? On Monday he was wearing a hat. No, it was more of a cap. And he was carrying a board thing, to write on, you know what I mean?"

"A clipboard?"

"Something like that. He went up the back steps, and then I couldn't see him because the way that door's set. I can't see the door, but he must have gone in. Then, after a while, out he came and went back out to the street. And then there wasn't anything until later, when the meter man came. I know who he is. He's the same one that comes here. He whistles all the time and he has that same thing, that clipboard. And then after he came, all hell broke loose again." She nodded her satisfaction at this. It had evidently been an interesting day. "After everybody was gone, after it got dark, you went over there. I saw you. I couldn't have told it was you except you came out of your own house. And then about half an hour after that, you came out and a man came and went in and flashed a light around, kind of dim. He was carrying something when he came out. The streetlight shone right on his face."

"Could you see who he was?"

"I think maybe he was there before, with the police."

"I suppose you saw me getting out of the doghouse."

"Is that where you were? I wondered. I don't see a doghouse from here. I didn't see where you went while the man was there, but after he left, I saw you go somewhere in your car and then come back. I saw you get something out of that house, but I won't tell on you. Way I figure it, when the police finally think about coming over here and asking me, I'm going to tell them I never saw you but that one time Sunday evening, going over to feed the dogs. If Agatha thought enough of you to marry you, why then you're likely not up to anything bad."

I sat there, thinking. "Nellie. If the police do get here, don't mention you saw the detective taking anything."

She stared at me, eyes like polished eggs in their wrinkled nests. "Oh, so it's that way, is it? A little on the side? My husband used to say that. 'He got a little on the side,' though I think he meant women, usually, not stealing. Don't you think I ought to tell somebody?"

"Yes. You should. But not now. We have to figure out who to tell."

"My, my," she said again. "Well, they're taking their time about asking, aren't they. Do you think I'll win my bet with myself and get my cat?"

"If the sergeant doesn't work harder than he has so far, you'll get a dozen cats. What if I get one for you?"

She flushed again. "I don't know. Janice has so much to do. She says she isn't going to clean any cat box."

"What if I find somebody to do it? You've been a help. It would be a way to repay you."

She shook her head, slowly, not meaning it.

"What kind of cat?"

"A white one," she whispered. "Oh, a white one."

Back at my desk, I made a note on my desk calendar to go to the animal shelter and get Nellie a cat. I thought I'd probably have to lie about it to get an animal since the shelter preferred to put animals to death rather than into "questionable" homes. Nellie's home would probably be questionable, considering her immobility and Janice's unwillingness, but she deserved a cat nonetheless. I'd be responsible for the cat. Mark would have to hire a cat tender for me. Mark had several remarkable talents, and finding people to do things was one of them.

"I'll find someone," Mark agreed, his eyes squinted in concentration. "Will Nellie care how old or what color?"

I replied. "If I know Nellie, she won't care. Janice may, but I'm not pandering to Janice's preferences. Anything happen this morning I should know about?"

"The two catalogues you asked for from Sotheby's arrived." He laid them on the desk.

I grabbed them and made smacking noises with my lips.

Mark shuddered and said, "Eugenia wants to know if she can have the second of January off. She wants a long weekend with her sister, I think."

"Tell her yes. Chances are there won't be anybody in that whole week. Anything else?"

"The annual fine arts seminar at the university—"

"I told them last year."

"They didn't believe you."

"All right, tell them again. I will *not* speak at their fine arts seminar because their chairman is a domineering ass who is rude to all his participants but particularly to those who make an actual living in decor. He grovels to painters, even bad ones, licks the feet of sculptors, accepts architects with a tiny moue of disgust, and attacks all the rest of us as Philistines."

"Should I quote you exactly?" Mark was trying to keep from laughing. He had met the chairman in question.

"Though I'd like nothing more than for you to quote me to him personally, just get the sense of it across. Anything else?"

"*Nada.* Before the Hoopers get here you've got a whole hour to gloat over possible acquisitions." Mark went across to the desk in his own office, his back to the open door.

There was something else I wanted to do before I gloated, something having to do with the want-ad section I'd retrieved from the laundry-room cupboard when I came in. I laid it on the desk, open at page 153. Perhaps the bomber had opened the paper to page 153 for a reason. Perhaps, when it came time to wrap up the bomb, he had set it down on the open page and wrapped away. Perhaps not, but I chose to ignore that possibility. If the choice of that particular page had any meaning, I might have a clue. If it had no meaning, which was a lot more likely, meaninglessness would inevitably emerge.

Beginning in the upper left-hand corner, I started reading the ads, one by one. Section 5004: Kennels and Pet Shops. Section 5006: Dogs. Section 5011: Cats. Section 5012: Birds. I worked my way through Fish and Aquariums, Pets and Supplies, and on to 5120: Livestock. Horses started on the reverse side, going on to Hay, Grain, and Feed. When I'd read through it once, I did it again, this time with a red pencil, ending up with half a dozen ads circled in red.

The first of these read: "Will the party who bought the Weimaraner from Mrs. Brown please call her." The dog ads were in alphabetical order, 99 percent of them starting with the breed of dog being advertised. This ad was under "W" for "will." The other circled ads touted a Siamese cat which was "extraordinarily talkative," a parrot which "speaks foreign languages," a type of catnip mouse "sold only in lots of 100," a load of "God's own Mountain Meadow" hay and an AQHA-registered quarter horse being sold "with saddle, tack, and stable companion."

I yelled for Mark, scowling at the paper until he came in.

"Do you remember the name of that kid you got through Kelly Girls last time we needed extra help? She was working to get money to go back to school?"

"Myra Sharp," Mark said calmly. "She lives over on Ash Street, somewhere in the three-hundred block, and her mother would know if she's available. What do you have, some typing do get done over Christmas?"

"I want her to go down to the newspaper office and read the Sunday want ads for the past year or two."

Mark tapped his teeth gently with the end of his pen. "I presume you want her to look for something. Or is it an endurance exercise?"

"I want her to look for ads that sound like one of these. Or all of these. I'm looking for a pattern."

Mark read, pondered, then said, "I'm afraid I don't see a pattern, Jason."

I looked at the circled ads again. Hell, I wasn't sure either. "I'm going on the premise that somewhere on this page there is something that somehow connects to the Whitney murder. It is unlikely to be part of a genuine advertisement. Since there's nothing on the page but ads, it must be a false one. In order for the recipient to know which ad pertains to him, the message probably should contain an agreed-upon word or phrase that stands out immediately. The ads I've circled all have words or phrases that sound to me like they could be arbitrary, chosen as a signal or a code. If you insert a word like 'cerise' in the middle of a cake recipe, it stands out. At least it does if you've read twenty or thirty ordinary cake recipes. If you read fifty or sixty of these ads, certain words and phrases come across as strange, stand-out, a little bizarre. 'Mrs. Brown.' 'Extraordinarily talkative.' 'Lots of one hundred.' 'Stable companion.' 'Foreign languages.' 'God's own Mountain.' "

Mark nodded, running his eyes down the Cats for Sale ads.

"You can see that, within categories, the ads are as repetitive as recipes. After reading a dozen, you can't remember any differences. Almost all the kittens are affectionate or playful or both. Almost all the female cats are spayed. Almost all the horses are healthy and well trained. But the words and phrases I've circled appear only once and they seem force-fitted. That's why they stand out." Maybe. I wasn't as sure as I sounded.

"Could be the people who wrote these are just trying to attract attention to their own ads."

"That's very likely. However . . ."

"You want Myra to look. You'll pay her by the hour?"

"Ten an hour and a bonus if she finds a pattern."

"You'll spoil her."

"Hell, Mark, would you spend hours and hours reading and rereading want ads?" I'd only done it for half an hour, and my eyes ached.

"Not unless my life depended on it." Mark's face was full of curiosity as he left, but he didn't ask what I was up to.

"Somebody's life maybe did depend on it," I muttered to myself, being interrupted by a tap at the door into my living room. I looked up, annoyed. People weren't supposed to come in that way.

"The woman downstairs told me I would find Jason Lynx up here." The speaker was pale, in his late fifties or sixties, dressed in a three-piece gray suit with lapels that had gone out of style twenty years ago. He had a full head of very white, rather long hair, a mustache that half concealed his mouth, and a short well-trimmed beard. He wore thick rimless glasses that distorted his eyes as he tilted his head forward to look at me through the tops of the lenses. "Mr. Lynx?" His voice was so mild and mellifluous it could slide right over you if you weren't paying attention.

"I'm Jason Lynx. Can I help you with something?"

The man fumbled in his breast pocket, withdrew a card case, and proffered a card. William W. Stimson, Attorney at Law. The firm had offices in Chicago, Denver, and San Francisco. I held the card between thumb and middle finger and raised my eyebrows.

Stimson nodded, as though reminding himself what he was

there for. "I'm intruding upon you because I've just seen the dogs at the Whitney house. When I went back to look at them, I saw a very similar animal in your back yard."

"I bought my dog from the Whitneys."

"I came to make some kind of preliminary arrangements about the Whitney house. The Whitneys gave our firm power of attorney long ago. They had no relatives. It hadn't occurred to me until I visited the house, however, that there would be—well, should one say, survivors?"

"The dogs."

"The dogs. Are they worth anything? I mean, aside from their undoubted sentimental value? I'm not sure how much trouble I should take to . . ." He looked around vaguely for a chair, and Mark brought him one. He sat across the desk from me, waiting, eyebrows raised expectantly.

"I would say the dogs are valuable, yes. Ladislav is an international champion of some kind; so is Eva. The puppy is only a young dog, a year younger than mine. The logical thing would be to put them in a kennel until you decide what to do with them, but I'd hate to have you do that. I know the dogs. Why don't you leave them with me?"

"That seems a dreadful imposition—"

"Not at all. My dog Bela is used to having them nearby. As a matter of fact, they stayed here last night, though I put them back in their run this morning. I didn't like leaving them in the run at night since they were accustomed to sleeping in the house." I leaned back and gave Stimson a long look. Something about him bothered me, but I had no idea what it was. Maybe just that suit. It looked like the kind of thing Jacob used to wear when I was a kid. "Would you like coffee?" I asked him. "Good." I poured us each a cup. "You're here very promptly, I must say."

"Someone in the firm heard about it on the news and got hold of me. We drew George's will, and we've acted for him in several other matters. We knew neither he nor Betty had any relatives to take care of things. Such a tragedy! Were you a witness?"

He said it almost eagerly. Aha, I thought, a disaster hound. I'd met his kind before. Mrs. Opinsky at the Home when I was a kid had been a disaster hound. She had loved to talk about earthquakes and hurricanes and murder.

I said, "Unfortunately, there seem to have been no witnesses."

"I thought, being right here, next door—"

"During the time in question Mark and I were either here, in this room, or running about taking care of business. So far as I know, no one saw anything." I sat back while my visitor shook his head sadly and made *tsk*ing noises.

"I don't suppose you have any idea why—"

I almost wished I had something juicy to give him. "None, I'm afraid. I haven't seen either George or Betty socially for years, and our acquaintance was pretty well limited to dog talk over the back fence."

"Oh. I had thought, since you say you bought your dog from them—"

Nosey Parker. I gave him another headshake. "They had a puppy they hadn't sold, and I was lonely. I gave them a check; they gave me the dog. Betty threw in a collar and a leash. I'm afraid that was it."

My visitor looked at me inquiringly, as though waiting for more. I didn't have any idea what he expected, so I decided to ask a few questions myself. "You'll make arrangements for disposition of the Whitney property?"

"Well, eventually, I suppose we will. I thought I'd go through the house today just to see what's there—"

"What's there are some remarkable American antiques," I interrupted. "When I went over Sunday evening to feed the dogs—at George's request; he left the door open for me—I saw that George and Betty have acquired about a million dollars' worth of furniture."

"They what?" Stimson splashed coffee onto the desk, almost dropping his cup. "Forgive me." He seemed at a loss for words. I handed him a tissue, and he wiped up the spill with a well-manicured hand. "I had no idea." He looked momentarily confused. "No idea at all."

Neither had I, but I didn't mention that. "I'm telling you this because someone needs to be responsible for seeing the stuff isn't stolen. I can do an inventory list for you this afternoon, if you like. It won't be an appraisal, though I can provide that too. An appraisal will take a good deal of time, and for that I'd need access to the pieces."

"Your—ah, that is, what would your fee be for a listing?"

"Five hundred."

He thought for a moment. "I suppose it would be a good idea."

"You'll have to get the police to take the seal off the door. And I have an appointment in five minutes which will take about an hour."

He looked confused again, but only for a moment. He smiled a bit oddly. "Oh. No trouble. No, no trouble at all. I can manage that."

I told him, "Give Mark a call when you're ready, and we'll set a time this afternoon."

As Stimson left, the Hoopers came in to talk about antiques as investments. Later Mark and I had lunch, prepared by Mark. Tuesdays and Thursdays were Mark's days. Wednesdays and Fridays were mine. Sometimes we got adventuresome and went out.

At two thirty, Stimson called to say he was on his way back. He arrived with a key to the house and a piece of paper saying he could cut the seal on the back door. I took my Polaroid camera and a tape recorder. Mark took a clipboard with NCR inventory sheets on it. We went across the cold driveway, through the dusty kitchen, and started upstairs. Stimson paid very little attention to what we were doing. He seemed to be more interested in what might be in drawers and cupboards. "Legal documents," he explained with a shrug, putting material from George's filing cabinet into his briefcase and then turning to the desk, opening each drawer and examining the contents as I watched. I thought about the pile of bank statements over in my bedroom. I'd have to bring them back eventually, and Stimson would know they hadn't been here today. There was no point in worrying about it, however. I went back to describing furniture into the recorder and taking at least two pictures of everything.

While I did that, Mark wrote a list, with brief descriptions, putting all the "ordinary" furniture on a separate list. When we'd finished, the lawyer ushered us out the back door and locked it, remarking that the police would be along to seal it up again.

I glanced down at Mark's meticulous list. "Assuming that close inspection shows all these to be genuine, I'd like to make offers on almost everything here—or, rather, as much of it as I could handle. I can give you the names of some honest dealers, but for heaven's sake don't let just anyone in here."

Mark folded one copy of the list and handed it to Stimson, who asked, "What would your estimate be, off the cuff?"

"As I said, close to a million. Could be more, could be less. I'd have to check the recent sales of similar pieces. And if I can find out the provenance of these pieces, that would help. There's some value in their recent furniture as well, though most of it depreciates very rapidly."

"I'm very grateful," the attorney said, handing me five new one-hundred-dollar bills. "I hope you don't mind cash. I didn't bring any of the firm's checks with me. I'll be in touch. You will take care of the dogs?"

I said I would, then watched as he got into his car and pulled away. When he had gone partway down the block, I stepped forward, saying something under my breath.

"What?" Mark said.

"He didn't ask for a receipt," I said. "First time I've ever known a lawyer not to want a receipt."

"Shall I type up this list?"

I shook my head. "File it. I'd rather you tried to find out where George bought the stuff. Start with the bombé desk in the dining room. There can't be more than one of those. Oh, and don't forget about the pet-sitter. I've got to get Nellie her cat!"

Despite ardent effort, it was two days before I located and succeeded in obtaining a blue-eyed short-haired white cat which, as an extra inducement to adoption, was already spayed and declawed and was not deaf, as most blue-eyed white cats seem to be. Normally I would regard a declawed cat as somehow unnaturally mutilated, but in this case it was probably appropriate. The cat bore a noticeable resemblance to Barbra Streisand, or perhaps Cher, particularly about the nose and eyes. The animal shelter said her name was Sphinx.

Janice warmed to the idea of her mama having a cat after I told her I'd hired a neighborhood girl to come around a couple of afternoons a week to sit with Nellie and clean up the litter box. "Your mother was a good friend to my wife," I'd said in my sincerest voice. "It would be a way to repay her. You could get out of the house while the girl is here. Your mother wants a cat very badly, and we both know she won't have many more years." I gave her my boyish look. People have said my boyish look is one of my better ones. Something inside me always has screaming fits of laughter when I intentionally become Prince Charming, but I ignore it.

"Well, if you've found someone to clean up after it," Janice agreed at last, unable to withstand boyishness.

Poor Janice. Nellie could probably be a handful on a daily basis. A pair of sharp eyes, a quick mind, and a good appetite, all caught in that aching, immobile body, all of it dependent upon Janice for everything and probably resentful of that. And Janice, her children gone, her husband often away, living in her mother's house, and probably resentful of *that.* Poor Janice.

Mark, with his customary efficiency, had found a girl. She was sixteen years old and wanted to be a nurse. She was indefatigably cheerful and competent and said she liked old folks. Her name was Jeannie Rudolph, she was black, and she lived one block away. For a modest wage Jeannie agreed to stay with Nellie at least twice a week for two to four hours at a time, so Janice got something nice out of it too. So did I. For the first time in years, I could think about Nellie Arpels without feeling guilty.

Jeannie met Nellie in Nellie's room, under my speculative eye, then I opened the carrier, and both Jeannie and Nellie met Sphinx—whose name Nellie promptly changed to Perky with Jeannie's full approval. I hid a shudder, but the cat didn't seem to mind.

Myra Sharp would not be available to read want ads until Christmas week. Until then, the only clues to the current puzzle were George's bank statements and the description of the man Nellie had seen: a man with a gray beard, which could be false. Not enough there to help me at all. This particular puzzle seemed to be stalled. Well, I'd been stalled before.

I'd worried about Sergeant Renard making off with additional items from next door, but I hadn't seen him around the place, and according to Nellie he hadn't been back. Stimson must have told the police why he needed to get into the house, and that had stymied Renard. All very well to take something if no one would know it was missing. It was a little more dangerous to steal something if it was likely to appear on an inventory list.

Mark kept trying, unsuccessfully, to find out who had sold the Whitneys their furniture. Ladislav, Eva, and Snowball settled into the status of permanent houseguests. Myron, in New York, sent a holiday basket from Zabar's, and I retaliated with locally produced honey, jams, and jellies. Not that they were any better than those Myron could buy, but they did have different labels. Mark decorated the showrooms downstairs with poinsettias and azaleas and provided cookies and eggnog for clients. Since "the accident," as I usually refer to the loss of my family, I hadn't really celebrated Christmas. My main acknowledgment of the season was to give Mark and Eugenia sizable bonuses and smaller ones to the cleaning people and the man who comes over to crate shipments. I also provided a special dinner for the attendants at the home and those few patients who knew what they were eating. I didn't intend to visit Jerry on Christmas, but Jerry wouldn't know it or care. Jerry didn't know or care that his father came for lunch every Monday. Jerry lay on a bed, eyes open, mouth drooling, his arms and legs completely immobile. If someone turned him over, he did the same thing face down.

I did plan a brief visit to Jacob on Christmas. When I was a kid, Jacob had made Christmases special. Jacob was Jewish, but he had assumed I wasn't—I'm not circumcised, for one thing—so he'd always played up the secular aspects of the holiday for me: the tree, the gifts. It wouldn't have been Christmas without a visit to Jacob. Except for that, I'd made no plans. There for a short while in the fall I'd thought I might be spending the holidays with Letitia "Chip" Harris, but Chip had gone back to New York and her former husband. "Not that I'm not terribly fond of you, Jason. I am. But you're still too sad." Chip had a sweet, meaningless line of chatter, a gamine face, and a body that invariably brought mine to attention, but Chip wasn't a girl for sad times. Chip wasn't even a girl for a little bit of melancholy. Chip was happiest with a tambourine in one hand and a brimming champagne flute in the other. I sent her flowers, regretting her absence without exactly missing her, if you follow me, and reconciled myself to another Christmas alone.

But then, only days before the holiday, I got a Christmas card from Grace Willis, a rebus-type card with a holly-decked horse and two embracing mice on it which seemed to decode to "Mare-y kiss-mouse."

It's hard to be alone on Christmas, she wrote at the bottom of the card. *If you are alone and want company, so am I, do I.* Both the dreadful card and the message made me grin.

Did I?

Maybe someone to have dinner with? A drink with? But a cop?

And why not a cop? Was I some Clayton Renard who didn't like women cops? My own response to that took some figuring out. I finally decided that cop had nothing to do with it, which I should have known right away. Snobbery had, and I regretted it.

"How about dinner?" I asked her over the phone. "I can't promise any wild pretense at Christmas cheer, but if the weather holds we could drive up toward Estes Park and have a nice dinner at La Chaumière if it's open, or some other place, with a little champagne and one kiss under the mistletoe and that's it."

She laughed. "Thank you for allaying my fears. One kiss under the mistletoe I can manage. What time drive? How fancy a place dinner?"

"Noon. And nice but not fancy." I hung up feeling modestly pleased about the whole thing.

Myra came home for the holidays and was hired to read want ads. Nellie sent a Christmas card saying thank-you-for-the-cat in a wavery old hand. Janice sent a card saying thank you in a firmer hand. I'd seen her a couple of days before, and she had a definite shape. Hair curled. Lipstick. Maybe even some eye shadow.

The shop did its usual runaway business the days before Christmas: wealthy men who didn't know what to get their wives, wealthy wives who didn't know what to get their husbands, and the lovers and mistresses of both; some not-so-wealthy people splurging on something special, looking at me trustfully, like Bela did, saying, Don't let me down, don't sell me something bad or wrong or false. I was careful not to. Jacob had noticed that about me and had laughed, telling me I'd come a long way for a kid who started out as a thief.

Peter Van Doorn came in on Christmas Eve, just as I was about to close.

"Don't tell me you forgot Kitty," I quipped. Van Doorn didn't look well. His face was gray and his eyes were bloodshot and weary.

"Didn't forget. Just haven't had any time," the big man said in a harsh voice. "Would you have a drink you could offer me?"

Eschewing Mark's eggnog, I went upstairs for the scotch. When I came down, Van Doorn was sagged onto a Federal sofa of which I thought highly, not seeming to care that his wet coat was spotting the upholstery. I kept my mouth shut, pulled over a small table, and offered him a drink.

"What have you got I can surprise her with?" Van Doorn begged.

I was familiar enough with Kitty Van Doorn's likes and dislikes to quote him a reasonable price on a pair of carved wood and gilt girandoles. "Dating around 1760," I told him. "They're English, not American, but Kitty won't care. She'll love them."

"I don't know. If you think so. Just so she'll like them." His mouth curved into an uxorious, adoring smile when he spoke of Kitty. It wasn't the first time I'd seen that look on his face. There was no doubt in my mind that he loved her to distraction, and this fact made me give my selection a second look. I'd been honest the first time. The girandoles were gorgeous and she would love them.

"I think she'll be crazy about them, Peter." The mood seemed to call for first names. "Is the price about what you'd planned to spend?"

Van Doorn snorted. "You go through stages, you know? In my life, the worried-about-money stage is over. Money isn't the problem anymore." For the first time I noticed that he'd been drinking before he arrived. "The problem is everybody always making demands, you know?" He gulped at the scotch. "Whatever you give them, it isn't good enough." He gestured angrily. "Like you. You get the best stuff available, right? It's not your fault if somebody wants something that just isn't available."

His tongue tripped over the "available," making a *la-la* in the middle of the word. "Shit."

"Every trade has its problems," I agreed, wondering what Peter Van Doorn's particular trade was. Investments, Kitty had said. Oil and gas. Something that required a lot of entertaining, at least. Kitty had told me they bought the huge new house so they could entertain more.

"Peter likes a lot of people around," she'd said. "I about went crazy down there in Colorado Springs. Nothing but party, all the time, and the house wasn't set up for it, besides being ugly. I told Peter I had to have more space and a little time to myself if he was going to entertain his colonels and his generals every weekend."

"Likes the military, does he?" I'd asked her.

"Oh, shoot, Jason," she'd replied. "Down there, there's nothing but military. Either active or retired. And it's hard for me to get up here to see my mom. She's in a nursing home, and I need to see her more often."

"Peter," I asked, "do you want me to wrap these for you?"

"Sure," he said. "Sure. Wrap 'em up. Send me a bill."

I took my time over the gift wrapping and then carried the cartons to Van Doorn's car, thinking I was doing the man no favor by letting him drive. The cold air seemed to sober him, however, and he was steady on his feet when we got to the limousine with its bar, phone, leather upholstery, and rosewood dash. I put the boxes on the front seat, next to the chauffeur, wondering why I'd thought Peter was driving himself. They weren't heavy. One tenth carved wood and gilt and nine tenths packing. Thank God for Eugenia's plastic worms.

I went back and closed up, ate alone, and went to bed early.

four

Christmas noon I put on my English wool gray flannel—the suit I wear only for special occasions—with a button-down white-on-white shirt and my favorite fake regimental-stripe tie and went to pick up Grace Willis at her apartment house. It turned out to be a bit of a surprise since Grace herself was the landlord.

"I've always coveted that house," I told her, staring out the car window at it while she settled herself. Sitting on a wide corner lot, it was a three-story Victorian brick with original stained glass, elegantly arched windows, and a beautifully understated paint job.

"It looks great on the outside," she admitted. "I got the color scheme out of a book. It doesn't look quite that great inside. It was my grandma's place. I inherited it, sort of. That is, my brother and I did, and if I ever get any money or sell it, I have to pay him off."

"You've divided it up? Into how many units?"

"Four, eventually. I've only got three finished. Two and nine tenths, really. Cops don't make all that much. I spent all the money I inherited to fix the place, but it wasn't enough to finish everything. You'd hate what I did to the bathrooms."

"Not if you tore them out and did them over. I think period bathrooms and kitchens are dreadful, except for some of those massive carved wood toilets and tubs with the marble or ceramic bowls and the wooden surrounds."

"These weren't. Even with bright towels and paint you still had little tiny white tiles with dirty grout, rusty pipes, and tubs with lion feet you couldn't mop around. The only way you could clean under those tubs would be to tie a soapy rag to a ferret and chase him in there."

"Yech," I remarked. "I hate wet ferret."

"That's what I thought," she said happily. "I said authenticity had to give way to cleanliness. My artistic friends—not that I've got many—tell me I ruined the place."

"Tell them to go jump."

"I usually do." She sat back and unbuttoned her coat. "If we're going quite a way, I'll take my coat off. No point staying bundled up in this car." She patted the leather fondly, as though the Mercedes were alive.

"We're going quite a way. Put it in the back seat." I cast a quick look at her out of the corner of my eye. A soft wool skirt, wide leather belt, and sweater that looked like cashmere. Heavy stockings and low-heeled, gleaming shoes. A softly shaped tweed jacket with a gold pin on the lapel. Her silver hair appeared more natural against the muted tweed than it had against the dark jacket I had seen her wearing before. "You look lovely," I said, meaning it, a little surprised at how well dressed she was. "Very appropriate."

"You expected maybe sequins and net stockings?"

I thought about her question, trying to be honest. If she had been Chip, she would have worn net stockings, though maybe not sequins. If it had been Chip, we'd have gone to the closest and most crowded restaurant, where she would have considered the meal a failure if she hadn't seen a least a dozen people she knew. I said, "One doesn't know, does one?"

"Sequins? With this hair? This hair is the hair I was born with, but I have to be careful about it. People seem to think this hair's an advertisement, but the merchandise isn't for sale." She blushed at my chuckle. "I had the advantage of you," she admitted. "I saw you in your home environment."

"I find your home environment fairly nonstereotypical, for a cop."

"Well, I told you I inherited it. Grandma didn't have anybody left but Ron and me, and Ron's in San Francisco, coming out of his closet. Or getting AIDS. Or something." She sounded bitter.

"Now, now. What was it you said about Sergeant Renard?"

"I said he was a bloody bigot. It's different when it's your own brother and you're worried about him. I know gays don't pick being gays; they're born that way. I've read everything I can about it, and I know they don't choose it anymore than someone who's born . . . oh, colorblind or who gets to be seven feet tall. It's all some kind of imbalance of maternal hormones, before they're even born. I know that. My unhappy feelings don't have anything to do with what he is. Just what may happen to him. It's like being bitter about a war. You understand about your father or your brothers being soldiers, but you mind like hell when they get wounded or killed. Or get mentally ill because of all the friends they saw get wounded or killed."

I drove without replying. She was in the mood to get things off her chest, so why interrupt? We were heading north on the turnpike with almost no traffic. The mountains loomed ahead, blue and pristine. For a wonder, the brown cloud which normally hovered chokingly over the city, obscuring the view during most of the winter, had blown away during the morning.

"Where did you learn about interiors?" she asked in a calmer tone, evidently having decided it was time to change the subject.

"That's a long story I can make very short. When I was about twelve, I stole something from a man named Jacob Buchnam. At that time he had an antiques shop over on Colfax. He usually kept the doors locked, but I slipped in when somebody was leaving. I didn't think he saw me. I stole a silver candlestick worth about five hundred dollars. He caught me."

"Caught you and turned you over to the fuzz?" she suggested. "Or called in your parents for a talk?"

"Neither of the above. There weren't any parents. I'd lived in a group home from the time I was three. He didn't call the police, either. He told me he'd hire me and teach me, and next time I'd know enough to steal the vase worth five thousand dollars that had been alongside the candlestick." I laughed as I always do when I remember that. "So I went to work for Jacob Buchnam, after school, then during vacations. He paid my way through college to a graduate degree in fine arts, minor in history. I went into the navy for a couple of years and then worked in a couple of big eastern auction houses during and after the time I got educated."

"Were you orphaned?"

"Damned if I know," I said. The question she had asked no longer hurt me, though it once had. "I was left on the steps of the home when I was three, with a note that said *Take care of this boy. I can't.* I don't remember who left me or why. I had health problems that took about four years to correct, by which time I was considered too old to be adopted." I can't remember the skin grafts, which had undoubtedly been very painful. Still, that pain probably made me the unadoptable brat that I'd been. If I'd been adoptable, I wouldn't have met Jacob. Something to be thankful for.

"Did the note say what your name was?"

"No, but I do know how I got my name. My hair stuck out over my ears, like my ears had tufts, so that gave one of the women at the home the idea to call me Lynx. I was clutching a yellow blanket, so she named me Jason."

"Of the golden fleece."

"Exactly," I said, a little surprised at her handy reference. No one learned mythology anymore. I did because I'd always read everything I could lay hands on.

"And the rest of the story of your life?"

"I got married when I was twenty-six, to Agatha Turning, a girl I'd known at college, where I studied about artists and she studied to be one. After she graduated, she took a job in Washington, D.C., to support herself while she went on studying painting. After I got out of the navy, I had a temporary job at the Smithsonian, and we ran into each other again. We stayed in Washington after we were married, and Agatha kept her job while I worked around, different places. A couple of years later, just after our son was born, Jacob Buchnam called and asked me to come back out here. He'd had a stroke and couldn't keep up with the business. We made an agreement that I'd manage the business and live in the house and he'd get an income from it. That was nine years ago."

I fell silent, remembering my visit with Jacob just this morning. Jacob lives in a pleasant apartment with a full-time male nurse. He is still ticking along, still reading auction catalogues, still inviting me to dinner every week or two, still teaching me things.

"Something happened to your wife?" Grace asked gently.

I took a deep breath and got it out of the way. "The year after we moved here, while I was in New York, my wife disappeared and her car was found wrecked in the mountains. Our son was in the back. He suffered a brain injury. He has never recovered and will never improve. He's at the home I told you about. He's been there for eight years."

Silence. "Ouch," she said at last. "That hurts."

"Not so much anymore. You get used to most things."

"You never get used to that," she said. "I had an uncle who was hurt in an accident. He lived for almost a year, if you can call it that, in a coma, hooked up to all the machines. No brain waves at all. We wished for him to die. It got so we couldn't look at each other, because the whole family wanted him to die."

"So you believe in euthanasia?"

"No, that's killing someone who's alive. My Uncle Bern wasn't alive. I think when the part that makes a person is dead, you just unhook all the machines and you don't feed what's left. You let nature handle it."

I nodded, saddened at her saying what I'd often thought. So many times I'd wanted Jerry to die. "Let's talk about something else. You said your uncle's name was Bern. Scandinavian?"

"Swedish," she said. "Towheads, all of them. That's where

I got the hair. My brother looks more like the other side of the family."

There was silence for a time.

"Tell me about the Whitneys," she said. "Let's solve the murder."

"Ah," I said, surprised. I'd fully intended to talk about the Whitneys, but not so early in the day. "Um. Well, before I do that, tell me something about Sergeant Renard. Is he likely to come up with any answers on this one?" A sidelong look showed her to be considering this, brows raised, lips pursed.

"Not likely," she said at last. "I don't know what's with Renard, to tell you the truth. He's done some good work in the past, everybody tells me. Well, it stands to reason; otherwise they'd have fired him. But now he's just going through the motions. There are at least a dozen things he should have done on this case, and he hasn't done any of them. I don't know what he's thinking about, but it's something else."

"He came close to burning down the Whitney house."

"How?"

"He left both the oven and the coffeepot on over there when he sealed the place up." I braced myself for the inevitable question as to how I knew. It didn't come. She gave me a knowing glance.

"He wouldn't let me near the scene at all. Told me to stay out of the way."

"Did he search the place?"

"I can tell you exactly what he looked for. He looked for drugs and he looked for money. If not money, then something that looked like money. Jewelry. Stolen credit cards. Something that would give him an easy motive for two people getting killed. And that's all he wanted. I can guarantee he never looked at paper. Sometimes I think Clay Renard hasn't looked at the printed word since he took his sergeant's exam. Except maybe the sports pages."

"Do you have any independence from him? Can you do any investigating on your own?"

"Me? Sure. Some. He doesn't like having me around, so if I give him some excuse for me to do something else, he probably wouldn't make any waves. We are assigned to this case, among others."

"Then let me tell you about Nellie Arpels," I said, swinging out to avoid an overloaded station wagon with gaily wrapped packages blocking the rear window.

When I'd finished telling her about what Nellie had seen, she was almost incredulous. "The old woman really saw the guy! I'll be damned. It never occurred to me to think of upstairs windows across the alley. You know, it was Monday morning. All the kids getting ready for school, all the mamas fixing breakfast. I interviewed the people along there myself. Damn. And I've watched the movie, you know, *Rear Window*, at least ten times."

"You asked Janice Fetterling if she saw anything, or if anyone else in the house saw anything, and she said no."

"Right! She said her mother was an invalid—"

I snorted. "Well, that's true. It's not the whole truth, of course."

"I'll go see Nellie tomorrow."

"You might try her with a police artist."

"Yeah, well, there're good police artists and awful police artists, and we've got one of the awful ones right now. He can draw a cow and you'd swear it's a van with legs."

"No talent."

"Our artist only knows straight lines and right angles. So what else do you know?"

"I know the Whitney house is full of valuable antiques. I wouldn't tell Sergeant Renard that. Not that he doesn't know it already."

She gave me another look and asked, "Have you solved the case yet?"

"Should I have?"

"People say you do. Solve things. I've asked about you. You've got a reputation for getting answers to things. That Rogers case a couple of years ago, the one where the man was supposed to have taken sleeping pills; you solved that."

"Balman Rogers was a client of mine," I told her, "and I liked him. I didn't like his wife."

"I guess you had good reason. The Rogers case wasn't the only one."

Puzzles were fine, but they were mine. Other people weren't supposed to horn in on them. I made a face.

She made a face back. "No, honestly! Like I say, you have a reputation! So what are you doing about this case?"

"If I told you what I had done, you might arrest me."

She thought about this for a while, putting two and two together. "Did you steal anything from the Whitney house?"

"Borrowed."

"Have you returned it?"

"Not yet."

"Are you going to?"

I sighed, still coveting the walnut desk box. "Probably." Of course I would. Jacob had taught me to be honest, among other things. That didn't mean I liked it.

"Then I wouldn't arrest you. Worst I'd do is give you a warning. What did you borrow?"

The result of part of what I'd borrowed was in the car. I'd put it there thinking she might be interested. "Reach in the back seat and get that blue folder. You'll find a computer listing of George's bank accounts and checks for the last ten years, in chronological order."

I kept quiet then, concentrating on my driving, letting her look at it. The top sheets listed deposits to George's checking account, going back over ten years. Small deposits at first, always the same amounts, twice a month, obviously salary checks. Then, after about a year, larger and larger deposits at weekly or even semiweekly intervals, in increasing amounts. Then in October, two years before, an abrupt stop to the variable deposits, though the salary checks went on.

"He lost his outside source of income, didn't he?" she said.

"His salary went on—I assume those checks every other week are salary checks."

I agreed. "It looks like he went about eight months last year without anything but salary. And then, the following June . . ."

In June there had been a cluster of deposits, made over a period of four days into three of the accounts. All the individual deposits were less than ten thousand. The total of all deposits was over a hundred thousand dollars.

"Well, well," said Grace, flipping the page. "In early June he hit some kind of jackpot, then nothing until the end of August."

"Twelve weeks. Then thirteen weeks later in late November," I said. "And again fourteen weeks later in February."

"And so on and so on," she said. "Every three months or so."

"The average is closer to thirteen weeks." I'd taken the trouble to figure that out, thinking it might mean something. If it did, I didn't know what, except that thirteen weeks was a quarter of a year.

Grace closed the folder and sat looking out the windshield. "Interesting figures," she said.

"I know what they tell me," I said. "What do they tell you?"

"Well, they tell me that ten years ago George started out small, on salary. The early bank statements look like mine— that is, bigger than mine but just two deposits a month, paychecks only. Then he found a reliable source of additional income, good income, and it got bigger and bigger. There were deposits one or two times a week. None of the deposits were over ten thousand, which could mean he didn't want the government alerted to what was going on, but it was steady money, coming in every few days. That went on until a little over two years ago, and then he had eight months without any income except salary again."

"After which George found a new source."

"Or resurrected the old one," Grace suggested.

"I don't think so. The original money came in constantly, all the time. The new money comes in lumps, four times a year. A different style."

"According to what you have here, he was bringing in around four or five hundred thousand a year before the break and about the same amount after. That's a lot for a man who worked for a religious station. I wonder what he did for it, and what he did with it?"

"He bought furniture with part of it. The house has at least a million dollars' worth of American antiques in it. What he did with the rest of it, he bought a lot of ninety-five-hundred-dollar cashier's checks. I ran a tape. The cashier's checks total over four million."

"Wow," she said softly, leafing through the copies. "What are you going to do with these?"

"Do with what? I never saw those. Detective Grace Willis must have left them in my car. Except for the copy I kept, of course."

"I'll have to go back and doctor my reports," she said. "I forgot to say anything about them." She turned and gave me a shining-eyed look of gratitude.

I felt abruptly happy. Not merely all right or vaguely contented, but happy. I hadn't felt that way in years. I took a deep breath, hoping it wouldn't go away. "Maybe you won't think of looking into George's bank accounts until tomorrow, after you talk to Nellie Arpels," I suggested. "Then you won't have to rewrite anything."

We got to the restaurant about three. We ate duck with brandy sauce, I abstemiously, as is my habit, Grace enormously, as was evidently hers. We drank champagne and kissed once under the mistletoe hanging in the doorway. It was a nice kiss, only gently spiced by lust. I was moving in an enchanted episode of quiet contentment, and I didn't want to disturb it. We drove back to town in humming quiet, the soft fall of snow outside the car windows only serving to separate us further from day-to-day concerns.

"It's been a nice Christmas," she said. "The nicest I've had for a long, long time."

"The nicest," I agreed, not wanting to take her home just yet. "Will you come over to my place for a nightcap? Or would you prefer someplace downtown?"

"My place," she said. "I've got some good brandy. Then you can see if the house is what you thought it was."

I went through her part of the house, approving of almost everything she'd done. I'm no architect, but I can tell good rooms from bad ones. She'd kept the size and shapes of the original rooms and had restored the woodwork. In the kitchen, instead of putting cabinets against windows too low for them, which most remodelers on a budget do, or raising the windows, which is almost invariably a disaster for the looks of the house from outside, she had turned her kitchen around and left the windowed side as a seating area behind the breakfast bar.

"Though I don't know why they call it a breakfast bar," she said, busying herself with the coffeepot. "I eat all my meals here except when I eat in front of the fire."

I pulled the stool close and leaned on the counter. "How many rooms?"

"Four. Living room and kitchen, the old dining room is my bedroom, and there's another little room, unfinished, that used to be part of a back parlor. My bathroom is in the rest of it. Then I've got one apartment on the second floor, and one that's partly on the second floor and the rest in the attic. They're both rented. I made some mistakes at first, got some bad people in. That's one advantage of being a cop, though. That kind don't stay very long when they find out you're a cop."

"And the fourth apartment?"

"It'll take up the rest of the first floor, plus part of the garage. But the garage is full of old furniture, there's no plumbing in there, and I can't afford it yet." She poured the brandy and gave it to me, lifting her own glass in salute. "Unless I find out who murdered the Whitneys. Then maybe I'll get a promotion and a raise."

"Is that how it works? I thought police promotions were all bureaucratic, taking exams, passing them, getting tapped for better jobs as openings came along."

She sighed. "It is. Sometimes I like to pretend it isn't, though. Come on in the other room. I'll make a fire."

We sat before the fire, thighs touching, hands touching.

"Why did you decide to be a cop?" I'd quit thinking about her as a cop. In my mind, she'd assumed some other role, something I wasn't able to define too clearly, certainly not law enforcement.

"Because there wasn't any money for college. Because I had to work at something. Because it always made me mad when people ripped other people off. Because Uncle Bern was a policeman, and I'd been around male policemen sometimes when they weren't too sensitive to crimes against women, and I figured I could do better."

"Do you like it?"

"When I get away from Renard, I'll like it a lot."

"Are you good at it?"

"Sort of. I'll get better."

We drank brandy. Our hands found one another and held on. After a time it seemed natural to touch more closely, more passionately. It wasn't anything I'd made a habit of since Agatha went away. It wasn't anything I'd meant to happen, nothing I'd planned on. After more time yet, it seemed wise to shut the curtains against the night, against eyes, against the world outside, for there was a world happening inside which took all of our attention.

five

Two days after Christmas, Myra brought the results of her research into the office, a few neatly typed pages. Myra is a skinny little girl with short dark brown hair, a little-boy face, and freckles.

"The guy with the hay advertises every week," she said, lolling in the chair by Mark's desk, legs extended as she flipped through her notes with stubby, short-nailed fingers. "The guy with the parrot evidently sold his bird. He ran that ad twice, and then nothing. Same thing with the horse with the stable companions." She shifted her weight to the other hip, stretching her feet even farther in front of her. I was on the window seat behind her, and I wondered how she kept her tenuous contact with the chair.

"OK. That leaves Mrs. Jones and the talking cat and the catnip mice. I thought for a while the mice might be it. They advertised kind of on and off, you know what I mean? Every few weeks there'd be this ad, then nothing. So I called them up and it's this old lady makes the things. She gets a hundred made, she runs an ad. I went out to see her, and she's straight. Weird, but straight. She doesn't want to talk to people, she just wants to make gray velvet mice and sell them all at one time with the least possible fuss. She told me I was a nice girl and to please go away and quit bothering her.

"The talkative cat, I checked out. I called the woman, and I went there, and she still had the cat and she's frantic. She's in an apartment and this cat talks all the time. Loud. Her neighbors are threatening to kill the cat, which is named Sally and is mostly Siamese. So I adopted it." Myra craned her neck around and looked through her eyelashes at me. "It's a business expense, right?"

"Can you keep it at school?" Mark asked doubtfully.

"No. Mom's got it. She's all alone most of the time, and we've got a big yard. The cat can talk all it wants to. Mom won't care, she'll just talk back. Better than talking to herself, and that's what she's been doing since I've been gone."

"That leaves Mrs. Jones," I told her. "I hope you haven't adopted a Weimaraner as well."

Myra shook her head, scrunching her face in concentration, putting one heel on the floor to give herself a bit more purchase on the chair seat. "That leaves Mrs. Jones. And every twelve or thirteen weeks, there's another ad like that. I wrote them down; they're on page three."

I took the sheet from Mark's desk and read it. "Will the person who left the long-haired dachshund at Mrs. Smith's kennel please call." "Mrs. McDonald wishes to talk with owners of Khomodors." With a phone number. And so on. Each ad mentioned a Mrs. someone.

"I called the phone numbers," Myra said, watching my face. "They aren't real numbers."

"Ah. The pattern is found in the use of a woman's name, then."

"Right. Always a Mrs. Somebody. Always in the dog column on Sunday. I checked the Monday papers on the dates following. No ads. Just Sundays."

"You have the dates?"

She handed me a sheet with a list of ads and their dates of publication and I took it into my own office, where I compared it to the dates of the deposits George Whitney had made over the last eighteen months. In each case, the clusters of deposit dates began within two or three days after the ad dates. The ads ran on Sundays, the deposits were never later than Wednesday.

I came back into Mark's office, humming to myself. I like things to link up. This might be a completely phony lead, but I liked the feel of it.

"You're humming," Mark said. "That means Myra found something."

I regarded Myra fondly. "Bonus. I owe you a bonus."

Myra sighed in relief. "God, you know, I thought so, and I went ahead and spent it on Christmas, so if I hadn't of found anything, I'd of been in real trouble."

"Pay her," I told Mark, waving my hand like a magician. "Pay the genius."

"Am I really?" Myra beamed, her little square face squinching in around her slitted eyes. "Am I really?"

"You are really. Next time you need part-time work, call me."

She offered her hand, shook mine with obvious pleasure, got her check from Mark, and sailed away down the stairs, talking to herself. The hallway echoed to the sound of her happy chatter.

"It must run in the family," Mark observed.

"I do it too," I admitted. "I think it has something to do with how we learn. Some learn by reading, some by hearing, some by both. If you read aloud, or explain aloud, the information seems to get where it's going faster. Or neater. Or something."

"You have some such information?" Mark asked.

"Some information about George Whitney. Within three days after each of those ads, George made big deposits into his bank accounts. Myra went back two years; the ads started eighteen months ago."

"Coincidence?"

"If the ads and deposits had been spaced differently, like exactly every thirteen weeks, or on some other regular schedule, I'd have said possible coincidence. But they were spaced sometimes twelve or even fourteen weeks apart, and the deposit intervals varied with the ads. I think coincidence is extremely unlikely."

"When you say 'big deposits,' what do you mean?"

"He had four accounts at three separate banks. His checking account and a joint account with Betty at one bank, a savings account at another, and an investment account at a third.

The investment account buys certificates of deposit and turns them over automatically. You can deposit into it just the way you can a bank account, but there are penalties for withdrawing from it except annually. With me so far? All right. For the last eighteen months, George has been making simultaneous deposits of just under ten thousand into checking, savings, and his investment account, repeated on the following day and then again, as necessary. No individual transaction was more than ten thousand, but the total deposit was a hundred thousand in any given sequence. Around six hundred thousand in the last eighteen months. However, he has also bought a lot of big cashier's checks, and his total balance is only around two hundred thou."

"And his salary?"

"About twenty-five hundred a paycheck. Say around sixty thousand a year."

"So what do you think?"

"So I want to know where he was getting his money. And I'd love to know what he was using it for, besides furniture. He's only spent about a quarter of it on furniture; where's the rest? Diamonds? A Swiss bank account? Money's a pretty good motive for murder, and big money should be a very big motive, don't you think?" I hummed, thinking.

"You're humming again," Mark said.

The office of the New Evangelical World Society was on an upper floor of a remodeled warehouse in lower downtown, one of a row of similar buildings. The turn-of-the-century structures had been sandblasted, their mid-twentieth-century accretions had been removed, new floors and stairs and windows had been inserted. The result produced light, air, and high ceilings at fairly low rents. The Evangelical Society occupied one side of the third floor.

The door was a simple slab with a brass plate identifying the tenants as GOOD NEWS. Half a dozen unmatched chairs stood inside the door before a desk holding nothing but a typewriter and a plastic sign that said RECEPTION. Fronting on the reception space were four small offices made of movable glass-topped partitions; a larger room beyond, where men and women sat opening mail and making entries at computer terminals; and, in the far back corner, a floor-to-ceiling right-angled partition which was unfinished but obviously soundproofed.

One of the male clerks was having a conversation with a short-skirted girl who looked up, made a face, and came toward the reception desk. "I'd like to see your manager," I said. She was a gum-chewing brunette of about seventeen. I hoped my manner conveyed that I was a possible contributor, though it didn't seem likely she would care.

"Mr. Daniel Beeman," she enlightened me, wrinkling her nose.

"Mr. Beeman," I acquiesced.

"Mr. Whitney was our manager," she confided. "But he got killed." She sat down at the typewriter and looked at it as though wondering what it was.

"I read about it." I shook my head, putting on a condoling expression. "It must have been awful for you."

"Not really. He wasn't all that friendly." She chewed for a few moments, blew a small purple bubble, then sucked it in hastily. "That's Mr. Beeman coming in now."

The man who had just come in behind me was solidly built and heavy-footed. He wore horn-rimmed glasses and a belligerent expression. His glare said that he had seen the bubble.

"This man wanted to see you, Mr. Beeman," the girl said hastily, fingering the keys of the typewriter.

I held out my hand. "Robert Argos, Mr. Beeman. I'm here representing a possible contributor to your cause. An elderly woman. She wanted me to check a few things before redoing her will. . . ."

The belligerent expression turned to one of affability. "Why don't we go in my office. Jill, the typewriter will work better if you put some paper in it and turn it on. How about getting us some coffee?"

"The coffee machine broke."

"Oh. Well, would you like a soft drink, Mr.—?"

"Argos. Robert Argos. No, thank you. I had a cup of coffee just moments ago."

"In here, then." He took me into the second of the glass-partitioned offices. It was small and cramped, the desk too large for the space without being large enough to hold what was on it: two calculators, a computer, several ledgers full of computer printouts, plus assorted other papers. Through the glass of the partition, I could see the back and side walls of the larger neighboring office, dotted with familiar-looking pictures of George and Betty holding dogs.

Beeman said, "Forgive the girl. She's the niece of a member of the board. We only promised to try her for a month, and Friday is her last day. I apologize for the clutter, too. Normally, I wouldn't see visitors in this office. Normally, I wouldn't see visitors at all. I'm the comptroller. I'm also acting manager, at least for now."

I weaseled my way into a chair, sucking in to get between the chair and the desk. "You do have tight quarters."

"I'm going to take out this partition between these offices. That will give me some room. Well, what can I do for you?"

I put on my most confiding, serious expression. "Mr. Beeman, my client wishes to give her estate to your cause. However, she does not want to find her name associated with any kind of scandal. First, of course, there was Mr. Whitney's murder. And you're aware of the recent revelations concerning certain evangelists?"

Beeman snorted. "Who isn't! Carnival barkers, most of them! My mother's family was carny, and I swear to God so are most of these so-called evangelists. How any responsible person could give money to some of those jerks is beyond me."

"You understand my client's caution."

"Of course I do. She wants to be sure her money is going where we say it is. She has a perfect right to assurances. And

I'll be frank with you, two years ago I couldn't have given them to her."

"You couldn't?"

"Not when the Society sent me out here to help George Whitney. George was a good manager, don't get me wrong. He did a first-rate job of programming. Sometimes I thought his wife Betty might have helped him some; the stuff sometimes seemed to have a woman's touch."

"Programming?"

"Everything's automated down at the transmitter. It's just a case of playing tapes. You understand?"

I shrugged, indicating that I really didn't.

"George made up the programs. The tapes came in here, and he reviewed them first, for content. NEWS buys almost all of its tapes from producers. You know, preaching, hymns, gospel singing, all that. George listed each tape with the time it was to be played. Then he taped the appeals for funds, back there." He waved toward the soundproofed area against the far wall. "And he scheduled the fund-appeal tapes to be cued in among the others."

"And that's all the Society is? A transmitter putting out tapes and fund appeals?"

"Oh, Lord, no! I didn't mean to give you that impression. No, there's a board of directors, and Reverend Allnight, he's the executive director, and his staff—they translate material into Spanish and into Portuguese for broadcast—plus the people working in the missions themselves. In addition to the tapes we buy, we broadcast taped reports from overseas and messages from Reverend Allnight and from other clergy members of the board. The board is the group that hired me. They're who hired George."

"Where do they hang out?" I looked around. There was no room for a board of directors to meet.

"In Houston. Near where the transmitter is."

"Then why is the office here?"

"It's cheaper here." Beeman nodded. "Texas was oil boom

country when the Society was set up. You couldn't rent space, you couldn't get workers. Here, you can get everything at about half to two thirds the cost. Wages aren't as high. Rent is comparatively cheap. Economically, it makes good sense to keep the office here."

"I see." I gave him one of my charming smiles. "You were saying you couldn't have given me any assurances two years ago."

"A little over two years. No, I couldn't have assured you of anything because the controls just weren't there. As I said, George was a good programming man, but he didn't know anything at all about accounting. Accountability, maybe I should say. Quite frankly, I think some of the employees were ripping him off."

"Why would you think that?"

"Well, we know a lot about the kind of people who respond to appeals like ours. I can tell you the average age, what sex, the religious background, the average amount, and how often the contributor will send a gift. We know, for example, that about fifteen percent of the contributions come from anonymous sources. That's true across the industry."

"Industry?"

"Well, that's accountants' talk. Money is money, and you handle God's money just the way a bank does—or you should. Anyhow, in response to broadcast appeal for funds, fifteen percent of the gifts come from people who don't want to be thanked or who don't want to be put on a mailing list. Anyhow, the reports George sent to the board indicated that only about five percent of the contributions were coming from anonymous sources. Which probably meant that someone was taking the money before it ever got recorded."

"I see."

"I can't assert that positively, but, as I said, the controls were sloppy. So the board hired me and sent me up here to help George out."

"A little over two years ago."

"Right." Beeman wiped his brow with a crumpled hand-kerchief and waved at the clutter before him. "It's taken a while, but the figures are where they ought to be, everything is properly controlled and separated, contributions are up, and George was feeling really good about it all. At first he was upset, you know? Thinking that some of his trusted employees hadn't been really trustworthy. That's upsetting for anyone. But after eight or nine months, when I started to get the controls working, he was very pleased. He deserved to have some time without problems." He shook his head, running one hand across the open pages before him, stroking them. "Especially the way he stepped in here when his predecessor died—on a moment's notice. It's a pity George died when he did. Things were really shaping up."

"Do you know how much was missing?"

He frowned, pursed his lips, and made thumping noises with his fingers on the edge of the desk.

"Can I guess?" I asked him gently. "Somewhere in the millions, maybe?"

He let out his breath in an exasperated sigh. "I do hope not. Possibly a lot less than that."

"Or possibly more?"

He frowned at his desk, not answering.

"Did you find out who was stealing?"

"Oh, hell, no. I'm sorry. Strike that. That kind of language doesn't go around here." He wiped his forehead and bit his lip. "It's so frustrating!"

"I take it you're not one of the . . . what do they say? Born again?"

"No, I'm not. I almost didn't get the job on that account, but the board chairman is a banker, and he said it was more important to get someone qualified to handle money problems than somebody with the right religion. He told me there was nothing wrong with the religion up here, just with the money, so they needed a money man to handle it."

"You said you didn't find out who . . ."

Beeman leaned forward earnestly, waving his finger at me. "I can't even prove *if,* much less *who.* How do you prove anonymous donations are missing? Somebody goes through the mail, takes all the envelopes with no return address, opens them, takes out the money, destroys the envelopes. How do you know?"

"There's no receipt."

"There's a contribution receipt form, but if you don't fill it out in the first place, who knows what disappears?"

"How have you stopped it?"

"Now the mail comes to a sort desk. Two people sort mail. The envelopes with no return address are counted and come into one of these offices and are opened by two employees, each checking the other. Each envelope has the amount noted on it, and those envelopes serve as a preliminary accounting tool. The envelopes come out of the room. Someone outside the room runs another tape, from the envelopes, and the tape has to agree with the one in the counting room. The room is glass, so even the counting is observed. No wastebaskets, no purses, no way to smuggle money out. We do more or less the same thing with named contributors, but there we have a receipt copy."

"And you instituted that change when?"

"The week after I got here. There was no trick to it. Accountants learn how to double-check cash, along with double-entry and cost-center accounting and all the rest of it. That isn't what took the time. What took the time was getting in a decent computer system, because the one they had was an invitation to steal. It couldn't put two and two together and get four twice in a row." He got up from the chair. "Take a quick tour around the office, five minutes?"

I went, without protest. I saw the mail openers, working in pairs. I saw the computer and heard Beeman talk jargon about how it worked. I saw the soundproofed studio in the back corner where George had recorded his fund-raising appeals. The recorders in the studio looked exactly like the one I'd seen in the Whitney house, with the same huge reels.

"Did he ever do any of this at home?" I asked.

"I don't think so," Beeman answered, looking puzzled. "Why would he? He had everything he needed right here."

"Well, my client's money would seem to be protected at this end." I patted his shoulder as he led me back to his office. "Now let's talk about what it does for the missions."

After learning a good deal more about evangelism in Latin America than I had ever cared to know, I took myself to lunch at the Rattlesnake Grill. I ordered lamb chops and artichoke salad without looking at the menu and told Bert to bring me a half bottle of whatever he thought would go well with that. I wanted to think about my puzzle.

George had been ripping off the New World Evangelical Society; so much was clear. The bank statements indicated he had skimmed off at least four million dollars. George had stopped ripping off the Society the moment Mr. Beeman had arrived. George had been, said Beeman, very upset. I could imagine how upset. Thereafter, George could not have resurrected his old source of income. The controls were still in place, and the figures were where they ought to be, said Beeman, and Beeman ought to know.

But, after eight or nine months, George had found a new source of income. Beeman had noticed that George was feeling better. So, what had George been up to recently? Something that made someone place an ad every three months or so, something that tied that ad to the receipt of four hundred thousand a year.

Did George place the ad? Or someone else? I sipped at the wine, hoping it would inspire me.

If George placed the ad, the ad was meant to say "I want money" or "Deliver the money."

I cut a chunk of artichoke bottom and dipped it in curried mayonnaise. It could take even a wealthy man a few days to

get together a hundred thousand in cash. But the longest inter-
val between running the ad and depositing the money had been
three days. Mostly the intervals were shorter than that. It was
unlikely that anyone could lay his hands on a hundred thousand dollars in less than two days, particularly since the first
day was Sunday. So the ad probably wasn't a demand for
money.

But if you looked at it the other way, the ad could be a
response to the money request. Let's say somebody told the
victim, "Every three months, you pay me a hundred thousand.
Every three months you run an ad telling me you've got the
money." Then, roughly every three months the victim ran the
ad, at which point all George had to do was arrange for delivery, which wouldn't take more than two days.

It made more sense that way.

It made more sense particularly if you considered what
reason anyone might have for giving George money. It was
very unlikely that anyone owed him four hundred thou a year.
Blackmail made the most sense. George had something on
someone, and George had been squeezing.

"Something wrong, Mr. Lynx?" Bert, the waiter, was standing by my table looking concerned.

"Everything's fine, Bert. Didn't I look like I was enjoying
lunch?"

"You looked as though you weren't tasting it."

"I was thinking about a current project. Say, Bert, can you
find out if I'm too late to make a reservation for two in the
Rattlesnake Club on New Year's Eve. Say about nine?"

He shook his head at me. The Club was a very different
matter from the Grill, and I knew it. "I'll ask Emil," he said.
"Will you be needing anything special?"

"Whatever's on the menu will be fine."

Bert gave me a tiny bow and went away. I refilled my
wineglass. Where was I? Oh, yes, George would pick up the
cash, take it home, and make a series of deposits.

And then George bought cashier's checks. Did he buy furniture with them or did he send them somewhere, like to a Swiss account? I got out my notebook and jotted down a few questions.

1. Furniture bought with checks or cash, from whom? And why furniture?
2. Furniture only amounts to one million. Where is rest of money?
3. How come auto accident, bomb, gun?

I finished the wine, received a message that I could be squeezed in on New Year's Eve, waved away the pastry cart, and then, on second thought, summoned Bert back.

"Can you give me two chocolate eclairs to go?" I asked him. "I'm calling on a lady."

While I waited I added two final points to the list.

4. Ask Mark to check want ads.
5. Did blackmail victim always know who George was, or did he find out just recently?

Nellie finished her eclair with a little sigh. "My, that was good." She handed me the little flowered plate Janice had sent upstairs. Janice had put her own eclair in the refrigerator for "later." I put the plate outside on the table in the hall.

"Reminds me of when Agatha used to come," Nellie was saying. "She used to bring me things to eat."

"I know," I said, remembering orange bread and cookies still warm from the oven and a fantastic pastry made from walnuts and filo dough and honey.

"I told you about her being here, the morning she disappeared?"

I felt the blood leaving my face. I've read about that, but I'd never felt it before. It felt like a bathtub drain had opened in my neck somewhere and my brain was flowing away through it. "Yes, Nellie, you did."

"She just came over, like she always did, to bring me some hot coffee cake she'd just baked. She showed me that locket you gave her for her birthday, the heart with the four-leaf clover on it. Just that morning she'd put a picture of you in it, and one of the baby. She showed me the pictures; then she put it back around her neck, proud as a cock rooster on Easter morning."

I turned away, swallowing, trying to get some function back. So Agatha had come over to show her the new locket. I'd made a little tradition out of giving her gold for her birthdays or on our anniversaries. Because gold never tarnishes, I'd told her. Because it always shines. Like our love. Like our marriage.

"I'm sorry," Nellie whispered from behind me. "I didn't mean to make you sad."

"It does make me sad," I admitted, still gulping for air.

"You're alone too much," she said. "You need to meet some nice woman."

"I've met some nice women." None of them had been Agatha.

Nellie didn't disagree. "Agatha was special," she said, snapping her fingers at the cat. The cat uncoiled itself, looked at me with ageless Egyptian eyes, and jumped into Nellie's lap as though to say, You see, I know my job.

"Agatha was special, but you should still find somebody, Jason. There are other special people out there, I know it. I was in love once, oh, Lord, so long ago I've more than half forgotten it. Sixty years, would you believe? He left me for a flapper with skirts so short you could see her behind. I thought there wouldn't be anyone else, but then, here in a couple of years came Mr. Arpels, and he was about the best man in the world."

"There may be someone," I said, thinking of Grace Willis. I'd sent flowers. I hadn't called her, though. Christmas day and night had been touched with something out of the ordinary, something miraculous from my point of view. There had been women since Agatha. There had even been laughter and good times and sex. But there hadn't been any of that quiet happiness I'd had with Grace. I hadn't wanted to call her for fear it would all fall apart into a lot of ordinary pieces. "There may be someone, somewhere," I said again, feeling guilty.

"Well, you have to look," she said. "Don't count on the good Lord to do it for you." She rubbed the cat's fur the wrong way, then smoothed it. The cat began to purr, loudly, ostentatiously, watching to see if I approved. "Did you just come by to bring me dessert?" Nellie asked.

"I came to ask if the police had been to see you."

"A nice girl policeman came yesterday. She did. I told her everything, who came and who went. All except a certain person going in and out through the doggie door. I didn't say anything about that."

"That's kind of you, Nellie."

"I did tell her about the other policeman, though. Even though you said not, I figured she wasn't in on it. I told about that other policeman taking something. She didn't seem real surprised."

"What did she say about that?"

"She said there wasn't much she could do. She didn't know what he took, and neither did I, so it was only my word that he was carrying something."

"That's right, Nellie. Don't worry about it. The matter will take care of itself. Now, listen to me. If a policeman by the name of Renard wants to talk to you, you just say you feel too frail, all right?"

"Is he the bad one?"

"He's the bad one. I'll tell Janice."

"She's been better lately, Janice has. She goes to movies and everything, now that Jeannie comes over."

"Why didn't she go before?"

"I told her over and over she could, but she wouldn't leave me here alone in case the house caught afire. And she wouldn't hire anyone in case she made a mistake and they took the silver, because she said Bruno would yell at her if she did. Bruno's my son-in-law."

I felt my lips quirking. "What would Jeannie do if the house caught fire?"

"She says she'd push the mattress out the window and drop me on it. She got it all figured out the first day she came."

"She's a smart girl."

"I like her," Nellie said, contentedly stroking the cat. "I like her a lot."

six

When I got back to the house, I knew I had to call Grace Willis. I wanted to see her again, and yet I didn't. If I did call, she would expect . . . and if I didn't, she would feel. . . .

Agatha had told me a lot about women's expectations and their feelings—their joys, frustrations, lusts, and guilts. So much, really, like men's joys, frustrations, lusts, and guilts. Except that men weren't supposed to admit the guilts and women weren't allowed to admit the lusts, and polite society frowned on either sex shrieking in happiness or bellowing at the constant stumbling blocks the world threw in their way. Agatha had told me that the closer people were to one another, the more often their feelings were hidden and their expectations were silent, but that these had to be assumed and acted upon anyhow.

They had to be, especially, when connected with that small handful of people who had a right to expectations and feelings where I was concerned: Jacob; Mark; Bruce Norman, my roommate from college; Mrs. Lear, the cottage supervisor at the Home, the nearest thing I'd ever had to a mother; William Sandiman, at the Smithsonian; Eugenia, probably; and now, perhaps, Grace.

Perhaps Grace. The words hung in my mind, making a line of poetry. Forgetfulness will come, and perhaps grace. I used to write poetry, more as a hobby than anything else. I'd given it up after Agatha's disappearance.

Around and around again. Should I call Grace or not? . . .

"I was going to call you," she said when I phoned. "I wanted to talk about the Whitney murder."

So much for feminine feelings! So much for sexual expectations. I laughed at myself. So much for guilt and lust, Jason. The girl wants to talk about murder.

I suggested she come over to the office.

"Can't," she said. "Renard has me buried behind this stack of records. He seems determined to keep me from doing anything about the Whitney case. All these records have to be done by the end of the year, and it'll take me every minute of that, and he's being an absolute bastard about it. Honestly, Jason, he's being really strange!"

"So when *are* you doing anything about the Whitneys?"

"On my own time, I guess. Such as it is. Tell you what. If you can make it to Enrico McGee's by five, I'll buy you a beer and pick your brain, but I've only got an hour, because Ron is coming in tonight from San Francisco, and I have to pick him up at the airport at seven."

"Your brother Ron?"

"The one and only. He needs money. He always needs money." She sounded momentarily depressed. "Anyhow, I've got an idea, so I'll see you at five."

At four I showered and changed. Forty-five minutes later I was sitting on the balcony at Enrico McGee's, looking down through the branches of the trees under the skylight at the madness called "Happy Hour." State law no longer permitted offering two drinks for the price of one. State law said nothing about the offering of free or incredibly cheap food, however, and McGee's was doing a brisk business in dollar plates of baron of beef and free tacos. I saw Grace come in and watched her for a few moments, trying to look through my visual impression of her to the real person beneath. What I saw was a cotton-headed waif, booted and scarved like a hundred others, her small face a little pinched from the cold. She looked up, saw me, and lighted up like a beacon. Something rusty inside me turned and creaked.

"I saw Nellie," she bubbled when we had ordered drinks and she had fetched herself a small plate heaped with tacos. "Did she tell you? That made the week. I got my report in and the lieutenant read it. Since he couldn't find any drugs, Renard's putting the whole thing down to religious fanatics, but it doesn't feel to me like a religious thing, does it to you?" She bit a taco in half, sauce dripping from her chin.

I shrugged. "I'm no expert in that field, Grace."

"Oh, I know. It's just . . . I know what it looks like to me." She scooped a double handful of popcorn from the bowl on the table and vacuumed it up like the front end of a snowblower.

"And what's that?"

"Blackmail! Oh, not at first. No, I think at first he was skimming off contributions. A lot of those religious broadcast shows are raking in the money and won't spend a dime of it on trained people." She wiped her chin on her cocktail napkin and looked resentfully at the empty plate.

"How do you know that?" I regarded her with astonishment. "Have you been down to his office?"

"No, not yet. No time. No, I know how they work. I had an uncle who was an evangelist. My mother's sister's husband. He'd pass the plate for the starving, and if it came back full, he'd send ten percent to the hungry and buy a new car with the rest. He paid his help starvation wages, and when they couldn't pay their bills, he prayed with them. Don't tell me. I know all about people like him. Only thing I can't figure out is why George stopped."

"He stopped because he had to," I told her, giving her an account of my visit to the New Evangelical World Society. "I think we can take it as a given that George was stealing from the till. Or, I should say, before it ever got into the till. When Beeman came, it had to stop. George would have been caught in a moment. There was a period of eight months with no extra income at all."

Grace waved the empty popcorn bowl at a passing waitress and received a full one in exchange. "And then, *powie!* something new. It has to be blackmail, Jason. And it has to be a very, very wealthy victim. Old George was pulling in lots and lots of money."

"Of course, there might have been more than one victim. I need to tell you about the want ads." I told her about catnip mice and Mrs. Jones, beginning to feel expansive and warm. She giggled and got another plate of tacos.

In the midst of our enjoyment she looked at her watch and groaned. "Got to go, Jason. Listen. I wasn't going to ask you, but I will, because you're honest and you'll tell me if the stuff is worthless, OK? Ron needs some money. I've already got the biggest mortgage on the house I can afford, and I don't want to sell the house. Grandma's furniture is still out in the garage. Would you come see if it's worth anything? Please? Maybe later this week?" She gave me time to nod before she was off, waving to me. I hadn't had a chance to ask her to dinner on New Year's Eve.

When I called her the next morning she told me she couldn't spend New Year's Eve with me. "It's Ron," she said. "He's too sad. He's decided to stay here with me for a few days. He's had so many of his friends die. I can't go off and leave him on New Year's Eve. You know."

I told her I knew. I should have called her before.

"You should have called her before, love," said the ghost, surprising me. I turned around, actually expecting to see her.

So on New Year's Eve I had dinner with Jacob, filling him in on the current puzzle.

"A William and Mary slant-top desk box," Jacob said. "I sold only one in all the years I was in business, and it was plain walnut, and the key surround was missing." Jacob was well rested. He was talking clearly and even looking well.

I described it, the base, the hinging, the glossy curves of the ball feet.

"What's it like inside?" His old eyes were bright with curiosity, and he leaned forward, wanting to know.

"Jacob, I never saw the inside. The thing is locked."

"Locked!" Somehow Jacob managed the "k" sound which gave him trouble when he was tired. "If I've told you once, I've told you a hundred times." He sighed in exasperation.

Jacob had said that picking locks was part of the trade. You couldn't sell them if you couldn't see them, so you had to open them, he'd told me. Old pieces were often locked. The owners had locked up their secrets and then hidden the keys. Later they'd died or been carted off to nursing homes.

"Open it, Jason. Bring it tomorrow and let me see it."

When I got home, I went down to the basement to fetch the box from the locked storeroom where I'd hidden it. It was almost midnight when I got it upstairs. My lock picks were in the chest in the living room, so I carried the box there and put it on the table in front of the fireplace. I broke out a chilled bottle of champagne and brought that in, then turned on the classical music station and built a fire. The occasion called for ambience.

With firelight on one side and lamplight on the other and a cold glass sitting at my elbow, I opened the leather flap of the case and began playing with the lock picks. I hadn't had to use them in over a year. The old lock was rusty, too. Unused for a long time.

I fiddled, the old tumbler clicking but not releasing. Then, at last, it *chunked* into place. I put the lock pick away first, delaying the moment, then lifted the lid.

The inside of the box had been painted. Old paint, faintly crackled by long time, that unmistakable crackle which really can't be successfully counterfeited. A soft blue. At the back of the box were two tiny drawers, and I just sat there, staring at them. I'd never seen a box of this type with drawers. But there they were, made of the same wood, their drawer fronts painted with the same paint, aged to the same degree, the edges showing the same amount of wear, the dovetailing at the corners in the same proportions as those joining the corners of the box itself.

The knobs were brass. I tugged at one of them, feeling the

reluctant slide of wood slightly swollen. The basement was humidified to keep old wood from cracking. Probably the drawer had picked up a little moisture. I tugged again, feeling it slide free.

Inside was a crumple of paper. I fished it out, feeling something solid wrapped inside. I unfolded it with one hand while picking up my glass with the other, sipping, unfolding, getting the thing out so I could see it, picking it up.

A locket and a gold chain.

I held that locket in my hand for a full minute before my eyes reported to my brain what they were seeing.

An old piece. Gold. A heart shape with diamonds set in a four-leaf clover, for luck. I'd spent weeks shopping for it, eight years ago. My thumb found the slit at the side and opened it.

Inside, a picture of me and one of Jerry, eight-month-old Jerry, grinning at the camera. I turned it over. On the back, the engraving: *To Agatha. All my love forever. Jason.*

It was the locket Nellie Arpels said Agatha had been wearing the day she had vanished. The locket which should have been up there, in the mountains, where the wreck had been. Or on her body, somewhere. Wherever she was. But the locket was here. Here. In this three-hundred-year-old box where it had no right, no business, no sense in being. I moved suddenly in a spasm of anger so deep and hot that it immobilized me, knocking the champagne glass to the hearth, where it shattered into diamond glitters in the firelight.

"Agatha!" I cried her name, feeling it all again, everything I had felt when I had lost her first, all the loss I had felt in all the years since then. "Agatha."

seven

Twelve years ago I'd been on my way to an appointment at the National Gallery when I'd seen a familiar pair of ears standing outside an exhibit of eighteenth-century painters. I'd stopped to peer at these familiar things my eyes had picked out among all those strangers, and then I was pushing through the crowd to touch the person with the ears and ask, "Aren't you Agatha Turning?"

She had spun almost into my arms, startled, the surprise passing as she smiled one of her open-mouthed, delighted smiles. "Jason. Jason Lynx. What are you doing here?"

I'd known her at school, though not well. I remembered her tightly curled little ears. It's a quirk with me to notice ears. My own left ear is a mess, has always been. Burned, the doctors said, when I was an infant, along with part of my head. Agatha's ears were perfect, the little lobes barely pendulous, not pierced, as sweetly pink as a baby's kiss, with a funny little pointy twist at the top. It was the ears I'd recognized. If she had had her hair down that day . . .

Sitting across the table from her, after that accidental meeting, I inventoried the rest of her, lost in the wonder of having recognized the part and missed the whole. I never thought of Agatha as beautiful. She was unusual looking. Extraordinary. Her forehead was low and broad with wavy light-brown hair sweeping up from it like grass in the wind. In the weeks that followed I saw her hair sometimes coiled into a topknot, sometimes braided down the back and tied with bright ribbons, sometimes curled and falling loose like a mane. She liked to fool with her hair, and with her eye makeup and her contact lenses. She had four pair of contacts in different colors. She looked different every time I saw her. It was like taking out a chorus line, all those different girls, but each one had the same empathy, the same immediate perceptions where I was concerned.

However extravagant she was with her makeup and hair, she didn't care that much for clothes. She wore her clothes over and over again. She told me that she bought only a few things and wore them constantly until she wore them out. "My head may be different three times a week, but my body always feels the same. I hate fashion," she said. "I hate thinking I have to look this way this year and some other way next year when I don't feel that way at all. When I wear a skirt, I like to feel it lashing around my legs, like a tail. I don't want it up around my bottom! When I wear pants, I want them to be soft and warm or skinny and cool, not gathered or cuffed or high-waisted or any of that garbage."

"You're an iconoclast," I accused her. "If all women were like you, the fashion industry would go broke."

"Let it," she said. "Mostly it's men, anyhow. I hate it when men tell women how they ought to look. I think women's shoe designers ought to be shot."

"I like the way you look," I offered.

"Oh, well, you." She'd snorted. "What do you know. If I were a piece of furniture, you'd know, but otherwise . . ."

After only a few dates, we found ourselves spending most of our free time together, but neither of us suggested living together. It was as though each of us needed a personal world to retreat to, even though neither of us used it much. Our increasing intimacy didn't bother Agatha, though it sometimes scared me to death. Scared me, delighted me, appalled me. She didn't even mind if I watched her painting, something as private and painful as I'd always thought giving birth must be.

"Where do you see that color blue?" I asked her. "I can't see it."

"I don't see it," she replied. "I feel it. What I see isn't always everything that's there. Isn't it that way with antiques? Is what you see all that's there?"

It wasn't. Often what one could see was the least part of what was there.

"You're an example," she had gone on. "What I see when I look at you isn't even half of what you are."

After we'd known each other for a few months, she painted my portrait. The narrow-faced man was in it, the one with the hard mouth. The bald little boy was there, as well as several other people too, dreaming, drifting, hiding. All wrapped up in the mirror stranger himself, with the mahogany hair and the strange almost yellow eyes. How had she known? I'd never told her.

"You ought to do portraits," I said, in awe.

She shook her head. "People wouldn't like it. I couldn't do you, either, if I didn't know you so well. Most people I don't know nearly that well."

And that was true, too. Many people she didn't see at all. Panhandlers on the street, she didn't see. "Why did you give him five dollars?" I asked her once about a shaking-handed, red-nosed toper who had been barely able to articulate his request for funds. "He'll just stay drunk with it."

"Oh, really, Jason? Do you think he drinks?"

I thought she was joking, thought she was being funny. She wasn't. She really did not see. It was almost as though she chose who to see and who not. She saw me. She saw a few people she knew as friends. Later, Nellie Arpels, Jacob, others would become friends, but some people she didn't see at all.

I'd worry about that sometimes. It left her so vulnerable. There was so much of the world she did not comprehend. She could hear its voices without understanding them, and the ugliness passed unnoticed.

"Don't you get tired of Betty's gabble?" I asked her.

"Gabble? I guess I don't listen."

"You always hear me, for heaven's sake?"

"Oh, Jason, even at school, I knew who you were. I've always heard you."

She took the apartment on Hyde Street, which Jacob had

furnished casually with castoffs and things he hadn't been able to sell, and in just a few months she made it warm and intimate and comforting. She sewed the curtains herself and made the coverlets for the beds. She upholstered the wicker chairs in our bedroom. She picked the rugs and the pictures. Though we had less than a year there together, when I look around I see her in every corner of it.

I proposed to her in Washington, in the Natural History Museum next to the towering skeleton of the Irish elk. Later I wondered what had possessed me. At the time I'd perceived it as a symbol of continuity—ages on ages focusing on the two of us in that echoing room where only brass railings separated men from time past. She had cried out in surprise, drawing away from me. A guard had started toward us, threateningly, and she had laughed, waving him away.

"He thought you were molesting me," she said. "He thought I was being abused."

"Well, perhaps I will," I said, suddenly terrified by the commitment I was making. "How do you know I won't? Perhaps marriage is an abuse."

"With some people, maybe. Not you."

The police had asked if I'd ever abused her. Was there any reason for her to run away? Was there any reason for her to abandon her child? No reason. Nothing. It had even been a joke between us. "When are you going to start abusing me, Jason?"

"Along about Halloween. I'm planning to shut you up in a pumpkin shell." And if only I had. In something safe.

We were married in September. Almost as though he knew we needed it, Jacob sent a check.

"He's the loveliest man," she bubbled. "He wrote me the nicest letter."

Sometimes she would come home weary.

"What have you been doing all day?"

"Filing damned photographs, with cross-references. Typing damned file cards."

"I wouldn't think the FBI would have enough photographs to keep you busy full time."

"There are several of us photo-file clerks. Would you believe it? And all we do all day is file faces."

"It sounds boring."

"If it were boring, I wouldn't get so tired. If I could ignore them, I wouldn't get tired. But I have to see them. All those people."

"Who are they pictures of? If I'm allowed to ask?"

"Pictures of people at demonstrations. Pictures of people at meetings. Pictures the CIA sends over, or Army Intelligence, or the British or Israeli intelligence people. Pictures of people in other countries doing incomprehensible things."

"Wow!" I said, miming awe. "My wife files spies."

"Spies? Do you think they are? Really?"

I spent hours trying to figure out how Agatha could be blind to people she saw in the flesh, and yet she couldn't forget photographed faces. Maybe with real people their humanity got in her way. Photographed people had no failings. They just were.

Two years later, Jerry was born. She planned to take only two months' maternity leave and then go back to the Bureau.

"Jerry sleeps all the time," she had said. "Except when he's eating, he's asleep. I'm eligible for free child care, and we need the money, Jase."

Which was true. She had medical benefits that paid for the doctor, the hospital, the pediatrician, but there were other expenses. Painting lessons and supplies and books. Rent and heat and lights and water. Food. More or less in that order.

But then Jacob had written, or rather, his attorney had written for Jacob—and a month later all three of us came back to my boyhood hometown.

"You won't mind?" I'd asked her. "Leaving the East Coast? "It may be harder for you to become established in your career."

And she had laughed and said that her career could wait for a while.

On her birthday in June, I had given her the locket. Five days later, she was gone. Now I held the locket tight in my fist and counted the days of our marriage: three years and a few days. The days of Jerry's life: nine months, after which Jerry didn't really exist anymore. The days of my own life: thirty-eight years. I would probably live forever, and I was not that sure I wanted to live without Agatha, not at all.

The New Year came in with Beethoven's Ninth from the local PBS station and a raucous explosion of shouting and singing from the street. I heard it through a fog of memory, a meaningless noise. The symphony went on to its culmination. I heard the grandfather clock in the showroom run through its chimes at one o'clock. The sounds of celebration had given way to a simple, repeated noise. The front doorbell, ringing insistently. I tried to ignore it and could not. I thrust the locket into my pocket and went down.

It was Grace Willis, brushing snow from her eyelashes when I opened the door.

"Surprise, surprise," I said, trying to smile and making a mess of it. I didn't want her. I didn't want anyone.

She stood in the door in her heavy coat and boots, looking puzzled. "Can I come in?"

I stood aside, letting her in. "I thought you were spending New Year's Eve with your brother."

"He went out with friends, people he knew from school when he lived here." She blushed. "He didn't even tell me until this afternoon. I had thought—well, you know what I thought. I passed up dinner with you because of him. I thought he came home because he needed me." She closed the door behind herself. "He needs me, but not to be with. So I called some friends, and they were having dinner at the Painted Cow, so I joined them, and we drank and blew horns and sang 'Auld Lang Syne.' Then when we came out, I said goodbye to them and watched them drive off before I found out my car had a flat and my spare's at home, because I took it out so I could use the trunk to move stuff."

"So you thought of me."

"Well, I looked and saw lights upstairs, so I figured you were up if you were home and I could at least use your phone. There was only one phone at the restaurant, and this guy was on it talking to his girlfriend in Los Angeles. The way it sounded, he was going to be there awhile. If you're busy or have guests, I'll go right away."

If I had guests. I had. A guest, if a ghost could be called a guest. Agatha. Every memory suppressed, every moment stored away beyond recall, every touch, every look had come back in one towering wave. Oh, yes. I had a guest, a phantom lover. And how to say that?

"I'm afraid I wouldn't be good company tonight," I told her, trying to sound natural. "So I won't ask you to stay, but I will drive you home. I'll come over tomorrow and we'll fetch your spare."

"Something's wrong," she said.

I ignored that. "Would you like some champagne while I'm getting my coat?"

"Really wrong," she said, sitting down on the stairs. "If you'll let me use your phone, I'll call a cab."

"I'll take you home." I went away to get my coat, away into that grief world I thought I'd left for good. Agatha. Jerry. Wife. Son. Gone, my mind kept saying, like a mantra. Gone, gone, gone. There wasn't anyone in that world but me and the ghosts. There was no room in it for this person, what's-her-name. Still, I had to take her home. There were certain things civilized people just did.

I didn't say a word on the way. She looked at me and said nothing either. I knew my face was rigid. I could feel it. We went in silence.

"I'll see you in," I said, ignoring her protests. I scarcely heard them.

I went inside with her, to help her with her coat. There were glowing coals in the fireplace but the room was cold. I went to put a log on the fire for her, still in my overcoat and boots. I leaned down over the small flames rising, and the grief came up and took me so I couldn't get up again.

"Jason, Jason," Grace was saying, holding me while I cried. "Jason. Tell me. It's all right, tell me."

I said something, sobbed something. Mystery. Horror. A person lost. The tears ran down my face and I couldn't stop. A person lost who had, perhaps, not been lost in that way at all. I laid the locket on the table in front of her. "Nellie says she was wearing it that morning."

"And it was inside this desk thing? Wrapped up in some paper?"

"Wrapped up in some paper. Inside the drawer. Inside the desk box. Which was locked."

"God. How did the Whitneys get it?"

"I don't know," I cried. "God, Grace, I don't know."

"I don't suppose it could have been there without their knowing?"

"How? Was it there when they bought the piece? That would be carrying coincidence too far. No." I wiped my face, stood up, took a deep breath. "Somehow, Agatha's locket ended up at George and Betty Whitney's on the day she disappeared. Which means that Agatha ended up there too. She wouldn't have lost the locket. Look at it. The chain isn't broken, the catch works perfectly."

"But the car . . . the car was found up in the mountains."

"Anyone can drive a car. She didn't have to drive it."

"And your son?"

"I don't know, Grace. I don't know. I need to know, God how I need to know, but I don't."

"Shhh, take it easy," she murmured, rubbing my neck, massaging my shoulders, as unself-conscious about it as an old friend, as kin. "Part of the problem we have is that you keep thinking of them as good old George and good old Betty. We have to remember this was George the embezzler. George the blackmailer."

I put my head in my hands, trying hard to be sensible. "The only picture I have of Betty is with a blue ribbon in one hand and a dog leash in the other."

"Who were they, really?"

"What do you mean?"

"I mean, who were they? People don't just start stealing when they're thirty-five or forty. How old was George, forty-five? Fifty?" She saw my nod. "And he'd been doing it for almost ten years. What about before that?"

I didn't know who they were. "They were here when I came. Jacob would know when they got here."

"Nellie would know too. And what about before? Where did they come from?"

"I don't know. I never cared. George never said; I never asked."

She looked at me, like a nurse looks at a patient, assessing whether I was well enough to get up, well enough to be told the truth about something. "That's where you'll have to look, Jason. You want the police in on it? Your wife's disappearance, I looked it up in the files. Renard worked on the case then. One of his first cases with the department here. It was never closed. I'm working on the Whitney thing. You could report the discovery of the locket to me. It could be a police matter."

I couldn't bear the thought of Renard messing about with memories of Agatha. "If they didn't find out anything at the time, they're not likely to find out anything now. I don't mean you, Grace. But this is the first clue I've had. There was *nothing* before, absolutely nothing. I want to do this myself. If I need help, I'll hire help. I have to know why . . . how."

We were interrupted by a loud singing at the front door, a fumbling with the lock. Grace got up and opened it. "Gra-cey," a bibulous voice said. "Little ole sis."

It was time to go. Time to let Grace sort her brother out. Time for me to sort myself out. Time to sleep. I waved at her over her brother Ron's dark curly head, going around behind him and out, unseen, while Ron spun a drunken story of New Year's celebration. She looked at me across her brother's shoulder helplessly, as though she wanted to come with me but could not.

I drove home, repeating what Grace had said, like a litany. Good old George. Good old Betty. All the way home I asked myself Grace's question.

Who were they, really?

When Mark arrived early the day after New Year's I was already at my desk, already working, already having my third cup of coffee. I drink too much coffee. I drink coffee like some people drink beer or chew gum or smoke cigarettes. One day I will have to cut down. But not while I have so much on my mind.

"Mark, I want you to do two things for me. First, go down to the paper and find out if anyone there knows who placed those dog ads. No one will know anything, I'm sure, but we should check. Then, call around and locate the best professional to trace people, to find out about their past."

"Some kind of private investigator?"

"I'm not sure. Despite the TV image, I think private investigators mostly watch people. They do surveillance. No. I need someone who can trace people and find who they really are."

"Maybe some former FBI type."

"Maybe. Somebody who works for insurance companies or lawyers or bondsmen. Somebody who goes after people who skip town."

Mark nodded. "Do you want to tell me what this is for? I might do a better job if I knew."

"Just between us, Mark. You're not to tell anyone, not even Rudy."

"You know me better than that, and if you don't—"

"I do know. Sorry." I took the locket out of the desk drawer and laid it in front of him.

Mark took it, opened it, read the inscription on the back. He had been a boy in school when Agatha disappeared, but he knew the story.

"Your wife's locket? Did you just find it?"

"The night after the Whitneys were murdered, I saw Sergeant Renard taking a valuable desk box from the Whitney house. The guy's a jerk, and it made me mad. Partly because he's a jerk, I guess. I followed him down to the station, and when he parked his car, I recovered the box and hid it here. The box was locked. I told Jacob about it. He told me to open it. New Year's Eve, I picked the lock. I found that inside." I turned my chair around to hide my hands. I still couldn't keep them from shaking, every time I told the story. Hell, Nellie was in better shape than I was. I cleared my throat and got on with it. "Nellie Arpels told me Agatha was wearing it the day she disappeared. I hadn't seen it since I gave it to her, not until it showed up in the Whitneys' desk box."

"So you want to know about them. Who they were."

"Exactly. Everything about them. While you're telephoning around, I'm going over to see Jacob."

"George Whitney?" Jacob slurred.

Francis, the nurse, murmured, "Jacob isn't very alert today." Jacob did look half asleep, his fine white hair puffed out on the pillow. He looked terribly old and weak.

I repeated the name. "George, yes."

"They came a year or so before you di'. Bought the ol' Peters place when Jem die'. Jem Peters and I use' to go to school together. Dora Moore School. It's still there."

"I know it is, Jacob. I buy most of my groceries right across the street from it." The red sandstone pile was a landmark. "What can you tell me about George Whitney?"

Jacob shrugged his left shoulder. The right side did not move at all. "Jem's daughter . . . she's named Dewen' now. Lives in Sal' La' Ci'y. She tol' me they pai' cash. She din' wan' a mor'gage to fool with."

"Do you know where he was from, Jacob?"

Jacob looked blankly at me. After a time he whispered, "George never tol' me." His eyes shut and he seemed to be dozing.

"Did he say 'Dewent?' " I asked Francis.

"I think so, yes. I think he has a touch of cold. I gave him something the doctor prescribed to help his breathing, but it makes him drowsy and affects his speech. I'm going to talk with the doctor about that, next time she's over."

"Francis, I'll come back when Jacob's feeling more chipper."

"Is there something you'd like me to ask him?"

"Just anything he remembers about the Whitneys, the people who had the house south of Jacob's, where I live now. Anything at all."

"We chat about all kinds of things. I'll make it a point to bring that into the conversation." He smoothed the sheet, tucking it lightly around the old man's neck. "Lots of people you take care of, you don't care that much for, if you know what I mean. Mr. Buchnam, though, he's a special kind of man. And he thinks an awful lot of you."

I knew what he meant. "I think an awful lot of him. If it weren't for Jacob, I'd probably be in jail about now. If not jail, in difficulty of some kind."

Francis nodded. "There's people that *do* good, and then there's people that do *good,* you know what I mean? Mr. Buchnam, he does both. He told me about your wife and boy. Is this something to do with that old trouble?"

I shook my head carefully, trying not to disturb the delicate balance in there. "Just a problem I'm having. I need to find out about the Whitneys, that's all."

Mark did not convey a sense of accomplishment.

"Nobody," he said in a sharp angry voice unlike his usual smooth tones. "Nobody wants this job. I found an ex-FBI man who says this kind of work requires travel, and he doesn't want to travel. I called a guy who finds people who skip out on bonds. He works mostly by using police records—known associates, known aliases, previous arrest records—and if the person doesn't have a criminal record, he says it could be impossible. I asked both these people how they would go about finding out where someone had come from, and they said the best way was through IRS and Social Security records, which they don't have access to. Otherwise they start by questioning friends and associates and co-workers of the person they were trying to trace. Hell, I can do that." He looked up from his notes, giving me an emphatic look. "I'd *like* to do that."

"Um," I thought about it. "You just said something interesting. Doesn't the IRS usually come popping up whenever somebody dies? Don't they get a big chunk of inheritances?"

"An estate would have to be over six hundred thousand before the IRS would be interested."

"Do we still have the papers with the stories about the murder?" he asked. "Was there anything in there to indicate that the estate might be big?"

The laundry room stack yielded the papers. Both dailies had reported the murder; both included interviews with the police and accounts of the attempted bombing. I had declined to be interviewed, and both papers said that. Nothing about an estate.

"I wish I could think of some way to get the IRS involved in finding out who they were," I said. "Except that they wouldn't tell me."

"If George had enough in the bank, the bank has already informed the IRS," Mark said.

"No," I told him. "George never let the total in the banks get above a few hundred thousand. His last bank statements totaled about two hundred thousand." Mark looked puzzled, so I told him what I'd done. "I took the bank statements out of his office. Grace Willis and I have been looking at them. This whole thing isn't just Agatha's locket. There are a lot of questions about the Whitneys."

"Grace Willis?"

"The cop. The detective. The one who was here with the sergeant."

"The little blonde." Mark had his head tilted to one side, the way he did when he first looked at a new acquisition, getting the idea of it. "The sergeant's a homophobe. He made that really clear the day he was here."

"I gathered that too."

"I asked around. He's got a reputation for being nasty. She seems all right."

"She's a nice person. Which has nothing to do with what we've been talking about."

"What we were talking about was my helping find out about the Whitneys. I can talk to people. I can ask questions."

"All right then. Start by finding a woman named Dewent who lives in Salt Lake City who was the daughter of Jem Peters, here in town, at the address next door."

"Because?"

"Because she sold the house to the Whitneys after her father died. They may have mentioned to her where they were from. Anything. Meantime, I have to get into the Whitney house again."

"For?"

"For returning bank statements and borrowing prize ribbons and pictures of dogs."

I "borrowed" all seven of the pictures on the office wall. One was of Betty with Snowball at a puppy show. There was nothing in the background of the picture that would help locate where the picture was taken. No city skyline, no mountain, no monument or road sign. Some exhibitors and some puppies in the background, anonymous. There was a picture of George holding Ladislav's leash in one hand, a red ribbon in the other. Behind him, a banner: TERN ST. Betty in the same pose, same dog, same ribbon. The angle was slightly different. The banner read TES KU. So. Western States Kuvasz something. Or Eastern

States Kuvasz something. Nothing to say where. Beyond the banner was only a parking lot.

Then the two Hungarian pictures. At least the banner was written in what I took to be Hungarian. George holding two blue ribbons and grinning from ear to ear. Betty holding the ribbons and the dog. I went through the ribbons in the pile. No ribbons looked like the ones in the picture. There were others: blues, reds, yellows; National Kuvasz Society, Kuvasz Fanciers of Great Britain, Société Kuvacs. No ribbons with that particular large rosette and that style of lettering. Surely, as proud as George appeared to be in the picture, he wouldn't have lost the ribbons? I made a note of the lettering on the banner, trying to tell myself I was getting somewhere.

The last two pictures were of another show. This time it was Eva being held and smiled over. No banners, no other participants, but looming clearly in the background was the spidery shape of the Space Needle.

Mark came in and leaned over my shoulder. He put his finger on the parking lot behind George and the banner. "Blow up the license plates," he suggested. "There are seven or eight cars there. It may tell you where the show was."

"That's one way," I agreed. "Do it for me, will you, Mark? In addition to that, we have to get hold of someone who attends these things. There must be someone else in the state who breeds Kuvasz."

"Didn't George have a phone directory on his desk? Some kind of a listing?"

"Damn."

"I'll get it."

"No." I sighed. "I'll get it. I'm getting good at burgling through a dog door."

No one answered at the number George had listed as Western States Kuvasz Association. I tried the number again and again while Mark went through George's appointment diaries, making lists of all the people George and Betty had met with, all the shows they had attended. If the places in the diaries were accurate, they had traveled widely.

"It might be interesting to know how George got the job in the first place," I said to Mark. "Why the board of the Society put him in charge of all that money. I'm going to call Dan Beeman and see if he can tell me." I gave up on the dog lovers and dialed the evangelists.

"Mr. Argos, I'm sorry I sound so out of breath," Beeman exclaimed when I got him on the phone. "But the police have been here, a detective who wanted to see everything. Old records. How the computers work. A woman. Detective Willis."

When I used the name Argos, my conscience bit me. The guy deserved to know the truth. "I'd like to see you too," I said. "I know it's late, but have you had your lunch yet?"

"I haven't had time. Is it about your client? Did she—"

"Not about a client. About a confession. I'll meet you at two thirty. At the Rattlesnake Grill."

"So you really aren't Robert Argos and there really isn't a woman who wants to leave us a lot of money in her will." Beeman didn't sound particularly upset.

"Sorry, no."

He gave me a long, level look. "And you think George was the one who was stealing from us, don't you?"

Since he seemed to be able to accept the idea, I took a deep breath and told him the truth. "I think George was the one who was stealing from the Society. Detective Willis has a good deal of evidence which would indicate that. Since I have an interest in the case, she's been kind enough to keep me informed."

"And you want to know something from me?"

"I want to know how George got the job."

Beeman put down his fork, took a tiny sip of the wine Bert had recommended, and looked slightly belligerent. "I hope you're not saying that you think some member of the board was involved."

"I'm not thinking anything. I just want to know how he got the job. George and Betty Whitney came here only ten years ago. The Society has been operating a good deal longer than that. Presumably there was someone else in the job before George."

Beeman nodded. "Ralph Jollaby. He was killed. Murdered. Shot, just like George, only it was a robbery and they found his body on the street somewhere. The board president told me all about it."

"Whoa," I said, half choking. "Jollaby was what?"

"He was murdered. He was mugged. Shot, on the street, and whoever did it took his wallet and his watch. It's a sad commentary on cities today, but it happens all the time."

It might happen all the time, but it came across to me as another coincidence, in which I didn't believe. I took a deep breath and made a mental note to come back to the topic.

"How did it happen that George was put into the breech?"

"I'm trying to remember what Mr. Bentworthy told me. He said George was a member of the board. A large contributor. He had made many helpful suggestions concerning programming. He'd been very affable and everyone liked him. And when Ralph was killed, George offered to fill in."

"How long had he been on the board?"

"I'm not really sure." Beeman chewed reflectively. "I guess from what you're saying, he hadn't been there long enough." He sighed. "How am I going to explain this to the board?"

"Don't try to explain anything yet," I suggested. "I'm not sure. It's all guesswork. I could be putting two and two together and getting seven or eight."

"They'll be really upset." He thrust his plate away. *"I'm* really upset." He shook his head at the hovering waiter and frowned at the tablecloth while I settled the bill. He didn't ask other questions, for which I was grateful. I didn't want to tell Beeman all I really thought about George.

eight

When I got back to the shop, I asked Mark to help me that evening. I wanted to keep my promise to Grace Willis concerning her grandmother's furniture. I asked Mark to come along, in my car, because I needed an excuse not to stay at Grace's. She might not expect it, but I didn't want to risk upsetting her or me. Though I'd always told myself I had a healthy libido, there'd been no evidence of it at all since New Year's Eve. I felt fragile and touchy, like an old piece of fabric, held together by dust. I told Mark he needed more experience in appraising furniture and left it at that.

We spent almost an hour in the musty garage, and then the three of us sat beside the fireplace in Grace's living room, Mark with his notebook and calculator, me with my pictures. The table was littered with Polaroid views of dirty old tables and beds. "I should think I could get twenty-five hundred for that country wardrobe," I said to Mark.

"It looks like it had chicken pox," Grace objected.

I agreed completely. The thing was hideous, a blocky cupboard built of pine, painted an ugly ochre and then sponged with blobs of dark gray. "I know. I think it's ugly too, but that two-coat sponged-on paint is valued by certain collectors. Where did your grandmother get the Shaker things?"

"From her mother. They lived near a Shaker community. I've got some letters where she writes about buying furniture from them. Ohio, I think. Or Indiana?"

That was good news. It established a provenance for the pieces and increased their value. "What do you make it, Mark?"

"If she's got letters about the furniture, and if she keeps the pieces here so we don't have to store them, we could advance her eighteen. Twenty-one if that Shaker table looks good after it's cleaned up."

"Hundred?" Grace asked in a disappointed tone.

"Thousand," I amended. "I don't do much consignment stuff. Jacob used to do quite a bit. Jacob always gave an advance against sales, if he thought it was warranted, and so do I. I don't think this stuff can sell for less than thirty, and it may fetch a bit more than that. Little things like the early glass and the spice racks can take a whale of a markup. And that Eastlake bed is a very good one. I like the little spindles. I can probably get three or four for that. One third of the total is going to come from that Shaker trestle table. My standard cut is twenty percent. Does that help you any?" My standard cut was forty percent, but Grace needed the money.

She sighed. "It gives Ron what he needs. He says he has a chance to buy into a business in San Francisco. Grandma's equity in this house was only fifty thousand, so I owe Ronald half of that. What cash Grandma left was split up between us when she died. I spent mine on the house. I don't know what Ron did with his."

"Didn't he inherit half the furniture, too?"

"No. She left the furniture to me. I guess she figured I'd need it if I lived here, but I wanted my own things. Furniture without so much . . . oh, I don't know. Memory in it, I guess. If I can give Ron fifteen or twenty thousand and a note for the balance, that will settle things between us."

"Good. Glad to be of help. Now we come to the quid pro quo."

"What quid pro quo is that?" She frowned.

"I need some official help. Police help."

"I hope it won't take clout. I haven't got much."

"It needs somebody to dig out a ten-year-old murder case, a man named Ralph Jollaby. It needs somebody to see—and this is the wildest hunch in the world, Grace—whether the bullet or bullets that killed Jollaby match the bullets that killed the Whitneys."

Her eyes opened wide. "What makes you think—"

I explained my conversation with Daniel Beeman.

She looked glum. "I never even thought to ask those questions!" She bit her lip. "Damn it, Jason. I thought I was doing a real good job on this."

"You would have asked. You gave me the idea. You asked who they were, really. And part of who they really were would tell us how George got the job in the first place. From what Beeman said, I'm guessing he got it because he went after it before the job was even available. Jollaby wasn't killed until George was ready to take over." I shuffled the pictures into a stack, put a rubber band around them, inserted them into a brown envelope, and wrote *Willis furniture* and the date on the outside. I gave the envelope to Mark. He's less likely to lose things than I am.

Grace stood up and moved nervously around the room. "I can ask the lab to look at the bullet from the old case, if there was one. If it hasn't been lost. If it wasn't too badly banged up. I know bullets were recovered in the Whitney case, because I did the paperwork. But Jason, people are going to want to know how I got the idea of checking the Jollaby case. Renard isn't going to sit still for many more discoveries from me. He was madder than hell about my report on George's finances. I thought he'd kill me. The lieutenant asked him, and he didn't know anything about it. It made him look like a ring-tailed idiot, which he is, but he doesn't like it being talked about in the squad room. And speaking of the Whitney finances, I've got to pick up George's bank statements."

"They're back in George's desk, in the upstairs office. You can go in there whenever you want to, can't you? Tell Renard you got the idea from me. You said I had a reputation. So, use it. If anyone asks, say I told you there might be a connection."

"You'll have Renard camped in your office again."

"I'll worry about that when the time comes." I kissed her on the cheek and went out to the car.

"You could have stayed," Mark said on our way back to

the office. "I could have taken your car and picked you up in the morning."

I shook my head warningly, and he shut up, exhaling sharply through his nose as though to point out how dumb I was. I was pretty sure he wouldn't understand, so I didn't attempt to explain. Mark had lived with Rudy for some time, so far as I knew, quite happily. He'd never lost anyone. Since finding the locket, I'd felt as though Agatha had disappeared or died all over again. All the original pain was back, and I didn't want to think about it with someone who didn't understand.

Mark evidently saw some of this in my face because he changed the subject. "Now what? What's the next project?"

"We have to get through to someone in one of these dog societies. I'm tired of trying a phone that's never answered, so I think we'll start with the American Kennel Club, tomorrow morning."

Morning brought two breakthroughs. One of Mark's friends, the amateur photographer, provided an enlargement of the parking lot in the background of the dog-show picture. The cars were, all but one, from Massachusetts. The second breakthrough came when the American Kennel Club provided a local source of information on matters relating to Kuvasz dogs.

"The Kuvasz is an AKC-registered breed," the starchy female voice told me.

"I know that," I said. George had told me when I bought Bela. "I'm asking if you know anything about Kuvasz people. Breeders' groups. Show groups. Anything."

"East or west?"

"West," I said. "Denver."

"Sophia Feathers," the voice said after a moment in a tone of surprise. "Sophia Feathers is the president of the Western States Kuvasz Society." She gave me a phone number.

I asked, "How about Massachusetts?"

She told me there was a New England group and gave me a name and a number.

I put down the phone and wiped my face with an open hand, feeling the tension there, as though I'd been gritting my teeth. Mark was watching me with an expression of concern.

"You OK?"

I pushed the memo pad across the desk. "Two people. Someone here named Sophia Feathers. Someone in Massachusetts named Colonel R. W. Makepeace, U.S. Army, Retired."

"Do you want me to start dialing?"

"No, thanks. I'll do it. You attend to business. Check on the valances for Kitty Van Doorn's place. I think that's the last thing—"

Mark shook his head. "The reupholstery on the dining room chairs."

I'd forgotten the damned chairs. "Right. Check that too. And that chandelier with the faulty wiring. We've sent it back twice."

"Can I pay the painter?"

The painter had finally quit talking long enough to finish the job, and I'd approved it. "Yes. He's finished. I checked it out Friday. Get our usual color cards from him. He hasn't delivered them yet." I kept a file on each client, and in a light-proof envelope I included a card for each wallpaper or paint color. I always got them from the contractor on the job so they'd be the colors actually used. Jacob had taught me that, among other things.

"The painter brought them yesterday."

"Carry on, then. I'm going to call Sophia Feathers."

"Soph!" the voice at the other end of the line cawed at me. "Nobody calls her Soph-ee-ya."

"Is she there?"

"She'll be here about two. Two thir-ty. She has to be here because Fluff is coming to be groomed."

"Would she have time to talk to me?"

"Fluff's at two thirty, and then the two Barret dogs, and then nobody. Four o'clock she doesn't have anybody. Not if you're selling anything. She won't talk to you if you're selling anything."

"I'm not selling anything," I assured the strange, cawing voice on the line. "Where will I find . . . ah, Soph?"

"Here," the voice said incredulously. "Right here."

"Where is here, ma'am? All I have is a phone number."

"The Pet Boutique. On Leetsdale Avenue. It's in the book."

The Pet Boutique was a converted gas station. The former garage was now a dog grooming center where Soph Feathers, the plump jeans-clad proprietor, was busy with a dog. The former office had been converted into a pet store which seemed to sell everything for animals though not the animals themselves. I remarked on this.

"I got sick of it," she said as she clipped the hair between the toes of a tiny neurotic poodle which kept trying to bite her as she worked. This was evidently the second Barret dog. The first Barret dog, already clipped, whined from a nearby cage. "Animals in bunches get sick. Puppies get sick. Kittens get sick. I don't care how clean you keep them, they get sick. Fish too. You go home at night with your fish all pretty and bright and the next morning you come in, they've all got ich and are floating belly up. And birds are the absolute worst. They're so pitiful. Dogs can at least curl up when they're sick, but a sick bird is just awful. So I quit selling them. I tell people to go to a breeder if they want a pet. Go to a fish store for fish, a bird breeder or importer for birds, a breeder for dogs or cats. Somebody you can hold responsible. Pet shops handling all kinds of animals just can't cut it. Hell, even vets specialize."

"But you have dogs? Personally, I mean. You seem to like them."

"These two I hate. There is no excuse for dogs like these. Dogs in general, I like. Oh, hell, yes. Dogs. Cats. A llama. Two donkeys, the little tiny kind. A miniature horse. Peacocks. Any fool thing you can name, I've got. Animal crazy, my husband calls me. I guess he's right."

"Was that your husband who answered the phone when I called."

The gray-haired woman burst into laughter. "I'll have to tell Cameron you asked me that! Oh, Lord. No. That was my workmate, Billy. He's a mentally retarded man who works for me, cleaning, putting prices on things, putting things away. He's getting pretty good with the dogs. I let him clip some of them, the easy ones. I taught him to read my appointment book, and lately he's been answering the phone. I've only had him for six months, and I don't know what I did without him. He works from nine until three. And he's funny! A laugh a minute with Billy."

"I'm afraid I called him 'ma'am.' "

"Well, he wouldn't mind that. He has a kind of high voice. You haven't told me yet what you wanted to see me about."

"Kuvasz dogs. Or, not really the dogs, more the Society."

"They are the nicest dogs. When I decided to get a new dog after my old Bouvier died, I said to myself, Soph, you have to groom dogs all day, you don't want another one to groom at home. Old Gentleman Jim, I just gave him a top clip to keep him neat, but still it took time. So I got me a Kuvasz, and he is a sweetheart!"

"I have one," I admitted.

"Well, then, you know! So you're interested in the Society? You want to come to the next show?"

"I want to talk about George Whitney."

She put down the clippers, blew the cut hair from between the dog's toes, and ran her hands over him while he snarled and nipped at her. "There you are, you nasty baby, all pretty." She lifted him from the table and put him into an empty cage beside his companion. "George Whitney. What about him?"

"He's dead."

"Well, I know that. I can read. It was all over the paper. Shot, wasn't he? Betty too." She didn't sound grieved.

"I'm trying to find out something about George and Betty. Where they came from, if they have any relatives. We know the Whitneys attended a lot of dog shows. We thought some-one in the Kuvasz Society might know something."

"You want some tea? I always make myself some tea about this time of the afternoon. We can sit down back here and have a cup." She bustled around the sink and the hot plate, putting a kettle on, getting out tea bags. "I ought to bring a teapot down here, brew it properly, but somehow I never think of it."

When we were seated at a minuscule table tucked away in a corner of the grooming space, she leaned back in her chair, booted legs wrapped around a table leg to anchor her. "George Whitney," she said, "was the most hopeless dog handler I've ever seen in my life. Betty was fairly good, but George was awful. I was really kind of glad when they quit coming to shows."

That surprised me. "Quit? So far as I know, they were going to shows up to the week before they died."

"Not local shows. No, sir. They haven't been to a local show in . . . oh, over a year. I don't know who they were try-ing to avoid, but it was somebody."

"Somebody in the Society?"

"Lord, no. No, we all know one another. This was some-thing else. Last show they came to, I saw Betty go running over to George and say something to him, and then the two of them went off, took the dogs, packed up, and left."

"And you think they were trying to avoid somebody?"

"Well, you know. Let me think now." Soph rocked danger-ously, sipping at her tea. The table rocked with her, creaking in protest. "It was the way she looked over her shoulder. Running up to George, talking to him, but looking over her shoulder. Just the way you would if you said, 'Here comes my mother-in-law; let's get out of here before she sees us.' You know?"

I could visualize the scene. "Where was this?"

"A show down in Colorado Springs. A year ago last fall. And they haven't been to a show since, not a local one."

I sipped my tea and forbade myself to make a face at the

strong chamomile taste. "You didn't see who they were trying to avoid?"

"I was in the ring when I saw them, standing there waiting for Hector Spence, who is an absolutely incompetent judge, to make up his silly mind. I looked back in the direction Betty was looking, but all I saw was a crowd there. We had two or three hundred people at that show."

I considered what she'd said, sipping again. The taste wasn't as bad as I'd first thought. Either that or the first sip had anesthetized my tongue. "Let's suppose—let's suppose that someone was looking for the Whitneys. Call this person X."

"Whoopee," she said dryly. "Mystery!"

"Call him John Smith then."

"X is all right."

"X is looking for the Whitneys. The Whitneys know X and don't want to be found. They see him, they leave, they don't come to any more dog shows. However—"

"However," she went on, "if X didn't see them go, X didn't know he'd been seen."

"Right. So, X continues to haunt the dog shows, looking for the Whitneys."

"You want to know if anybody has been hanging around." She grinned at me, rocking dangerously, the table swaying.

I got my legs out of the way in case she went over backward and asked, "Has anybody?"

She nodded thoughtfully. "There was someone, yes. There was this man, big man. I saw him at the Colorado Springs show. I saw him a couple of times after that. He wore dark glasses and a cap. I sat next to him once outside the refreshment trailer. He was drinking coffee."

"Why do you remember him?"

"Because he wasn't with anyone, I guess. I spoke to him when we were there at the table. I asked him if he was showing, and he said no, he was just interested in the dogs. I remember, he asked me if there was a certain kind of dog that had a soprano bark. I thought at the time what a silly question."

"This wasn't a Kuvasz show?"

"Oh, no. This was a multibreed show with what's called an 'other' category for non-AKC breeds."

"And you couldn't think of a dog with a soprano bark."

"Sure I could. Any little dog. Any young dog that gets a little hysterical. I used to groom a Norwegian elkhound—not that they take much grooming—who always barked soprano when he got excited. He sounded like an opera singer reaching for high C. I told the man that. He just sat there, making butterflies."

"Making butterflies?"

"He was having coffee. And he used artificial sweetener, in the little envelopes, you know? I watched him use three or four of them. Each time he'd tear off the end, put the torn-off part in the empty envelope, fold the envelope in half longways, then twist it into a butterfly. Like a bow tie. And he made dents in his cups—those Styrofoam cups—with his thumbnail. All the way around, like a design. I must have sat there for an hour, waiting for my friends to get their dogs in and out of the ring, and he was right there the whole time. Watching everybody. Decorating cups. Making butterflies."

"I suppose everyone goes to the refreshment trailer during the course of a show?"

"At that kind of show, you do. Those little shows are run cheap. We don't rent exhibition halls. We hold them out in some pasture where the barking and the mess won't bother anybody. We put up a rented tent, in case the weather turns iffy, but that's it. You groom your dogs in the back of your station wagon or your van. Unless you bring your own thermos, your own sandwiches, the trailer is the only place you can get anything to eat or drink. They have hot dogs and barbecue on a bun and cheese sandwiches, that kind of stuff. Heat it up in the microwave."

"You didn't ask the man's name?"

"No. I didn't tell him mine, either. We talked about dogs, mostly him asking me questions about different kinds of dogs."

"If I had a sketch artist work with you, could you picture what he looked like?"

She shook her head. "I'm no good at that. Oh, I'd probably remember him if I saw him again. And if I heard his voice, I'd remember that. I'm good with voices. But all I can really tell you is he was big and wore dark glasses."

"You've been a lot of help, Soph."

"Hope so. If you're trying to find the man who killed the Whitneys, I'd like to help. Like I said, George was hopeless, but I kind of liked Betty. Whenever one of her dogs did well, she'd light up kind of like a candle. I always felt sorry for her, married to him. He wasn't a nice man."

"Why would you say that?" I was really curious. I'd never thought George a nice man either, but it was hard to say why.

"Something about his eyes. Something about the way he handled the dogs. He had a cruel streak in him somewhere. I just know he did, that's all."

When I got back to the office it was almost six but Mark was still there.

"What are you doing here?"

"I waited. I needed to tell you that Sergeant Renard came by." Mark's face was very pale.

"Did he give you a hard time?"

"I told him you weren't here. He accused me of lying. He told me he was going to search your apartment. I told him he needed a warrant, and he told me he didn't need anything to get by some pervert with two limp wrists."

I sat down hard. "And then?"

"And then I told him he'd have to get by me, and if I got even slightly injured in the process, he would have an assault charge on his record and a lawsuit that wouldn't quit. I may have mentioned my father's name."

I felt heat around my neck and ears. "He left?"

"He insulted me a few times and said you were to call him as soon as you got back."

"Did you gather what stirred him up?"

"I gathered the bullets from the Whitney murder matched those from some other killing back, in the sergeant's words, 'when that little cunt Willis was wearing diapers.' He was a very unhappy man."

I took a deep breath the way Jacob had taught me to do when I was fourteen and out of control, ready to slaughter someone, anyone. When you grow up in a home for lost and hopeless kids, which is how I always identified the place, there are numerous occasions for anger. There hadn't been many as effective as Renard. He was a walking incitement to violence.

"Bull's-eye." I managed a reasonably calm voice. "Well, well, well."

"I'm not sure I understand what all this means."

"It means that the person who shot Jollaby is also the person who shot George and Betty. At least, the same gun was used, so there's a connection, whether it's the same person or not."

Mark rubbed his forehead and jaw, bringing some color back into his face. "Or part of the same group."

"Why group?"

"The broadcasting station, I guess. Why would somebody kill in order to make a job available? It has to be something about the specific job. Not just the money."

I shook my head. "Mark, you've always had money, so you don't realize how important it is to some people. Money is enough for a lot of people. George was in the job for ten years, and he managed to steal during most of them. He got away with over four million. Only a quarter of that went into the furniture next door. Where do you guess the rest of it is?"

"Swiss account. If it were mine, that's where it would be. I still say it could be something more than money."

"If there was some motivation besides money, what would it be?"

Mark shrugged. "In the first murder case your shooter worked for George and in the second case he worked against him. We might think in terms of a falling out. George and Mr. Shooter were in this thing together, then Mr. Shooter got peevish about something and wiped out George and Betty."

"Because of something George did?"

"Or Betty. Though I guess it's more likely it was George."

"The only thing we think he was doing was blackmailing someone," I commented.

"If Mr. Shooter approved of skimming, why would he object to a little blackmail?"

We looked at each other, frowning.

"We need more pieces for this jigsaw," I said. "We could be off the wall with this. The only things we know for sure are that the same gun that killed George's predecessor also killed George, that George was stealing from the Evangelical Society up until two years ago, and that George found some other source of income since that time."

"And that your wife's locket was found in their house."

"And that, yes."

"What are you going to do now?"

"I'm going to call Daniel Beeman's board president in Texas and the retired colonel in Massachusetts. You're going to look into the want-ad matter, which you haven't done yet, and how about the Dewent woman? The daughter of Jacob's old neighbor?"

"I have three numbers in or near Salt Lake City. One of them isn't it. Neither of the others have answered yet." He stood poised, as though for flight. "What are you going to do about Renard?"

"I'm going to ignore him, for now. Try to do the same."

One of Mark's hands rubbed the other in a way that told me he was seriously upset. "He's really angry. He said you had no right to interfere in police business."

This remark heated me up again, but I said, "Let it go, Mark. For now. I wouldn't put it past Renard to do something unpleasant, so I'll be careful for a while, and so should you. No alleys. No dark garages. No letting people into your apartment unless you know them."

He nodded, reluctantly.

"I'm interested in seeing what he'll do." And I was. The man was strange. Another puzzle.

nine

Colonel Makepeace, U.S. Army, Retired, of Boston, Massachusetts, President of the New England Kuvasz Fanciers, was suffering from a very bad attack of gouty arthritis, according to his wife. She suggested that I call Anne Bibleton. "Anne knows everyone," she said, in a careless, breathy voice that reminded me of wind moving through rushes. "She knows a lot more people than my husband does. If you have any questions, Anne will know."

When I called Anne Bibleton's number in Scituate, Anne's niece told me that Anne Bibleton might well know something that would be of help to Mr. Lynx, but that Anne could not talk on the phone. Anne was deaf. Anne read lips. Hadn't Mrs. Makepeace told Mr. Lynx that?

I vented a silent sigh and persevered. "Would you ask Ms. Bibleton, please, whether she knew George and Betty Whitney. If she did, I will come to Massachusetts to speak with her."

A long silence with murmurs in the background. "She knows them," the niece said. "They were at the last show. She doesn't like him very much."

"It doesn't really matter," I told her unfeelingly. "They're both dead." After a shocked silence and a few more murmurs, we settled upon an arrangement whereby I'd call Mrs. Bibleton again, via her niece, when I got to Boston.

I called Daniel Beeman and got the name and home phone number of the president of the board of NEWS. "Bentworthy's a gawdawful busy man, Bob . . . ah, Jason. Sometimes I try for three or four days to get hold of him," Beeman warned me. When I called Bentworthy's home and said I was seeking information concerning George Whitney, however, I got an appointment for the following afternoon. Seemingly Mr. Bentworthy was not too busy to talk about George.

"While I'm away," I told Mark, who was watching all this long-distance work with a bemused expression, "write a letter to Stimson and ask him if he wants us to do the appraisal he talked about. I hate having that furniture just sitting there. His card is in my file. You may have an answer by the time I'm back."

"You'll be traveling for a while, then?"

"Houston. The transmitter is located on Galveston Island, but most of the board members seem to live in or around Houston. When I leave there, I'll go to Boston. Anne Bibleton lives on the South Shore below Boston. Then, since I'm on the East Coast, I'll go down to New York for a day or two and pick up some trinkets for the Van Doorn place. Kitty's having her open house the end of next week. Can you hold the fort, Mark?"

"If Renard will stay out of here. That man scares me. He's not rational."

"Does your dad's lawyer represent you?"

"Usually. I've never needed him for much."

"Call him. Alert him. Give Eugenia his number, just in case. If Rudy's back, give him the number, just in case. Give Grace Willis his number, just in case."

Mark managed a smile. "I'm not naturally combative, Jason. It's one of the things my father seems to find most objectionable about me."

It was not the first time Mark had mentioned his father's attitude, usually in a way to evoke sympathy, which I was not about to give him. Mark is a good assistant, a good person, but every now and then he tries to get me to be a substitute father while he plays little boy. He would never think of playing shrinking violet among his friends, and if I'm not one of those, I don't intend to be a father surrogate, either.

"There's no point in acting weak-kneed with me, Mark. Being self-protective isn't being combative. I know you play hockey, and when you're goalie you wear a mask. When you ride in horse shows—and I know you do—you wear a helmet. Protecting yourself is mostly foresight and the rest good sense.

If you think Renard is going to make trouble for you, just because of what he is, then protect yourself. Don't go anywhere risky. From what Grace said, he is capable of senseless brutality."

He nodded. "There's the shooter, too."

I agreed. "There's the shooter. So far we've got George, and his blackmail victim, and the shooter. The last two could be one person. George is no threat, but the other one or two could be. Be careful."

"You be careful too," he urged.

"Maybe we're overreacting," I said in unthinking self-confidence. "Whoever we're after doesn't know we're chasing him. Yet."

The president of the board of the New Evangelical World Society was also the president of a Houston bank. It was a monumental edifice, with enough marble in the lobby for a mausoleum and three ranks of elevators. The office of the president was on the fortieth floor. I spent about half an hour at that altitude in the reception area, looking across traffic and the tops of lower buildings toward a distant sparkle that I thought might be Galveston Bay. I'd never been to the Gulf before. I had no idea how far one could see from where I was, but then, what you can see from four hundred feet in the air is undoubtedly more impressive than what you can see from the ground. I wished I could find such a crow's nest to look over the rest of this puzzle. If I could get above it and look down on it, some of the tangles might vanish.

When I was finally escorted into Mr. Martin R. B. Bentworthy's office I found that gentleman seated behind a quarter acre of polished walnut, watching expressionlessly as I waded through fifty feet of oriental rug. He gestured me toward a chair, and he didn't smile when he did it.

"I have very little time, young man, and very little patience. If you have something to say to me, get it said."

I sat down and unbuttoned my jacket. Most people had

quit calling me young man about five or six years ago. I guessed that to Bentworthy everyone under forty was young.

"We have reason to believe that George Whitney stole somewhere around four million dollars from the Evangelical Society." I paused to let that sink in. "Starting almost the day he took the job." I squirmed back into the deep leather chair I'd been invited to occupy and gave myself time to observe Mr. Bentworthy's reaction to that. The man looked slightly like a frog, broad and bald and low-centered. He blinked once, very slowly, making a froglike though dignified noise as he swallowed.

"We would like to know how George Whitney got the job in the first place," I continued. "Particularly, where he came from, how he was introduced to the rest of the board, how he ingratiated himself."

The frog eyes blinked once more.

I shut up and left the next leap to the frog.

After a long silence, Mr. Bentworthy asked, "Is that all?"

"That will give us a good start."

"As I understand it, Mr. Lynx, you have no official status. Under the circumstances, I don't think I care to answer any questions about the matter."

The back of my neck got hot. I felt a familiar wave of frustrated fury rush up my backbone. I sat very quietly and let it subside. "Well," I said, "I had thought you'd be interested in keeping the whole thing quiet. It will make quite a story. The papers will have a field day. One more revelation of scandalous goings-on among evangelicals. The widows sent in their mites and Good NEWS robbed them blind. Your refusal to answer questions may be taken as a sign of guilty knowledge by some."

"There are laws against slander and libel, Mr. Lynx."

I kept my voice quiet with some difficulty. "There is freedom of the press, Mr. Bentworthy. And truth is the best defense against charges of either slander or libel. I wouldn't threaten to make this matter public if getting information weren't terribly important to me, but it is. Personally important. This matter has to do with the unexplained death of my wife. Believe me, I will tell the press nothing but the truth. I won't speculate. Let the public draw its own inferences."

Silence again. The man strummed his fingers on his walnut football field, making a sound like a tiny horse galloping away. When the horse had gone, he said, "What do you want to know?"

"I want to know how George Whitney got the job of Manager."

"He got it because my wife was susceptible to flattery."

"Excuse me?"

"George Whitney opened an account with this bank, a fairly large account, several hundred thousand. He introduced himself to me and told me he knew my wife was involved with NEWS and he wanted to get involved too. He claimed to have belonged to an evangelical group in the East. Lila was president then, and I gave George her number. He made a large contribution to the Society and she nominated him to the board."

"No one objected?"

"Why should they? The man had money. He talked a good line. He listened to the programming, which is more than most of them did—or do. Don't misunderstand me, Mr. Lynx. The people on the NEWS board are sincere Christians, and I include myself in that number, but they don't have eight to sixteen hours a day to listen to all the programming. Lila often had it on when she was in the house, but she was no expert."

"You're telling me that George was an expert?"

"According to what Lila said, he talked like one. Oh, she used to go on about all the things George said, in addition to the sweet things he said to her. Nothing personal, nothing indelicate. He was too smooth for that. Just how sweet she looked and how hard she worked and how much he was sure Jesus loved her for what she was doing. Then, when he had her feeling happy, he talked about scheduling fund appeals for certain times in the day when people are most receptive and about varying types of programming, so the audience wouldn't get tired of the station and turn it off. Oh, he talked well. Lila was ecstatic. She used to tell me how much George wished he could do the programming himself."

"What about his wife?"

"I never met his wife. I don't think Lila ever met her. I was surprised when I heard from Beeman that George's wife had been killed as well, because I'm not sure we ever knew he was married."

"You didn't know him well?" I was asking the same question Renard had asked me.

"The board doesn't socialize a lot. Oh, they have meetings every month and some committee meetings in between, but that's it. According to Lila, George was at every meeting. And when Ralph Jollaby was killed, George was right there. He told the board he owned a house in Denver, that he'd move there at his own expense and run the station until they found someone else. Lila thought it was an answer to her prayers. When she told me about it she was in rapture."

"When he'd been there awhile, didn't anyone notice that the contributions had decreased?"

"Lila's term as president ended the year George went up to Denver. Her board term ended then, too. I wasn't on the board at that time. I didn't go on the board until two and a half years ago. First thing I did was haul all the audits out for the last fifteen years. Nobody else had bothered to do that. I did some research, and then I insisted we hire Dan Beeman because our statistics didn't match up to the industry profile."

"The board members in between your wife's term and yours hadn't seen anything wrong?" I suppose I sounded a little incredulous.

"A president's term is two years. There were four good Christian people served as president between the time Lila left the board and I came on it, and none of them had any experience with money management. Like setting sheep to guard the henhouse. If you want to blame somebody, blame the accountants. They should have called it forcibly to someone's attention. After George went up there, the bottom fell out of contributions for one year and then went up a little squinchy bit each year for the next seven. Anybody looking at the current year would see an improvement over last year. Now, since Beeman's been there, they've gone through the roof. I was surprised to hear you say it was only four million. I'd say it was over five."

"Didn't Beeman give you an estimate?"

"Said he couldn't prove anything. I did my own estimate. Based on what's coming in now."

"What does your wife think?"

"She died three years ago. Cancer. I miss her. Lila wasn't long on practicality, but she was a dear good lady and I miss her." The frog face became abruptly sorrowful, human, worn. "I went on the board honoring her memory, because she believed in the Society. I'm not nearly as sure as I used to be, but Lila always was. Not that it's any of your business, but when you mentioned your wife, I thought you might understand. Now. Are you going to spread this all over the papers and give a lot of good people a black eye?"

"I don't plan to. I can't guarantee that someone else may not come asking the same questions I did, but I don't think anyone is interested in making a scandal out of it."

"Who's likely to be asking?"

"Police. What George did is what ended up getting George killed, and they may be interested in that. Now, I need to know where George came from. When he opened the account here, did he give you any references? Did he talk about his previous home? Anything at all?"

"He said he came from Boston, I remember that. His funds were from a Boston bank, I don't remember which one. I'll have someone check the records and let you know if we can get closer than that."

"Any reason given for moving here?"

"I just don't remember. The one person on the board that George talked to almost as much as he did Lila was Lila's best friend, Horty Lemoines. I can give you a note to Horty."

"I'd take that as a kindness, Mr. Bentworthy."

"And I apologize for my manner there at first, but you came on a little strong. All I could think of was somebody maligning Lila's name—"

"It's forgotten."

Horty Lemoines was a violently red-haired woman in her near sixties dressed in too-youthful clothing and all too willing, once I'd given her Bentworthy's note, to invite me into her parlor to talk about George Whitney. The parlor was a sunporch with patio furniture, woven wood blinds, and a huge cage in the corner with half a dozen small bright birds in it.

"Lila would go on about him," Horty said. "Lila was nutty about him. A woman her age!" She sat down in a rocker and set it moving with a touch of one sandaled foot. The other foot was crossed over her knee. Her toenails were mauve. They made her feet look bruised.

"Martin Bentworthy said George talked to you a lot." I smiled, drawing my fascinated attention away from Horty's feet.

She flushed, an ugly reddening of her nose and neck. "Not a lot, no. Oh, he talked to me some."

"The only thing we're interested in learning is where George Whitney and his wife—"

"His wife?" Horty blurted, turning redder. "I didn't know George was married."

"He may not have been married when he was here," I soothed, realizing I'd made a wrong step. "Come to think of it, I believe his marriage was later. What we're interested in knowing is where George lived before he came here."

"I don't hold with this talking about people behind their backs," she said, wiping her mouth with a tissue. Her eyes were wet. I wondered what had gone on between Horty Lemoines and George.

I said, "Martin Bentworthy asked you to talk to me, Mrs. Lemoines. It's important."

"Well, if Martin hadn't sent that note asking me to talk to you, I wouldn't do it. George came from Boston. Some little town around there. I forget where."

"Can you remember anything he said about the place he came from? Anything he said about what work he had done?"

"He said he had a rich relative who left him his money," Horty offered unwillingly. "I don't think it was his father. He laughed when he said it, and I don't think he would have done that if it had been his father."

"Did he ever talk about his education? About hobbies? About anything like that?"

"I remember he said once that Maine lobster was a revelation from God."

I kneaded my forehead between thumb and forefinger, feeling that I was losing the trail. The birds in the cage twittered and danced among their perches. I stared at them, trying to think. Horty got up and went to the cage, reaching a finger through the bars to touch the seed bowl. Evidently there was enough food there to satisfy her. She turned back to me, her cheeks wet.

"He liked Mexican food. He said it reminded him of his grandmother's cooking. I asked him what his favorite dish was and he said chicken paprikash." Horty gestured, a meaningless wave of one flabby arm. "I like chicken paprikash, too. The chef at the club makes it. Maybe that's where we were when he said it." She turned back to the birdcage, hiding her face.

"Did he ever talk about dogs?"

"No. He talked about pigs once. He said the pigs here in Texas were bald. The pigs where he came from had long hair." Her voice was weepy and unclear.

I got out one of my cards. "Mrs. Lemoines, if you think of anything else he said, anything at all, will you call me or write me at this address?" I put the card on the table, the one that said simply *Jason Lynx,* with the address and phone number.

I got up, ready to find my own way out, when she turned all at once, eyes red, to ask, "How is George? I keep meaning to write to him." She was staring hungrily at me, as though I might produce George out of a hat.

"I'm sorry, Mrs. Lemoines. I thought you knew. George was murdered about three weeks ago."

"Oh," she yelped. "Oh, oh!" Her eyes filled with tears. Her eyes squeezed shut around the tears flowing from them. Her hands were clutched at her breast like little paws, fingers spread to catch the tears that were dripping from her chin. She couldn't see me. She had forgotten I was there. As I left, I could hear her exclaiming, over and over, like a drip of icy water. "Oh. Oh, oh."

When my flight came into Logan Airport that night, I watched the rim of the bay and the rivers cut black holes and strips in the lighted cityscape beneath the plane. It was late, so long after Boston's notorious rush hour that I decided to rent a car and drive to the Copley Plaza. Once in my room, I called Mark.

"Everything holding together?"

"Renard was here late this afternoon."

"What did he want?"

"You. I told him you were out of state and wouldn't be back for several days. He demanded to know where, and I told him you'd started out in Houston. I told him which hotel in Houston, but I presume you're no longer there."

"The man I saw says George came from Boston, which, coincidentally, is where I am now. The guy from Houston may be calling you with the name of a bank. I'll call again tomorrow and pick up that information. Thanks, Mark." And I hung up.

My last call before falling into bed was to Anne Bibleton's niece, making a date to see Anne in the morning.

The shore south of Boston is packed with charming little New England villages, each with its churches, its town common, its twisting roads leading everywhere but where you want to go. Even with good directions, I made wrong turns twice before I found the half-hidden side road and turned in at the proper place.

It had been, perhaps still was, a farm. The tall red barn, though slightly dilapidated, testified to that much. I could hear dogs barking as I drove up, that deep, chesty bark the Kuvasz males have. Snow dusted the ground and shifted around in the cold wind. A young woman hailed me from the farmhouse porch, hugging herself in the chill. "Are you Jason Lynx?" I told her I was, and she invited me to come in and join Anne Bibleton for coffee.

Anne met me just inside the house, a tall, erect woman in her mid-forties who might once have been a model or an actress and who still carried that experience with her. Her immaculate shirt was tucked into tailored trousers over boots. Her smile was practiced. Her hair was shining and sculpted. When she took my hand, I felt calluses. Her hands were square and hard with very short nails. Only her eyes betrayed her handicap. They remained fixed on my mouth.

"I am almost totally deaf," she said. "It happened in an accident when I was in my twenties. I always tell people that immediately, to get their curiosity out of the way. I read lips very well, but no one can read them completely. If I seem not to understand, please write the words down for me." Her voice was clear and soft, though almost unaccented, a monotone. She handed me a pad and pen, then led me to a chair beside the window where the light fell on my face. She sat down opposite me.

From the adjoining kitchen, the young woman said, "Tell Aunt Anne I'll bring the coffee in a moment."

I faced those hearing eyes and told her.

"Thank you, Selina," Anne called, raising her voice only slightly.

"I need to know everything you can tell me about George or Betty Whitney," I said, sitting back into the light as she obviously wanted me to do.

"George Whitney knew nothing about dogs," she said in her uninflected voice. "Didn't know and didn't care. I could never understand why he came to the shows. Not merely regional and national ones, you understand, but foreign ones. Even shows to which one cannot bring one's own dogs because of health regulations."

"George and Betty went to shows where they didn't bring their own dogs?"

She watched, being sure I'd stopped talking. "Yes. It isn't that uncommon. If we are interested in a particular breed, we may wish to import that breed, so we go to foreign shows to see what dogs are available. The Kuvasz stock comes originally from Hungary. There was a show a year and a half ago in Hungary. We can take our own dogs to Hungary, though we can not take them to England. The English have stricter quarantine regulations, but the Whitneys went even to English shows."

I remembered the ribbons on George's wall. If he couldn't take his dogs to England, how had he won a "Kuvasz Fanciers of Great Britain" ribbon? Obviously, he hadn't.

"George and Betty were at a show in Hungary eighteen months ago?"

"It was in the spring. A little over a year and a half ago. They were there, yes. And although they could have brought their own dogs, they did not."

Selina brought in a tray. Coffee, toasted split muffins. "Are you ready for elevenses?" she asked me. She looked enough like her aunt to be her daughter. "Aunt Anne usually has a little something about now." She poured me a cup, while her aunt munched greedily at a muffin.

I left the muffins alone. I had no idea whether Anne Bibleton could lip-read while I chewed, but I didn't want to test it.

"George and Betty did not take their dogs to Hungary?"

"They did not."

I fished out the copies of the pictures from the Whitney house and leafed through them to find the two with the Hungarian banner. I put them on the table. Anne Bibleton looked at them and nodded, then shook her head.

"I remember when they took those pictures. We thought they were very silly," she said. "George said he had a sick little boy back in the States who would be made very happy if his dog won, so he was going to pretend his dog did win. He borrowed the ribbons for the picture."

"But they didn't even bring their dog?"

"George told someone the animals got sick. He left them in a kennel, he said."

"Let me see if I understand this correctly. He said his own dogs got sick, so he left them in a kennel. He said he had a sick little boy at home. He borrowed the ribbons from the winner to have his picture taken with them."

Anne, her mouth full of muffin, nodded firmly. When she could speak again, she said, "Borrowed the ribbons, borrowed the dog. In this picture, Betty is holding a dog. It is not her dog."

And probably borrowed the ribbon from England as well. "George and Betty had no children that anyone knew of," I told her.

"I don't find that surprising. One always had the feeling that George was lying about everything he did or said. Betty— well, sometimes one rather liked Betty."

"Is there anything else you can tell me?"

"The Whitneys showed their animals here in Boston. I saw them at several other shows, other places. They had good animals, though badly handled and getting a bit old now. Big dogs do not live as long as small ones. I wish I had had that big dog of theirs five or six years ago. The bitch was a good animal, too."

"I bought one of Eva's pups. He's a good dog."

Her face lighted. "Have you ever been to a show?"

I shook my head.

She stared at me for a long moment. "Still, if you have a dog, you will understand. People who show dogs are quite silly about them, you know? They want ribbons. Best of Breed. Best of Show. When the judging goes on, they hang around like flies, buzz, buzz. In between classes, they wander around, looking at dogs, muttering to one another. They talk about dogs. Since I read lips, I can tell what people are saying, here, there, and I know what people at shows talk about." Her eyes darted as she mimed herself listening to people. "They talk about dogs. Everyone. Only George and Betty did not talk about dogs. They did not covet ribbons. When they won ribbons, it was almost by accident."

"Did you—overhear anything you can repeat to me?"

"I watched them sometimes. Curious. Their talk was often of picking something up. Picking something up at a certain place at a certain time. Furniture, perhaps. There were furniture words. Sometimes they talked about investments. He would say, 'It's a good investment, Betty.' Several shows I saw him saying something like that."

"In Hungary?"

"No. In Hungary George said it was good to eat chicken paprikash again and to see pigs with fur. It made me laugh, hearing that, and I thought I had not read him correctly. But there was an agricultural show there at the same time we were, and the pigs did have fur." She shook her head. "Woolly. Almost like sheep."

I smiled to myself. So George had come originally from Hungary. Or at least spent some time there. Horty Lemoines had quoted him correctly. "Is that all they talked about?"

"No. In Hungary they talked of a person coming to meet them at the show. They did not want to meet this man, even though they had come all that way. They had to explain something to him, and they thought he would be unpleasant. George said, 'He'll have to understand. It wasn't my fault.' Things like that. The man they expected did arrive, and they went away with him."

"Do you remember the man's name?"

She shook her head. "It was not a name I know. It may have been a foreign name. One cannot lip-read foreign words. So much of the sense comes from the context. I'm sorry." She smiled at me. "Sometimes they said things I could not understand at all. In Boston they said they had to pick up a type at the drape."

"Type at the drape?"

"I tried it several ways. Type at the droop. Teepee at the droop. I don't know what they said. They were so strange I made up stories about them, just for my amusement. At the shows in this country, I made it up that they were drug smugglers."

"Why smugglers?"

"They were secretive about their van. Sneaking in and out of it, as though someone were watching. As though they were smuggling something inside it."

"In Hungary too?"

She thought about that, finishing her muffin. "No, not in Hungary. They did not have a van in Hungary. They were just there to meet the man."

"I see." I drank the last of my coffee. Her thought of them as smugglers had set off a small chain reaction in my brain. "Ms. Bibleton, when they were talking about picking something up at a certain time, could they have said, 'Pick up the tape?' "

She frowned, puzzled. "That's what I said. 'Pick up the type at the . . .' "

I wrote it down for her. She nodded, mouthing it. "Oh, yes. They could have said tape. But what does it mean?"

"Just another alternative." Except that George worked with tapes, I had no idea what it meant. I changed the subject. "Just for my own curiosity, how do you manage to show dogs? Don't you have to hear what the judge says?"

She held up her wrist. I had thought she was wearing a

watch, but it was some other kind of device. "A signaler," she told me. "It was developed for deaf people as a doorbell. When the doorbell is pressed, the thing on the wrist vibrates. Selina goes with me to the shows. Selina listens to what the judge says. She has a button which she pushes in code, and I feel it. The judge says run. Selina pushes one long, and we run. The judge says walk, Selina pushes one short. Many of the judges know me. They wait until I am facing them to say anything." She looked at me expectantly.

I knew what she was waiting for. It had been inevitable from the moment I had admitted owning a Kuvasz. "May I see your dogs?" I asked.

ten

Martin Bentworthy was unable to find a record that named any bank in Boston as the source of George's original deposit, said Mark when I called him. So that was a dead end. I went on down to New York on Saturday morning. The two days I'd planned there turned into four, including the weekend. I got theater tickets for Saturday and Sunday and luxuriated in an anonymous hotel room with no memories. There was an auction on Monday that I wanted to attend, and that night I checked with Mark by phone, being noncommittal about my return. I spent Tuesday shopping for a few final items for the Van Doorn house and having them sent air freight. Tuesday night I tried unsuccessfully to call Mark at home. Finally I got hold of Eugenia and asked her to tell Mark that I'd be back at noon the following day.

"Mark's probably hiding out. That sergeant has been hanging around," she said with distaste. "He was up in your office yelling at Mark this afternoon. He's a very unpleasant man."

"I'll be there by noon," I said, giving her the flight number. "Tell Mark."

I was there by eleven. The direct flight had taken four hours, but I'd gained two hours on the clock.

When I got to the house, Eugenia said something again about Renard. I went on upstairs and Mark said, "There's an interesting letter on your desk."

"Are you all right?"

"Why wouldn't I be?"

"Eugenia said Renard was here again."

"Same as last time. He came in in the late afternoon and wandered all over the downstairs and the basement. Then, just as I was getting ready to shut up and go home, he came up here. Alone. He evidently doesn't want any witnesses to these encounters. He threatened and blustered, working himself up into a rage. Funny. Almost as though he wants to startle me into doing something or saying something. I told him I'd informed my attorney about his previous visit, about his threatening me. Interesting reaction to that. He shut up and got out, just like that."

It made no sense to me. I said, "I worry about Grace. She says she can handle him, but I wonder. The man's like a bomb, ticking, ready to explode." I took off my coat. "What's this about an interesting letter?"

"On your desk."

"It's from Stimson." I read it aloud. " 'Dear Mr. Lynx: Thank you for your letter,' et cetera. 'We cannot find any record of having asked you to make an inventory or appraisal of the Whitney property. We have no connection with the Whitney property. The Whitneys were not and are not clients of ours. No member of this firm recalls meeting with you on the date mentioned or on any other date. [Signed] William Stimson.' "

I put the letter down. "I'll be damned."

"Who do you think he was?"

"I don't know," I said. "Except that it was someone who preferred to impersonate an attorney rather than act covertly and possibly get caught at it. He did get an authorization to enter the house." I turned to the desk drawer and took out a brown envelope with the words *Whitney furniture, December 12* written on it and spilled the pictures onto my desk.

I knew I had at least one. No, two. "Here they are." I pulled them out triumphantly. The pictures were of a corner chair which I had pulled into the middle of the room to get three views of. In two of them Stimson appeared in the background peering into the drawer of a secretary, oblivious, his mane of hair standing out in the dim room like a candle flame.

"I'm going to run downtown and see if I can catch the real Stimson," I said. "No time like the present."

The real Mr. Stimson, caught just as he was returning from lunch, was at least twenty years younger than the false Mr. Stimson, much more stylishly dressed than the false Mr. Stimson, and was, at first, very suspicious. I gave him references, told the story, showed him the pictures, showed him the card.

"That's our card," Stimson averred. "Of course, anybody can use a card—"

"Somebody did," I assured him. "Not only with me, but I imagine with the police."

"Wouldn't the police have asked for some other form of identification?"

"Maybe they did. Maybe he had it. You'd have to explore that with the police. It might be a good idea. Just in case the imposter wants to use your name again."

Stimson gave me a speculative once-over. "I don't recognize the guy in the picture. With that beard and hair—I suppose it's occurred to you it could be a disguise."

"It occurred to me when I got your letter, but not until then," I admitted. "If it was makeup, it was expert makeup. The whole episode had a very professional air to it. Quite perfect. No wrong moves. I didn't doubt the man for a moment." I thought of the false Stimson's failure to get a receipt for five hundred in cash and amended my remarks. "At least, not while we were looking at furniture."

"You're saying . . . ?"

"It wouldn't have been the first time this man has pretended to be someone else."

"But no damage done?"

"Not so far as I know. Of course, I don't know what he was after or what he took from the house. Some papers, but I don't know what they were or what they implied."

"Why was he there? Why did he drag you into it?"

I had been wondering about that since I'd read Stimson's letter. "I don't think he intended to have me go through the house with him. I think that just happened. What he really wanted was for somebody to take care of the dogs so no officious animal control officer or neighbor, including me, would make a fuss and draw attention to the place. Then I surprised him when I told him the Whitneys had a million dollars' worth of furniture in that house, and while he was a little confused I told him I'd do an inventory list for him, and he pretty well had to take me up on it. It would have been natural to do that, so that's what he did. It was worth it to him to make me think he was real. If he'd just vanished at that point, I might have been suspicious."

The real Stimson furrowed his brow. "From your account of the conversation, he may also have been trying to find out what you knew about the Whitneys, if anything."

I admitted that was possible.

"Would my following up this matter with the police assist you in any way?"

"It could," I admitted. "There's an officer in charge of the murder investigation who isn't doing much. All the pressure that can be brought to bear is useful. And then, too, calling attention to the matter thwarts the person who used your card. You might get some satisfaction out of that."

The real Mr. Stimson scowled at the picture of the imposter and thanked me for bringing it to their attention.

"I have a report," Mark said when I got back at two thirty. "First, the paper has no record of who placed the dog ads. I went down there while you were in New York, but I forgot to tell you this morning."

"Well, I really didn't expect any help there."

"Also, I reached Susan Dewent, Jacob's old neighbor's daughter."

"Did she remember George?"

"Vaguely. She said he told her he came from Boston. The check for the house was drawn on a Texas bank. Houston, she thinks, but she's not sure. When George bought the house, he told her he and his wife and their dogs wouldn't be moving into the house for six months."

"Six months?"

"That's right."

"Then he bought it before Jollaby was killed!" The two things were connected, had to be connected.

"Some time before. The check was for the full purchase price. She never returned to the house. She never saw George's wife. She never heard another word from George. She sends her best to Jacob."

"That doesn't take us any further, does it."

"Not much. But I have more. In one of George's old desk diaries there was a sales slip from an audio store. After I went to the paper, I went down there with a picture of George and asked around. They knew him. He bought tapes there all the time."

"It must have been for his work," I said. "There was no audio system next door except that big reel-to-reel player."

"I know. I asked about that. According to the guys at the audio shop, they had modified a machine like that to record without erasing."

I had no idea what Mark was talking about. "I don't understand."

Mark dropped into a chair. "Look, Jase. Most tape recorders, if you put them in RECORD, the tape is erased just before it runs through the recording head. If you wanted to tape a voice over music, for instance, you'd have to use a recorder that didn't erase the tape. George had one modified to record without erasing."

I considered that. "Of course," I said in my alert voice. "He recorded fund appeals over the music."

"According to what you told me, Beeman said he did that down at the office. Why did he need another modified recorder at his house?"

"I don't know."

"I don't either, but he could have recorded anything over anything, you know. It didn't have to be voice over music. If he did it at home, it was because he didn't have time down at the office or didn't want someone down there to know about it, maybe?"

"When did the people at the audio shop fix the recorder for him?"

"A little over two years ago."

"When Beeman arrived."

"I did notice the coincidence." Mark grinned happily, the way he did when he bought cheaper or sold dearer than he'd planned on.

"He had been doing something at the office, but when Beeman came he thought he'd better do it elsewhere?"

"It looks like that, doesn't it?"

"And those big reels? That meant it had something to do with the station, didn't it? He wouldn't have needed a machine like that otherwise."

"Of course. The big reels are necessary because some of the programs are an hour or more long. An ordinary tape deck won't hold that much tape. If all George had wanted to do was listen to the programs at home, he wouldn't have needed to modify the recorder."

"He had a little cassette deck too," I said. "It was in his desk. I turned it on, but all it did was squeal at me."

"Squeal how?"

"A high-pitched squeal. A long one."

"Jase! Honestly, the things you don't know!"

"What don't I know?"

"If it squealed, that could have been a speeded up transmission. Information, speeded way up and then transmitted all in one burst to keep anyone from hearing what it was. Spy stuff!"

"Information?"

"It has to be information. Information that someone wants to get out of the country. Is that cassette recorder still there?"

When I told him I didn't know, he dashed out. He'd been dying for an opportunity to try that dog door for himself. In five minutes he was back. "Gone!" he said. "I didn't see Stimson take anything like that, did you?"

I hadn't. As a matter of fact, I had been watching the desk self-consciously every minute the phony Stimson had been near it. "No." I shook my head. "I didn't see him take it."

"Well, somebody did. And you can bet that's what it was. Some kind of speeded-up information that George was smuggling out."

"Something that can be transmitted in sound," I said. "So, presumably, no graphics of any kind."

Mark shook his head. "Not true, Jason. If you transmit data to a computer at the other end, it can be graphics or documents or maps or diagrams. Just like the space probes beam pictures back to earth. If it's only information you're after, you don't need paper anymore. All you need are numbers a computer can read."

"Anne Bibleton said they behaved suspiciously," I told him. "She said they talked about picking up the tape at the drape, or droop—."

"At a drop?" asked Mark impatiently. "As in drop shipment?"

"As in where something is dropped off? Is that spy talk?" He nodded. "Amazing. At the time Anne Bibleton thought they were smugglers."

Mark nodded. "They were picking up a tape at a drop. A safe place where a tape could be left for them. And the Bibleton woman was right; they *were* smugglers, but only of information. They must have been picking up tapes around the country when they went to dog shows and then mixing them in with the religious stuff and transmitting them." He actually bounced up and down in excitement. When he said it, it sounded logical.

And yet, of all the things I'd suspected George of, I'd never thought of him as some kind of agent for . . . well, for whom? Some foreign power? Or could it be some kind of industrial espionage? Mark read all the suspense novels, I didn't. I felt at a loss.

"Do you have any idea what a bonanza that would be for spies?" Mark asked. "A captive radio station that could transmit anything they needed to get out! No couriers to worry about. No wonder they took so much trouble to get George into that job! It wasn't the money at all."

I disagreed. "It was at least partly the money, Mark! It had to be. Anne Bibleton said that in Hungary, George was worried. He didn't want to meet the man there because he had to explain something, and he said, 'It wasn't my fault.' "

Mark frowned. "He had to explain something that had happened?"

"Right. And the only thing that had happened at that point was Beeman's arrival. Beeman's arrival shut off the money. If George said, 'It wasn't my fault,' he meant it wasn't his fault the money had shut off. That money is important."

"All right," he agreed unwillingly. "Both the transmissions and the money were important."

We could have gone on talking about it, but I needed to let the recent information settle and connect to something real.

It was only three thirty. I told Mark I was going over to see Nellie to see if she knew anything else about the Whitneys. Actually, all I wanted to do was sit down somewhere quietly for an hour or so and figure out what was going on. Self-indulgence once again. Which was once again about to be thwarted.

"The Whitneys?" Nellie asked. "The murdered people? I never saw them very much, Jason. That summer when Agatha was here, she used to have coffee with the woman sometimes, out on the back porch. That was before they enclosed it to make a room. I was sorry to see them do that. Porches are such nice places, and when you go and shut them up inside the house, they just aren't porches anymore."

"I think they needed an inside room for the dogs," I said.

"Sometimes it gets pretty cold, even for furry creatures like Ladislav and his family."

"You've got them now, don't you? Are you going to keep all four of those big dogs, Jason? They must eat a lot." Her words sounded more like Janice than like herself, but with something a little wistful in them.

"Are they fun to watch?" I asked, suddenly perceptive. She could watch every move the dogs made, now they were in my yard. Better than watching an empty alley.

"Oh, yes. They play," she said. "Your dog never had anyone to play with before."

I wondered briefly if Bela had been lonely, living just with me. "How's . . . ah, Perky doing?" I asked, looking around for the cat.

"She's wonderful. She's in the back of my closet asleep. That's where she likes to sleep in the daytime. At night she sleeps on my bed. You can get her out."

I got her out and put her on my lap, where she curled into a purring ball, tail twitching, eyes fixed on my face to be sure I approved.

"She climbed out the window yesterday," Nellie said. "Got almost all the way down to the ground before Janice heard me yelling and caught her. There's a hole in the screen she got out through."

I told her I'd send someone over to fix it.

"Getting back to the Whitneys," she said, "all I know about them is that Agatha thought she knew them from somewhere."

I felt that brain drain again, that leaking away. "What do you mean?"

"She said so. Not long before she disappeared, I was talking to Agatha about *her* one day, the woman . . ."

"Mrs. Whitney?"

"Her. Yes. And I said Mrs. Whitney looked a lot like Mabel Montefiore, Mabel Monty we used to call her. She had the little store down on Colfax, across from the high school? Oh, it's gone now, but it was there for thirty or forty years." She fell silent, remembering.

"And?" I urged.

"Oh. And Agatha said she must have a familiar face, that both of them must, because she'd seen them before. She laughed. She said she was going to tell Betty—that's right; she said, 'I'm going to tell Betty I filed her picture and George's.' Then Agatha said it wasn't really them."

"Wasn't really them?"

"Couldn't be them, I guess she said. She said she'd seen their picture, but it couldn't be them." Nellie examined my face. "What did she mean, Jason, it couldn't be them?"

I tried to manufacture a smile. "I don't know, Nellie. Just some resemblance, I guess. She thought Betty and George looked like someone, just as you thought Betty looked like Mabel Monty." I went on sitting there, petting the cat, not saying much, letting her talk. After a while, I told her goodbye, promising again to send someone to fix her screen and to keep at least one of the dogs so that Bela would have a playmate. And all the time what she had said was bouncing around in my mind like a loose cannon on a ship, banging into the sides of my brain, threatening to go through the rail of my sanity at any moment.

Janice Fetterling met me as I was going out the door, a changed Janice, with a new dress and her hair in crisp curls. "I wanted to thank you for the Christmas box of fruit, Mr. Lynx. We've all enjoyed it."

I said a few inane words and then asked, "Mrs. Fetterling, would you say your mother's memory is good?"

The woman laughed, a little harshly. "Good? It's perfect. She remembers everything anyone ever said to her. She remembers anyone she ever knew or even met. It's all she has to do, now, is remember, and she does it. Why?"

"Oh, just something she remembered about my wife."

"Well, if Mama remembered it, it happened. You can be

sure of that. She doesn't make things up." She shook her head. "I forget things, Mr. Lynx—"

"Jason."

She flushed. "I forget things, Jason. Mama doesn't. Sometimes I feel like she's the child and I'm the old mother."

"No." I shook my head at her. "You look younger every time I come over, Janice. Don't worry about forgetting things. I do it all the time."

I left her standing in the door with an expression of almost childlike pleasure on her face. As for me, I couldn't think of anything except that the Whitney murder was no longer a matter that Grace Willis and Mark and I could handle alone. It had become, all in an instant, something bigger.

I couldn't remember the name of the man Agatha had worked for in Washington. I'd met him once, at a cocktail party, a fortyish, dark-haired man who wore horn-rimmed glasses and had a funny laugh, like a honk. What had we talked about? Agatha, of course. What else? The man's wife, Mrs. blah-blah, who had recently taken the blue ribbon in some kind of equestrian event. The man had laughed and said she had only married him because of his last name.

Rider! Now, what had Agatha called him? Old something-or-other. Old Bill. Bill Rider. William Rider. Because there was another William Rider in the department, and they called them Old Bill and Young Bill.

"Are you going to use that phone?"

I was seated at my desk, my hand on the phone where it had evidently been for some time. I looked up at Mark. My face felt like a mask.

"God, Jason. What happened?"

"I'm not sure," I mumbled. "Nellie remembered something."

"Tell me."

I tried, repeating myself, the words stumbling over each other.

"You think your wife really had seen those two? That they

were in some FBI file? And that your wife told them? Would she have done that?"

I nodded. Yes. Oh, yes. It was what she would have done. Laughing. Never for a moment considering that it might be true. Innocent. Not seeing. Not looking at George at all. Only seeing in Betty what she wanted to see.

"Jason, you have to tell someone!"

"I know. I finally remembered the name of the man she worked for. But it seems such a betrayal." My voice faltered.

"Like telling on her?"

It *was* like telling on her. It was like saying, You know what my stupid wife did? She got herself killed. She was so dumb, she told those people she knew who they were.

Who were they? Really?

I reached for the phone again, punching for information.

The man from the local office of the FBI was Gower Hodgson. He had a long nose, a narrow chin, and a thin mouth. From the neck up, he looked like Punch. Below that he looked like a Brooks Brothers mannequin. He had come from the local office, arriving only an hour after I'd succeeded in reaching William Rider. During that hour, my world had moved from day to night. Mark had gone home. The world was dark and cold once more, outside me and inside me. I was the only one who noticed the cold inside as I explained and explained while Hodgson took notes.

He went over things and then over them again, making me repeat. I told him things I'd forgotten I knew. When almost two hours had passed, he said, "You seem to have accumulated a good deal of information." His voice was a surprisingly vibrant baritone.

"A lot of it's guesswork," I said.

"A lot of it usually is in the beginning. My guess would be the same as yours, however. I don't think George's predecessor died by accident. You say you've got pictures?"

"Of George and Betty, yes." I went into the office, dug them out of a desk drawer, and brought them back into the living room. "I took them out of the frames before I took them to Massachusetts." I put them on the coffee table.

Hodgson shuffled the pictures, looking carefully at each one. "It was your assistant, what's his name—Mark—who suggested that George was transmitting information?"

"He knows more about computers than I do. What they can do. He knows about electronics, too. I don't. Besides, he reads spy stuff."

"His suggestion raises the question of what information was being transmitted."

"Naturally."

"We wouldn't want you to speculate about that. To the police. Or to anyone else."

I raised my voice. "I hadn't planned to go running down Colfax shouting that George Whitney was a spy! The only people who know anything about this are Mark and Grace Willis, the police detective I told you about. I doubt very much if either of them has mentioned it to anyone."

"And you say these pictures taken in Hungary are fakes?"

"Staged, I think I said. According to Anne Bibleton in Massachusetts, the Whitneys didn't actually take their dogs on that trip."

"Would you have any speculation concerning the reason for the pictures?"

I surprised myself by saying, "Sure. Every time George went somewhere, he took off from work. When he came back to his office, he hung pictures of his dogs winning ribbons, or the ribbons themselves, and that showed all his employees where he'd been and what he'd been doing. All very innocent. If he needed to explain why he went to Hungary, he'd point to the pictures and say he'd gone to a dog show. Isn't that what you guys call a cover? The pictures over at his house were surplus. There are duplicates of these two Hungarian ones on his office wall. Or were. Beeman has probably thrown them out by now."

Hodgson accepted that and noted it down. "Bill Rider may want to talk to you."

"No more than I want to talk to him," I said fervently.

"You seem terribly involved in this."

I snarled at him. "I told you—"

"Of course. Sorry." He flushed uncomfortably. "For the moment I'd forgotten about your wife's disappearance." He looked over my head, out the window, his fingers still shuffling the photographs. "The police had no leads on your wife's case at all?"

"None. The car went off a side road not far from a busy highway. She could have been going for a drive. She could have been going to visit someone. We never found her."

"And now you think that Betty and George Whitney were responsible?"

"I don't know what I think. George probably didn't kill Jollaby, because George was in Texas then. George didn't kill himself and his wife. There's someone else. Someone I call the Shooter."

"And you think this Shooter could have killed your wife."

I stood up, moved around, tried not to shout. "Could have killed my wife, yes. Worse than killed my son, yes. Or it could have been George who did that. Whoever the Shooter is, he was connected to George. The locket turned up over there."

"Why do you think they would have kept it?"

"I don't know. For later. A clue. Something to plant somewhere else if they thought someone might be getting close to the truth. Who knows?" I was tired. I wanted him to go away.

Hodgson nodded, then rose. "Thank you for your time, Mr. Lynx. And for the work you've done on this. We'll be transmitting these pictures to Washington. The files are huge, as I suppose you know. We have a considerable computer capability, but nothing yet surpasses the recognition ability of the human eye. It will take a while." He took his topcoat from the chair by the door and put it on. "We'll be in touch." He went out and down the stairs, leaving me staring at the door where he had been, unable to decide what to do next.

The air in the room smelled of White Linen. Agatha had always used it. Bath soap, cologne, perfume, it was her smell. I got up and went out into the hall. The door to the front bedroom was open. That's where the smell was coming from. From the sheets on the bed, the curtains, the little bottles still standing on her dressing table. I called it a guest room, but no guest had ever stayed in it. I went into it, turning on the bedside lamp and shutting the door behind me.

The curtains were English chintz, colorful branches of tropical blooms decked with vivid macaws, all on a dark green background. The walls were a paler green, slightly blued, the color of the sprawling leaves in the print fabric. The chairs and bed were old wicker, soft brown, upholstered in the bright colors of the parrots. On the wide oak floorboards, grass-green rugs lay beside the bed, making a warm place for bare feet. Through the broad south window, light from the streetlamp outside poured into the corner where she used to sit reading in sunlit hours.

"I want something different," she had said. "Not in all the rooms, Jason. Just in our bedroom. Something that doesn't look like an antique shop."

We had honeymooned in the Bahamas, in a room very much like this one, though not so carefully done. She had shopped for the furniture herself, not letting me help. "I want this one to be mine."

Perhaps I should never have left this room. Perhaps the ghost who haunted the house lived here, in this room, and only wandered because she was lonely. Perhaps if I slept here again, she would be content.

Or perhaps the ghost wandered because Agatha had never been buried, never truly mourned, never truly grieved over. There had always been that thin edge of hope, like a knife's edge, cutting me away from finality, making me doubt that she was gone forever.

Or perhaps she lingered because of Jerry. Jerry who was neither alive nor dead. Perhaps she stayed to watch over him, to be there if he needed her.

I closed my eyes and heard her voice, quiet, the way she used to speak to me late at night when she was half asleep. "Find out," she said. "Somebody killed me, Jason. Find out!"

I turned and left the room, wiping at my cheeks. In the back bedroom I fell face down on the bed, trying to think of nothing at all. When I woke, it was to the sound of the phone. I groped for it blindly, still lost in dreaming.

"Jason. It's Grace Willis."

"Grace," I acknowledged. "What time is it?"

"About ten," she said. "Were you asleep?"

"I guess I was."

"I called to tell you the FBI has been in, at the precinct. They've taken the files on the two shootings, the Whitneys and the Jollaby one. They took the file on your wife's case, too. Renard is madder than hell."

"Why?"

"He had that file out. I think he was trying to find a way to blame it on you. I think he's decided you took that thing out of his car. He wants to get even."

"That's why he's been harassing Mark." I was awake, aware of what she was saying. "Trying to get even. Or maybe just trying to make sure. Mark says he charged through this place yesterday. Maybe he was looking for it."

"Well, are you going to tell me?" she asked.

"Tell you?"

"What is the FBI doing in this?"

"Tonight? Tell you tonight?"

"If you've had enough sleep," she said. "Or tomorrow. Or the next day. But I'm dying of curiosity."

"Tonight," I assented, knowing I wouldn't be able to go back to sleep. "Have you had supper?"

"No. I've been working since noon without a bite."

"Where?"

"Enrico McGee's?"

"Not my favorite place."

"They have good steaks."

"Oh, all right." I wondered why it made any difference. "I'll meet you there in about an hour."

I ate part of a small filet and a salad while I watched Grace dispatch two plates of vegetables from the salad bar, a twenty-four-ounce porterhouse steak, blood rare, a side order of spaghetti, and one of fried onion rings. Only when she had dipped the last shred of garlic bread into the final drop of spaghetti sauce and said a reluctant farewell to the steak bone did she sit back and demand to be told. I didn't particularly want to talk about it, but she deserved to know.

"You'll have to be discreet, Grace. The FBI man doesn't want a lot of talk."

"Oh, sure, I'll just tell Clayton Renard about it. No one else. He'll be so excited. It will do my career so much good." She searched the bread basket for another crumb, shaking her head at finding none.

"I wasn't suggesting you were talkative. I was just passing on what I'd been told."

"So, what did you find out?"

"Nellie Arpels remembered a conversation she'd had with my wife not long before she disappeared. My wife said she'd seen George and Betty before, that she'd filed their pictures. She said she was going to tell Betty about it. She laughed. She thought it was a joke. She didn't believe she had really seen their pictures."

"Pictures?"

"When we lived in Washington, Agatha worked for the FBI. She filed pictures."

"Pictures," she mused. "What kind of pictures?"

"Oh, Lord, I'm not sure, Grace. I suppose if I were to visit a known terrorist, someone would take my picture. If I traveled to some communist country and visited somebody in the hierarchy, somebody would take my picture. If I took part in a demonstration against the United States—or even for it, for all I know—I'd probably get my picture taken. The pictures, or copies of them, would end up at the FBI in the hands of a clerk who'd fill out a card on them, cross-index them, and file them. That's what Agatha did."

"You told me your wife was an artist."

"She was."

"I suppose that's why. They would hire artists, wouldn't they?"

I had never thought of it until that moment, but it was perfectly true. They would hire artists. People who could distinguish shapes, features, coloring. People who could remember faces. She would have had to remember the faces. It had not been a quirk that made her remember the photographed faces. It had been a requirement of her job. "She did fine portraits," I said inanely.

"So she filed this picture of George and Betty with information that said they were spies or terrorists or something. But you're saying she didn't really believe it?"

"No. She didn't really believe in spies or terrorists or any of it. They were just words. It wasn't real, not to Agatha."

"Damn," she breathed. "That's horrible. What are you going to do?"

"Nothing," I said. "I've run out of leads. We know there are at least two other people besides Betty and George. We don't know anything significant about either of them. I have no idea how to go about finding them. Him."

"Or her."

"Or her," I agreed.

"There's the man the pet shop woman saw at the dog show," Grace reminded him.

"How did you know about that?"

"Mark told me. He came over the night before you got back to give me a check for Grandma's furniture. He didn't figure you'd care if he told me, since I already knew about the other stuff. We talked about the case for a long time. And we talked about Mark. He has the same kind of problems Ron does, so I can be sympathetic. He didn't want to be alone that night, and I didn't either."

I wavered between anger and acceptance. What right had the two of them to discuss me? And if they didn't have the right, who the hell did? "I guess it doesn't matter if you know," I said finally. "Except that it'll get you in even deeper with Renard."

"Poor Clayton. Every which way he turns, you've got him stopped. He wanted you for the Whitney murder, and he couldn't pin that on you. So he wanted you for your wife's murder, and the FBI stepped all over that."

"Hatred at first sight," I quipped, without humor.

"Well, it's mostly that way with Renard," she said. "Most guys, even rotten ones, they have some good days, you know? Not Clayton. He's always playing himself, right to the hilt. Anyhow, there's the guy the pet shop woman saw. The one who sat next to her at the dog show."

"Wearing dark glasses," I said. "Though Soph Feathers said she'd probably know him if she saw him again. Definitely if she heard him again."

She grunted. "Well, at least we know there is somebody else. I feel very frustrated. Usually I can think of something to do next, but this time I can't."

She sounded so pugnaciously annoyed and her face was set into such bulldog lines that I laughed. "You look like an ornery pup," I said.

"That's what my mother used to say." She grinned. "I'm not really very pretty. I guess your wife was beautiful."

I shook my head at her. "I've never seen much sense in comparing people. Some are beautiful, some are cute, some are ugly but charming. You're changeable. One minute you're a gamine, the next minute you're as sleek as velvet."

"But she was, wasn't she? Agatha? Beautiful, I mean."

"Not really," I said. "But yes. Agatha was beautiful to me. And I loved her terribly. There had never been anyone else before her. There has never been anyone for me since. I have no experience of there being anyone but her. I loved her. And I guess I still do."

"I know." She nodded, her eyes barely slits. "I figured that out New Year's Eve. It's because you've never really thought she was dead. You couldn't grieve and get over it, not with her just gone that way."

This was close enough to what I'd thought earlier to make me aware of her sensitivity. "There was never any reason for Agatha's disappearance, Grace. She had no enemies. She had no large sums of money. There was nothing to explain the wrecked car. It wasn't icy or snowy the day she disappeared." I had been speaking too loudly, too vehemently, and people were looking at me curiously. I tried to calm down. "There was never any reason until today. Now I have a reason. It hurts, but at the same time it helps that awful burning itch I had. The itch to find out, to know why. Of course, a lot of what I'm supposing is just that—supposition. I want to know for sure, but I have to let someone else take it from here, because I simply don't know what else to do."

"Well, when I've got a case like that, sometimes it helps just to get away from it for a while. Sometimes if you do that, you wake up with a new idea, you know?"

"I guess."

"So. Do you have something else to do?"

"I should finish up the Van Doorn job. Kitty's having her open house the end of this week, and if it isn't finished, she'll be annoyed, to say the least."

"I met her when I was checking your story. She's kind of nice." Grace's eyes were fixed on a neighboring table where the diners had just been served huge constructions of ice cream with thick brownies on the bottom and slathers of syrup. "She reminds me of Marilyn Monroe. In the old movies on late-night TV, you know. I don't like her husband, though. That one's got cold eyes."

"That one's got a lot of money. And a gorgeous house.

Speaking of which, would you like to go to the open house with me on Saturday? I have to show up. Kitty says black tie."

"If you're sure you really want me to go."

"I'm sure." I gave her a lopsided smile, the best I could manage. "You know where I stand, Grace. I'm not over Agatha. I think you're right: I never got to grieve over her. I don't seem to have any emotions left over to make commitments with. But I like you. I'm fond of you."

"Right." She flushed, eyes on her plate. "Before you tell me we'll always be friends, are you fond enough of me to buy me dessert?"

Five scoops of ice cream later, we left the place, and since Grace had taken a cab to the restaurant, I drove her home.

"I'm not going to ask you in," she said firmly. "When we get all this mess figured out, then we'll see. I don't want any sad lovers. A sad brother is enough."

I didn't know whether to be amused or annoyed or grateful. I contented myself with kissing her lightly on her sweet lips and saying good night.

As I came down the block to my own alley, a car came out. I only caught a glimpse of it as it crossed the street and disappeared in the alley there, but it looked familiar. I turned into the alley, stopped outside the garage, and got out to open the garage door.

Just as I started to open the door, I heard a pathetic meow from the row of garbage cans along the fence. A silver shadow slipped between the cans, coming toward my feet. Perky. Nellie's cat. I looked at the window above me, and it was still lighted.

Leaving the car where it was, I picked up the cat and went through the back gate of Nellie's house, through the back yard, and around to the front door. Janice would probably be asleep and would be very angry to be wakened, but I couldn't help that.

Evidently she was up because she answered the first ring,

lips tightly clenched. When she saw it was me, her mouth dropped open. I held out the cat. "Sorry, Janice, but I found Perky in the alley—"

The words were swallowed up in a crashing thunder of sound. As the noise faded, I heard windows slamming open, people shouting at one another. I left the cat with Janice and ran back the way I had come.

When I came though the gate into the alley I could see there was almost nothing left of my garage. The side toward the house was still whole, but the door and alley end were simply gone. My car had boards resting on it, but the force of the blast hadn't been in that direction. If I'd gotten out of the car, if I'd been raising the door of the garage, if I'd driven in . . .

When the bomb squad came this time, I told them I'd seen a car driving out of the alley. I didn't tell them where I'd seen it before, because I couldn't remember.

eleven

Mark found the bug in the phone the following morning, after I'd told him what happened, and after he'd asked me how anyone knew I was going to be coming home about that time.

"Somebody knew you were going out to have a late dinner with Grace," he said.

"How did they know I wouldn't stay at Grace's all night?" I asked him.

He shrugged. "You haven't been."

"You mean somebody's been following me?"

He didn't know. I called Gower Hodgson and told him about the bug. He didn't know either, but he sent two men over to look for more of them. They didn't find any. Gower suggested that someone didn't like whatever I was doing and maybe I'd better stop. As far as I was concerned, I had already stopped. I couldn't think of anything else to do.

Saturday, the evening of the Van Doorn open house, I got myself into dinner jacket and black tie and went to pick up Grace at her place. Once more, she surprised me. She was wearing a slender, glittering sheath of rose lamé, her silver hair was piled high on her head, and her eyes were extravagantly made up. She looked like an escapee from the cover of *Vogue*.

"Wow," I said inadequately.

"I spent six months' savings for this dress," she said. "I hope you approve. I'm a lot more dressed up than I usually get." She slipped her coat on, searching the pockets for her gloves. "You look wonderful. Very handsome. I don't think I've ever been out with a man in a dinner jacket before. I had to look up what black tie meant, you know. I wasn't sure what it implied for women, but the book I bought said it meant this kind of thing. I hope I'm dressed up enough."

"Kitty Van Doorn will be hard put to it to compete with you," I told her. "I think ravishing is the word." I watched as she locked the door behind her.

"Well, good. I hope I stay that way. I hope my mascara doesn't run or my hair doesn't fall down or anything. It kept slipping when I was doing it. I've got a whole can of mousse on it, and that may not be enough. The thing I worried about most was whether I should carry my gun, because we're generally supposed to, off duty or on, but I figured in an evening bag, where would I put it? And I hope they have lots of food because I'm starved."

"If they don't, I'll take you to dinner, after," I promised, thinking of the enormous buffet that Kitty had described to me when I'd delivered the last of the small items. "They won't have anything at Van Doorn's but filet mignon, prosciutto, chicken Kiev, a hot lobster dish, hot crab puffs, about twenty gallons of shrimp, pâté, plus cheeses and little things on toast, stuff like that." I opened the car door for her. "Not to mention the quail eggs in aspic and the pastries."

When I got in beside her, she still seemed to be considering this. "It sounds like it might be enough, depending on the number of people invited."

Despite my somber mood, I laughed. "Grace, have you always eaten like this?"

"No," she said seriously. "Only since I was about nineteen. Before that, I ate more. Grandma always had trouble keeping up with my appetite. I'm just always hungry."

"How much do you weigh?"

"A hundred eighteen. Sometimes I get up as high as a hundred twenty, but something always happens and I lose it. I'd like a little more bust, to tell you the truth."

"I think it's fine, whatever size it is," I said, not thinking about what I was saying.

"You ought to know what size it is," she blurted, then turned bright red. I could see the color in the lights from the dash, dark against her dress.

"It was dark," I deadpanned. "Come on now, Grace. If you start in on me this way, we'll never make it through the evening. The Van Doorns are important clients. I have to look respectable. Not like some—"

"Prodigal?" she suggested.

"Libertine," I amended. "Despite your provocative dress, your lovely face, your elegant hair, and the voluptuous rest of you, tonight I have to be professional."

"Sure you do," she assented. "Because everyone will be asking who did the decor, and you'll be introduced, and you'll be modest and everything, and not mention your prices, and everyone will just fall over themselves hiring you. I think I'll just drift around saying, 'Did you know Jason Lynx did this beautiful room? Isn't he wonderful?' "

She actually might! "You do and I'll drag you away from the buffet table, foodless."

"I'd die," she said. "No, I'll be good. I do know how. I have very nice manners, I think, except being a cop I get out of practice. How's your garage coming?"

I told her the garage was coming fine. There was some controversy over whether insurance would pay for a garage destroyed by a bomb, but it was being rebuilt.

"Do you know who's out to get you yet, Jason?"

" 'Stimson,' " I told her. "I think that's fairly clear. Whoever he is, he doesn't like me messing about in his affairs. If it hadn't been for Nellie's cat, I'd have been mincemeat. Well. What about your nemesis? Is Renard still giving you trouble?"

"No. He's lying low, Renard is. The lieutenant had a few words with him about sex discrimination, so Renard's decided to do some work instead of picking on me. It's a funny thing, too. When the guy wants to work, he really can. I thought he was a total loser, but he can be smart. Nasty, but smart. Besides, I don't have to work with him anymore. My six months was up this week. They've got me teamed with another guy now. He's OK."

"Who's going to work with Renard?"

"God knows. I don't care, as long as it isn't me. I'm glad the work he's done on this case isn't an example of what the department usually does, or I'd quit." She sniffed, as though that was something she had wanted to say for some time.

We rode in companionable silence broken only by my occasional growls and mutters at the traffic. When we finally turned off the main road and started down the winding driveway, she rubbed a clear circle in the frosty window beside her and gasped.

"Is that the house?"

"That's the house. I thought you interviewed Kitty and her husband."

"Well, yeah, but not here. I was at their Colorado Springs house. It was an ugly house, big, moderne with an 'e,' you know, but nothing like this. I guess they've just moved here, huh?"

I said they had.

"This one is beautiful. Will you look at the lights! He must support Public Service all by himself."

The house was garlanded with twinkling holiday bulbs, too late for Christmas but definitely within the season. Light spilled from the many windows and darted from the flashlights being used by the parking attendants.

"OK, cop," I muttered to her. "On your best behavior." I turned the Mercedes over to an attendant and offered Grace my arm.

"I don't have a fur coat," she growled, looking around her at the other arrivals.

"Nobody will, once they're inside," I said. "Once we're divested, no one will know the difference." And when we were divested, no one did. There were at least a hundred people already there, and more arriving. I snagged two glasses of champagne from a smoothly scurrying waiter.

"Look at all the uniforms," Grace whispered over the edge of her glass. "What's two stars?"

"Stars are generals," I murmured. "The more stars, the higher the rank."

"Where did the Van Doorns get them all?"

"ENT Air Force Base. Fort Carson. Cheyenne Mountain."

"Oh, yeah. Where they watch for missiles. Who's minding the store?"

One of my former clients tapped me on the shoulder, and I made introductions. "Wilson Trotter, Grace Willis. Agnes Trotter."

"Well, Jase! And where did you find this charming creature?" Agnes, being her usual needly self, still peeved at me for not having responded to an attempted seduction while I was redecorating her townhouse.

"Ah'm just visitin'," said Grace in a perfect southern drawl. "Ah'm Jason's cousin."

"Oh? Where from?" Agnes wanted to know.

"N'wawrlens." Grace smiled. "And wheah ah y'all from?"

Agnes began talking about Chicago. Wilson saw another acquaintance across the room and dragged her away.

"What's this N'wawrlens business?" I demanded.

"I grew up there. When my folks died, I came here to live with Grandma. Sometimes I just like to try it on again. Like for size."

"Now you'll have to keep it up all evening."

"No problem." She grinned at me. "Don' you worry abaht li'l ole me. Besahdes, it's easiah to have nahce mannuhs in a suthen drawl."

There was much circulation of champagne. The buffet was as extraordinary as Kitty had promised, with twin pyramids of shrimp and flower-decked ice sculptures. In one of the large back rooms on the ground floor, originally a billiards room and one I hadn't redecorated—yet, I told myself, yet—there was a seven-man group playing stuff that occasionally sounded like music. I hadn't been on a dance floor in a while, so I rather tentatively asked Grace to dance. I had visions of stepping on her elegantly sandaled feet. She melted into my arms as though she had been there for years. The crowd was old enough that I didn't have to do gymnastics and could just hold her. We danced and ate and danced and ate. About every twenty minutes Grace suggested that we visit the buffet. Her accent held up flawlessly, and when I wasn't dancing with her, she had more partners waiting than she could accommodate.

While Grace was otherwise occupied, I was introduced to a number of people who I hoped would become future clients. I danced with the women, talked sports with the men. I've never been a team sports fan but I try to read the sports pages so I can talk to people who are. I hadn't been keeping up lately, however, and a few of the conversations limped a bit. I was reduced to saying nonspecific things like "How about those playoffs!" in an enthusiastic tone. Everyone had enough to drink that no one noticed.

Along about midnight, waiters began circulating with coffee. I found myself at a small table in the ballroom *cum* billiard room, sitting next to Peter Van Doorn while Grace danced with an attentive and overly attractive young officer.

Peter was a little drunk. "I want a billiard table in this room," he said. "If we need a ballroom, we can build one."

I said, "I can get you a table, Peter. You play billiards?"

"Oh, sure. A lot of these people do." He gestured at his guests. "Billiards or pool. I guess if you're an officer you'd play billiards. Pool is for noncoms."

"Looks like the whole U.S. military establishment is here tonight," I remarked.

"Well, you get to know one or two, and they introduce you to a few others. Frankly, down at the Springs there isn't much else. Military and retired military. A few academics, I guess, from the college. A few snooty folks up Broadmoor way. That's about it." Peter raised a finger at a passing waiter and took coffee and sweetener.

"Kitty did herself proud tonight," I said, knowing he would relish the compliment.

"Isn't she the prettiest thing? I'll tell you, that lady does love a party," Peter growled, tearing the end off the packet of sweetener and dumping the contents into his coffee.

"She says you do," I commented.

Peter put the torn-off strip into the empty packet, folded it once lengthwise, and then twisted it into a tiny bow tie that he laid on the table beside his saucer.

I swallowed, painfully. "She told me that's why she wanted to move up here to Cherry Hills, because the house down in the Springs was ugly, and besides it wasn't big enough to do all the entertaining you wanted to do."

Peter laughed, a pleasant chest-rumbling sound. "Well, she accuses me and I accuse her, and I guess we both like it better here. The real reason is that this is nearer the nursing home where Kitty's mama lives. Kitty likes to see her mama every day, and that meant quite a drive from the Springs, especially in rotten weather. Now, what I like is to have a few folks stay for the weekend so we can do some serious golf. I've got a good foursome for tomorrow, and that's what I'm really looking forward to. Excuse me." He rose to speak to someone, taking his cup with him.

I picked up the tiny pink bow tie and dropped it into my pocket. My hands were cold.

I cut in on Grace and her partner, telling her that we had to be going. She took one look at my face and agreed. We picked up our coats and retrieved the car. Only when we were leaving the driveway did she ask, "What happened?"

I steered with one hand while I unbuttoned my overcoat, reached into my jacket pocket, and dropped the pink paper into her hand.

"What? Oh. The thing the man made! The pet shop woman called it a butterfly."

"Right."

"Who, Jason?"

"Peter Van Doorn. It's obviously an unconscious habit, something he always does. He didn't even notice he was doing it. It doesn't prove anything at all, of course. There could be dozens—hundreds—of large men with the same little habit. But it's just too coincidental."

"I know," she said. "What are you going to do?"

"Call William Rider again. Or the local guy, Hodgson. Tell him about it."

"I'd do it tonight," she said, looking at the grim set of my jaw. "I wouldn't wait for morning."

Gower Hodgson, roused from his sleep by a night operator from the bureau office, told me that William Rider was flying out from Washington on Monday. "Bill has put some ends together, Jason. I suggest you just sit tight until he gets here. You're savvy enough to know that this little trick of Van Doorn's doesn't mean much at this stage."

I didn't feel very savvy. Mostly I wanted Soph Feathers to get a look—or a listen—at Peter Van Doorn. Soph Feathers and Nellie Arpels. I wandered around the house, Bela whining at my heels. I went into the front bedroom and lay on the bed, the scent of Agatha in my nostrils. I heard her saying, "You're getting close, Jason. Just a little more. Find him. Oh, find him." It was her voice, not some kind of internal monologue tricked up to sound like a ghost. It was her. I convinced myself of that and then fell asleep on our bed and awoke at dawn to wander around for an hour, like a ghost myself, starting at every sound.

I knew I was in serious danger of losing it. I called Grace.

"I can't sit here until tomorrow morning," I told her. "Let's do something, I don't care what. Let's go for a drive or to a museum or something." I picked her up and we spent the Sunday meandering, going to shopping malls and the Natural History Museum and to four different restaurants for breakfast, lunch, tea, supper. When I dropped her at her house, it was almost midnight.

"Thank you," I said, hugging her almost impersonally, like a teddy bear. Something comfortable. "I'm sorry I was such lousy company." She'd tried to distract me all day, but I'd kept losing track of the conversation. I had the feeling I'd been silent for hours, hanging around her neck like a dead albatross.

"Waiting's always the hard part," she said sympathetically. "I know that, Jason. Call me as soon as you know something." In the rearview mirror I saw her standing on her porch, looking after me.

Back at the house, I walked through the showrooms, stopping in the south bay window to look out at the Whitney house just as Peter Van Doorn had done when he and Kitty had been here, the Wednesday before the Whitneys were killed. I had known he was uninterested in the conversation Kitty and I were having; I hadn't known the fascination of the window was what was outside it.

What had he seen?

Outside in my back yard, Ladislav barked, his voice rising to a squeaky soprano. He couldn't see me from where he was, and he was lonely. If he'd been in the Whitney run, I could have seen him.

Peter had gone to the window because he had heard what I had just heard.

A dog that barked soprano. Wasn't that what Sophia Feathers had said the man at the dog show was asking about? Peter Van Doorn was looking for a dog that barked soprano . . . because? Because he had heard such a dog? On the phone perhaps, when the blackmailer made contact with him? Peter had gone on a fruitless search for that dog, or that kind of dog. And then on that Wednesday a few weeks ago, he had come into my shop and heard the same bark, the same strange squeaky bark.

What else?

I rubbed my head, trying to remember. Peter had walked to the big bay window. There had been sounds. Dogs barking. A door slamming.

The door had slammed because George or Betty had come in or gone out.

"Are those your dogs?" Peter had asked. He had known

they weren't. He could see they lived next door. But the question served to make me answer him.

"The Whitneys' dogs," I'd said. And Peter had come back to the table, looking distracted. I had given him a name.

Now I stared at the house next door, not thinking of anything, listening for a voice just outside my hearing. I could almost tell what it was saying. After a long time, I went upstairs to bed.

William Rider was just as I remembered him except for a little gray in his hair, not much. He still had his honking laugh and wore horn-rimmed glasses. He took off the glasses when he sat down beside my desk, however. Took them off and put them in his pocket. "I'm nearsighted," he said. "I can see these pictures better without glasses. I want you to look through them, Jason, and tell me if there's anyone you recognize." He handed me a thick packet and sat back, exchanging meaningful looks with Gower Hodgson and two stolid, expressionless men who had been introduced only as Al and Joe. Mark stood silently by the door. I had insisted that he be present. It was the first Monday I could remember that I hadn't had lunch at McInery House with Emilia Montoya. It was twelve fifteen, and I hadn't even called her to say I wouldn't be there.

The packet held over a hundred pictures. They were photographs of a town. A street, a grocery store, a post office. A dry cleaner's. A school. People, moving around. A newspaper boy. A magazine stand on the corner of Forest and Main, the street signs showing up clearly, as well as the titles of the magazines and papers: *Atlantic, The New Yorker, Playboy, The New York Times.*

"Where were these taken?"

"I'm not supposed to tell you," Rider said, casting a significant glance at Mark. "But I will on condition you don't mention it to anyone else. Anyone at all." Mark nodded, eagerly. I nodded, more slowly. "They were taken at a school in one of the iron curtain countries."

"A school?"

"A school where selected people are taught to act like Americans. To talk the language. To behave just as we behave."

"It's a whole town!"

"One of several."

"How did you get these?"

"That I can't tell you. I can tell you that they were all taken on the same day. That makes a difference."

"Why?"

"Because all the people in those pictures were there at the same time, and we can therefore speculate that they could recognize each other."

I went on looking. The phone rang. Mark went to answer it. I heard him making excuses for me: Emilia, wondering where I was. I leafed through photographs. Some of them were long shots, with several people at various distances. One of them was of a bus stop, with people waiting. I looked at it twice before I saw them. "Betty," I said, pointing. "And George." The woman was wearing a hat and had a dog on a leash, a small brown dog. Unmistakably Betty. George was a lot thinner than I'd ever seen him.

"We thought so too. Keep on. Go through them again." Gower Hodgson took out a pack of cigarettes, looked around for an ashtray, didn't find one, and put the cigarettes away with a sigh. I found another one with Betty in it. Then another with George standing in a butcher shop, lower lip out in his habitual pouty expression. "George," I said, nodding. "I am absolutely sure. That's George."

"Keep on looking," Rider told me. He got up and had a low-voiced conversation with Al and Joe as I plowed through the photographs. There was a man half hidden behind Betty at the bus stop. I wished I could see all of him. There was something funny about his ear, but I couldn't identify why I thought so.

I kept stopping at the butcher shop picture. There was a

man in the background who looked familiar. I beckoned to Rider. "This looks like Peter Van Doorn." I said. "Without his glasses and mustache and with his hair cut really short."

"Do you think it is?"

"I think it could be, but I'm not sure." The more I looked at it, the less it looked like him. "I'm not at all sure."

"Ah. Well. Then we need to try something else, don't we?"

I flipped through the pictures again. "Maybe Kitty is in here."

Rider said, "No, she won't be in there. We're sure Kitty is home-grown. Just her misfortune she fell for someone who may not be quite what she believed him to be."

"But, my God, why would Van Doorn . . . he has money coming out of his ears!"

"George stole at least four million, and his furniture stash accounts for only one million of that," Hodgson remarked. "Hadn't you wondered where the rest of it went?"

"Not to Van Doorn!"

"We think it's likely. To set him up in style and then to pay for information."

"All those military men!"

"His informants are probably of considerably lower rank," Rider murmured. "Usually it's the technicians who know the kinds of things Van Doorn pays for. Most generals don't know that much about details, quite frankly."

"But it doesn't make sense! I figured George was black-mailing Van Doorn! They were both on the same side!"

Hodgson said, "Maybe the ideology wore a little thin after a few years. George had been busy setting something aside for his retirement, and then his income was curtailed. Then, out of the blue, he sees Van Doorn coming into or leaving your place. He recognized Van Doorn as being a colleague of his, a convivial type who must be working on something very hush-hush. All George needed was Van Doorn's license number. If he had that, he could get the name. And once he had the name, he did a little more checking and knew what Van Doorn was up to. At that point, he saw his way to a few hundred thousand more, so he put together a blackmail scheme and to hell with taking sides."

Rider said, "He may even have realized that the money he'd been raising had been going to Van Doorn. In any case, he'd have known Van Doorn had access to money, lots of it, to keep up his lifestyle and pay for information."

"But after George's source of funds dried up, where did Van Doorn get money to pay a blackmailer?" I asked. "He told me once that money was no problem for him."

Hodgson shrugged. "It wouldn't be any problem for Van Doorn, however much of a problem it might have been for whoever he's working for. They wouldn't take all that trouble to set him up here and then cut off his support just because George's money tree wilted. Whoever is back of Peter Van Doorn found the money somewhere."

"Wouldn't George have worried that since they'd recognized Van Doorn, Van Doorn might recognize them?"

"Van Doorn's showing up here was a fluke, Jason." Hodgson waved the fingertips of one hand, as though dusting something away. "Up until a few days ago, Van Doorn lived sixty miles away in Colorado Springs, not here. He could have lived there for twenty years and the Whitneys could have lived here for that long, and their paths would probably never have crossed. George must have thought they'd never cross again."

Rider said, "One thing that concerns me. If Van Doorn was being blackmailed, he'd have known it had to be someone who'd known him when those pictures were taken. Why didn't he get in touch with his control and tell him about it?"

I thought I might know why, but I didn't say anything. If I had been Peter, I wouldn't have told anyone either.

Rider pursed his lips. "However, we're getting badly ahead of ourselves. Most of this is conjecture; we have no proof of any of it. We haven't positively identified the man in the picture as Van Doorn. Which means we need to go a step or so further." He stood up, stretching. "We have to find out if Van

Doorn is really the man your pet shop lady saw. That will tell us if he was hunting for George, which will be some confirmation. If he's also the man your woman friend across the alley saw, that will tell us he killed the couple and we can stop looking for anyone else. So our next task will be to find out whether the women recognize him and do it without alerting Van Doorn. Maybe you could help us, Jason. Do you think you could get him to come here? Could you have some kind of—oh, I don't know. A showing or something?"

"You want Soph Feathers and Nelly Arpels here?"

"Here seems the easiest to manage."

I tried to think. There had been too many revelations. My mind was blank.

Mark had been standing quietly. Now he said, "There's the billiard table, Jason. This morning you said there was dancing in the billiards room and Van Doorn talked about a table."

I stared at him blindly. "The table . . . of course."

"What table?" asked Hodgson.

"I've got a billiard table in the basement. An auction house in New York made a mistake and shipped it instead of the dining room table I'd bought. They keep saying they're arranging to have it shipped back, but no one's picked it up yet. The thing's still in the pieces it arrived in. Peter Van Doorn mentioned he wanted a billiard table. I could invite him and Kitty over to look at it."

"Just him, if you can."

"We'd have to set it up. I'd need some help. It took three men to get the parts down there in the elevator."

"How long will it take you?"

"If we leave it in the basement, a couple of hours, I suppose. If we bring it up to the first floor, longer. I'll have to make room for it."

"Call him. See if he'll come over to look at it tonight."

"Tonight?"

"Tonight, Jason. Along about eight, maybe?"

When I spoke to Peter Van Doorn, my voice sounded

strained. Evidently Van Doorn heard nothing wrong with it, however. He left the phone to ask Kitty if she wanted to see a pool table. Rider grimaced when I said it was all right, and I turned my palms up. I couldn't prevent Kitty's coming with her husband if she wanted to.

"He says they're having dinner downtown," I explained. "He says he should be finished around nine, and I told him that wasn't too late."

Rider frowned.

"Now what?" I asked him.

"Now get your table set up. Al and Joe'll help you. Gower'll help you. I'm going to find out if your two lady witnesses can come over this evening. I'd like to have a woman available to talk with Mrs. Arpels."

I told him that Grace Willis already knew about the whole mess and suggested I call her for him. I did, and she talked to Rider and agreed to meet him somewhere. Then Joe and Al and Gower and I headed for the basement.

The billiard table parts were stacked along the wall just outside the elevator. Each individual leg looked monumental.

"Nobody wanted to carry those any further than necessary, did they?" Al asked, his long face sagging. "I suppose you're going to want them moved a hundred yards due east." He took off his jacket, disclosing a very workmanlike shoulder holster.

"I think we'll set it up right here," I told them. "It's no showroom, but then, Peter won't expect a showroom. We'll have to start with the legs."

When Eugenia opened the showrooms at noon, I locked the door to the basement and we went on working. It wasn't as easy as I'd thought. There were long bolts that went through the legs into the crosspieces, and two of them were missing. I had to run out to the hardware store and find something that would do. By four we had the table set up, and Mark and I took some time to rig a light over it. At five, Rider returned with Grace Willis to say that both Sophia Feathers and Nellie

Arpels could be present. He looked around the room where the table was set up. It was frankly basement, with a concrete floor and walls. "I think over there," Rider said, pointing to a recessed area where a coal bin had once stood. "Nelly and Soph can sit over there, in that corner. Have you got some kind of screen? If you turn all the lights off but this one, the women will be in the dark but they'll be able to see him."

Grace said, "This isn't safe. We ought to have the man in a lineup, Mr. Rider. This is just not good procedure."

"If I could get him in a lineup without spooking him, I'd do it," Rider said patiently. "If I were planning on arresting him, it would be easy. I'm not sure we can do that; he may not be guilty of anything I can charge him with right now. And there may be other players, people we don't know about yet."

"You could have the two ladies outside," I suggested. "In a van or something."

"Then they wouldn't be able to see him up close," Rider said. "Mrs. Feathers saw him up close before."

"How about upstairs, in the showroom? She could see him as he comes in."

"Try it my way," Rider urged. "Mrs. Arpels is in a wheelchair. We can bring her into the elevator from outside and directly here, without any stairs."

It was an arguing point. As it was, they would have to carry Nellie down the stairs in her own house. I quit arguing with them. Mark found a couple of screens in the attic. They looked unconvincing, so he threw a few fabric samples over them and scattered some pieces of disassembled furniture around. With the addition of a roll of old carpet and a couple of half-unpacked crates with excelsior sticking out, the whole assembly looked more natural. There was just enough room in the alcove for Soph Feathers and Nellie Arpels. I sat on the chair back there and checked the holes in the screens. With the light over the table and the other lights off, I could see the whole table and all the men around it. At night, in the dark basement, no one would be able to see where I was sitting. Still, it bothered me.

"I don't think this is a good idea," I said.

"What's the matter with it?" Hodgson asked.

I couldn't tell him. I didn't know. It should work. we'd put the two ladies behind the screens at about eight, just in case Van Doorn showed up early. I'd bring him down here to see the table. He'd look at it, and then, since it was obviously dusty and uncomfortable down here, we'd go back upstairs to talk about it.

When Hodgson brought Nellie Arpels over in a van, Grace was with her.

"I told her I wanted her," Nellie said. "I haven't been out of that house in twenty years, Jason. Something might happen where I'd need a woman."

Rider harrumphed, glaring. There wasn't room for three people behind the screens the way we had them arranged.

"Peter knew Grace was with me at his open house," I said. "It would be natural for her to be here." Actually, having Grace there made me feel more normal. As though the evening were just a regular evening, during which a client was dropping over to see a possible purchase.

We unloaded Nellie in her chair and pushed it into the elevator, which has an outside door off the driveway. Grace and I went with her as the old machine made its slow, grinding way down. At the bottom I heaved the solid old door aside and we went out. Meantime, Soph Feathers had arrived and we introduced the two ladies and showed them where they'd be sitting during our little show.

About a quarter to nine, Mark called down the stairs that the Van Doorns were driving up. Grace and I went upstairs to meet them. Soph and Nellie were in place. The four FBI men were in the furnace room where they could see everything through the partly opened door without being seen themselves. The light over the billiard table was on, plus a few lamps to light the way to it. The rest of the basement was dark.

Mark was chatting with Peter and Kitty when we got up there. Grace remembered to use her accent, and we talked about N'wawrlens while they got their coats off. Peter had been drinking enough that he was flushed and laughing very loudly at everything.

I said, "Peter, let's you and I go down and see that table. It's dusty down there, Kitty. Why don't you and Grace stay up here?"

No chance. Kitty bubbled about how she loved to play pool and just had to see the table herself. I gritted my teeth and led the way down. The four of us found our way to the lighted area and I pointed out the features that would make the table a good buy, inventing most of them. I knew absolutely nothing about billiards.

"I thought maybe you'd have a cue and some balls," Peter said. He leaned over the table looking at it, with Grace beside him. I was watching from across the table, and Kitty was behind me. "Damn, Jason, you can't try a table without a cue and some balls."

"I never thought of it," I told him while I mentally cursed Rider and Hodgson. Damn it, they should have thought of it. "I suppose you're right. Well. Why don't I get some, and then you can come back?"

I don't know how Kitty got away from the rest of us. She was right behind me, and then she wasn't. I turned around, and there she was, reaching for one of the fabric samples Mark had thrown over the screen. I should have known. She pulled. I think I yelled, maybe not. The whole screen came over, in slow motion, revealing the pale figures behind it. When the screen went, Soph stood up and leaned forward, probably to try and catch the screen. There was enough light to show Peter her face.

The rest of us were frozen, but I don't think it took him more than two seconds to recognize her and realize what was happening. He grabbed for Grace, pulling her in front of him as a shield. He had one arm around her throat, the other at her

side. Grace reached for her gun, actually got her hand on it
before he jerked her off her feet, snatching the gun with his free
hand. He backed away toward the elevator, dragging Grace in
front of him. Kitty had moved across the room when the screen
fell, and as he backed away she started toward him. He didn't
see who it was, only the motion coming out of the dark. He
fired once and she went down. "Don't!" he screamed at us.
"Don't, or I'll kill her!" He pulled the elevator door shut, and I
heard it begin to grind.

I saw Rider moving toward the back stairs. Soph was
bending over Nellie Arpels. I didn't stay to see if they needed
help. As soon as the elevator door started to close I ran for the
stairs. I'd pushed the wrong button in that elevator too many
times to think that Van Doorn would push the right one. He'd
hit the middle button, and the middle button would take him to
the second floor. Rider and the others would be on the first
floor or outside. I went up the basement stairs like a scalded
cat, around the corner into the hall, across the hall and up the
stairs, into my office. My handgun was still in the lower drawer
of my desk. It wasn't loaded.

I don't know what made me think I could climb two flights
of stairs, get my gun, and load it before Van Doorn arrived.
Maybe just thinking of that old elevator as slow had misled me
to the actual time it took to travel up two floors. It had been a
vain hope. Stupidity. I was coming out the door of Mark's office
with the gun in my hand when Peter came into the far end of
the hall. He saw me and fired once. I felt my right leg go out
from under me as though it had been chopped in two.

Grace screamed. I don't know what she said. I don't know
what happened. Everything was black and red, and there was
a lot of my blood spurting. Then she was there, pressing a
towel tight on my leg, saying, "Press it, Jason. You'll bleed to
death." Van Doorn was standing over her, the gun at her head.
Then he dragged her away again.

I heard men yelling. Grace was hollering that I'd been shot.
Van Doorn was telling them he wanted a TV traffic helicopter

out in front of the house in thirty minutes or he'd kill Grace. For some ridiculous reason I looked at my watch. Then there was a blank spell.

I came to with Grace yelling at me to press on the towel and stop the bleeding. Evidently I'd been doing that, even though I didn't remember it. Suddenly things were very clear, sharp-edged.

"Why, Peter?" I asked him. He was standing there in the hall, Grace in front of him, only about ten feet from me.

"You damned idiot!" Van Doorn snarled. "Why did you have to stick your nose in this?"

It wasn't really a question, but I accepted it as one nonetheless. "Because either you killed my wife or George did."

He gaped at me from across Grace's shoulder. "Your wife! What the hell does she have to do with anything."

"My wife was a file clerk for the FBI. Eight or nine years ago in Washington she saw George's picture, and Betty's. Not that she really believed she had. She thought she'd seen someone who resembled them, that's all. She told them about it, probably the same day she disappeared."

"I didn't kill her. I knew nothing about her."

"You killed Jollaby, didn't you?" Grace asked him.

"I don't even know the name."

"George's predecessor. The man who used to run the radio station."

"That was before I came here. At least a year before. I know nothing about it."

"But you killed George." It was a statement, not a question.

"Damned fool. Greedy idiot. Here he'd been passing money to me with one hand, and then he started snatching it back with the other."

"Did you know he was supporting your . . . your work?"

"Not until a few weeks ago. There was no contact between us at all. Up until then I didn't know George was within a thousand miles of me. I didn't even know where the money came from. All I knew was when it stopped."

"What did you do then?" I asked. Pain grabbed at me, a wave of blackness. I pressed harder on the towel, feeling the warmth of the red soaking through it against my hands.

"I got what I needed elsewhere."

"George blackmailed you, didn't he?" Grace asked the question, keeping him talking.

Van Doorn snarled. "I got that damned phone call. Somebody saying he'd turn me over to the authorities if I didn't pay him. Saying he had evidence of who I was, what I was doing, that he'd blow the operation." His voice was thick. He had drunk enough to make him talkative. I wondered why it hadn't been enough to slow him down.

I tried to focus through the waves of pain. "I don't suppose your boss liked that much."

"I didn't tell him. He'd have wanted to pull me out. After seven years, working my damn butt off, just leave it all, leave Kitty." There was something suspiciously like a sob in his voice. "I couldn't risk that. I had to find out who was doing it myself."

"Is that why you went to the dog shows, Peter?"

"That time he called, that time I heard a dog in the background. A dog with a funny bark. I thought maybe—"

"You went to dog shows. But that didn't get you anywhere?"

"Nowhere. A waste of time. It took me a year and a half to find out who was doing it, and when I did it was a complete accident. I heard the dog bark and I looked out the window. There they were, next door to you, Jason. I saw them. I recognized them. Right then I knew who was blackmailing me."

"So you killed them."

"No, I didn't have to kill them."

"The gun that killed George is the same one that killed Jollaby," Grace gargled around the choking arm.

Van Doorn shook her. "Once I told them what George was doing, they took care of it."

"They?" she asked. "They who?"

"I don't know who. I wouldn't tell you if I did." An expression of crafty awareness came over his face. "When I get out of this, I'm going back. I want to have somewhere to go."

"One of 'them' goes by the name of Stimson," I said, my mouth dry. Too dry. Too cold. I knew I was going into shock. "At least, he did."

"We have a lot of names," Van Doorn muttered. "All of us. Lot of names." He stiffened at a sound from below. "Where's that helicopter?"

I took one hand off the towel to look at my watch. "You gave them half an hour, Peter. It's only been fifteen minutes." I stretched my leg out on the floor, trying to ease the pain, but the motion made me grunt. My leg lay out there at an impossible angle and the towel was soaked with blood. I tried not to think about it. "How did George blackmail you? I would have thought you'd have followed the man who picked up the money and found out who was doing it long ago."

"George was clever," he sneered, dragging Grace to a chair where he sat down heavily, pushing her onto her knees, the gun to her head. "Clever George. He only called that one time. He said he wanted a hundred thousand every three months. When I had the money, I was to run an ad in the Sunday paper. Then, on Monday night I was to drive downtown late, after all the businesses and offices were closed."

He shut his eyes for a moment. He looked sick, sweating.

"What happened then?" I asked.

"My car phone would ring and this computer voice would say, Go to such and such an office building, take the elevator to the tenth floor, or the fifteenth or twentieth, throw off the package, and return to the lobby. The voice would give me five minutes, or three, just time to do it from wherever I was. A few times, I went right back up, but the money was gone, he was gone."

"Don't those buildings have guards in the lobbies?" Grace asked. I heard her through a haze.

"Of course. I signed in, I signed out. He didn't. He was already there. He went there in the daytime and hid out. Bastard. Sometimes he wouldn't call on Monday, and I'd have to do it on Tuesday."

"How much money did George supply you with before it stopped?" she asked.

I fumbled with my belt, took it off. If somebody didn't do something pretty soon, I was going to bleed to death.

"Four million and something." He didn't seem to mind telling her. Maybe he knew that most of what he was saying no longer mattered. Maybe he needed to keep on talking to keep from falling apart himself. I thought of telling him what he had done to Kitty and discarded the idea. He might go crazy if I did that. Crazier.

Grace kept after him. "Four million! That's enough to buy a lot of information. Who from? The generals from Cheyenne Mountain?"

I got the belt around the towel and tightened it.

He grinned like an animal, all teeth. "Wouldn't you and your friends downstairs like to know." We had finally come to something he wasn't willing to talk about.

I heard a low hammering sound, growing louder. The *whap-whap-whap* of rotors.

"There's your chopper," she said.

I wondered how in hell they were going to get it down in the street outside. The utility lines ran down the alley, but there were streetlights. I concentrated on getting the belt as tight around my leg as possible.

"Are you going to let Grace go?" I asked. I sounded like Jacob. Old.

The feral grin again. "When and if I can, Jason. I'm not a killer by nature, but I will if I have to."

Rider's voice came from downstairs, amplified. "All right, Van Doorn. The chopper's down in the street."

Peter edged down the hall, keeping the gun at Grace's head, dragging her. She wasn't helping him, but she was a small woman and he was a big man. He started down the stairs, bellowing at the men below. "Back. All of you. I don't want to see any of you." I heard people moving around.

I crawled after him, coming to the head of the stairs just as Van Doorn reached the foot. To get to the front door he had to cross the hall. I clawed my way up the wall, balancing on my good leg as I tore at the gold-covered cable that supported the chandelier. It began to slip while it was still twined around the cleat, and I hung onto it, letting it slide through my sticky red hands. The belt around my leg slipped and blood spurted. I felt the black surging up, swallowing at me. Just as Van Doorn and Grace came beneath it, the crystals chimed and he looked up. I couldn't hold it. It burned my hands as it tore through. I heard it crash. I said, Grace, Grace, to myself, trying to believe it had hit him first.

A rifle shot, only one, cracked sharply in the hallway. Echoes bounced around inside my head. Men started yelling. I got my head over the banister somehow. Below me, Van Doorn lay sprawled beside a glittering cascade of broken prisms. Beneath him Grace squirmed and howled. William Rider moved toward the bodies, entirely too slowly to suit me.

"Will you get her the hell out from under him?" I cried, trying to pull myself up by the banister. Then everything turned a velvet black and I quit worrying about anything.

twelve

The next clear picture I have is of Bill Rider sitting on the foot of my hospital bed a day later while a starchy nurse insisted I take several pills.

"That was one of the more interesting maneuvers I've seen in my time," he remarked. "I've seen all kinds of weapons, but this was my first capture by chandelier."

I looked up at the container of blood dripping into my arm and thought briefly about AIDS, hoping the blood donor had been a priest who took his vows seriously. Then I decided not to think about it. "The chandelier?" I asked, my voice sounding like wet tissue paper, all glop and sob, with no fabric to it. There had been some surgery done to fix my bullet-shattered leg bone and sew together a torn artery. I knew about this in a sort of dreamy way, but I was not entirely with it. "The chandelier didn't kill him, did it?"

"Oh, no. It didn't even hit him. No, our sharpshooter did that. He was hunkered down in a window across the street and sighted in through the open front door of your place. The helicopter fly-by was just for sound effects. No way we could get a copter down through the trees and telephone wires in that street. If he'd been sober, Van Doorn would have known that. The chandelier distracted him long enough for our man to get a good shot at him without risking Detective Willis. I'm sorry he's dead. There were a lot of questions we wanted answered."

"Was Grace hurt?"

"Not badly. Bruised a little when he fell on her. She says she used to get hurt worse playing football with the neighborhood boys. After you were taken care of, when we asked what we could do for her, she told us she was hungry."

"That's Grace." I sighed.

"I bought her dinner while you were being sewn up," Rider

said. "The girl eats like an elephant. Man might not be able to afford to feed her, but she's fine otherwise. Not a hysteric out of her."

"No," I agreed. "Grace wouldn't have hysterics."

Rider nodded his head, ticking off points to himself. "Mrs. Feathers and Nellie are both all right. Van Doorn was the man Sophia Feathers saw. Nellie will probably never stop talking about helping us catch a murderer. Even though he wasn't. At least not by intention. Kitty Van Doorn died last night, but he never knew he'd killed her."

It might have killed him if he had known. It was love for Kitty that had made him seek his tormentors by himself rather than calling for help. "I still don't know—" I tried to sit up so I could see his face.

"Know what?" Rider asked. "You've earned the right to know what happened, Jason."

"Was George really sending information through the religious broadcasts?"

"Yes. He was. We picked up some tapes from the station in Galveston. The speeded-up sections are still there, and we're getting them decoded now. Preliminary results tell us there's no question about it. George was a spy as well as a thief."

Old George a spy. I started to laugh. I couldn't stop. Rider got out of his chair and shook me by the shoulders, gently. He didn't hurt me as much as I was already hurting myself, jerking the leg around.

"This is crazy," I said, choking down the laughter. "Spies. Cold War stuff. For God's sake, Rider, the Russians have pulled out of Afghanistan. Gorby has declared glasnost. Everything our scientists or military does is in the newspapers or the technical magazines. What is so compelling right now that we're still being spied on here? We don't have any Star Wars research going on."

I didn't intend it as a question, but he took it as one.

"Jason, this all started years ago. This operation might have been planned twenty years ago. The agents were trained then. Each move was decided on, one, two, three. It's like trying to stop one of those huge oil tankers in mid-ocean. Even if you shut down the engines, you go for fifty miles before the thing stops. Even if Mr. Gorbachev gains total control of the Supreme Soviet and gets infected with the peace bug and tells everybody to stop all surveillance everywhere—which you've got to admit is pretty unlikely—it would take years before things wound down. People have to be debriefed and pensioned off. People have to be called in from the cold and warmed up for retirement. Records have to be made and filed. And even though we're in the habit of thinking of the Commies as the bad guys, Russia isn't the only player. There are intelligence-gathering organizations in every country in the world. It seems George was from Hungary, originally, but who in hell paid him? I don't know. Who paid Peter Van Doorn? We know where they were trained, but a lot of people from a lot of different places are trained there, or have been. Terrorists, even. For all I know right now, Peter Van Doorn could have been working for the Ayatollah Khomeini."

He sighed, and shook his head at me. "Maybe someday I'll find out who was running George Whitney and Peter Van Doorn, but right now I haven't a clue. The players are dead, and I can't ask them."

"Don't we monitor broadcasts?" I asked, still worrying about the unlikelihood of the whole thing. "Wouldn't somebody have heard those squeals, somebody who knew what they were?"

"No," he said, his mouth making a grim line. "No, we don't monitor broadcasts routinely, and the reason we don't is we aren't given the money to do it with. Our own intelligence organizations haven't been in great favor with Congress recently, and do you know how many radio stations there are in this country?"

It all seemed to come down to money. All of it. Money and what people did with it. Which brought another question to mind.

"Why didn't George just put the money in an account? All this . . . this traveling about, buying furniture here and there, bringing it home in his van, all that seems so—"

"Unnecessary?" he offered. "Not really. We believe Van Doorn was not George's only source of information. Every time George traveled he was given bits and pieces of tape to transmit through his religious broadcasts. If I had been running him, I'd certainly have made that resource as widely available as possible to other agents. That's why George went to dog shows. It's so easy at a dog show for someone to bump up against you and slip an envelope into your pocket, or go sightseeing and pick up something that's been left for you."

I admitted it made sense.

"At the same time, because George was handling so much money, if I were running him I'd have kept an eye on him. I'd have wanted to know if he went into a bank or a diamond exchange or mailed money to Switzerland. I don't mean daily surveillance or bugged phones necessarily, but I'd have someone watching to see where he went and what he did.

"But suppose my watcher reports that George is buying furniture. Would I care? He makes a good income. He's entitled to furnish his house if he likes."

"Nobody would know the furniture was valuable, was that it?"

"Exactly. No one would know. The phony Stimson was probably controlling both the Whitneys and Van Doorn, and he didn't know until you told him. Eventually, George would have been allowed to 'retire.' When that time came, the Whitneys would have moved their household effects to California or down to Florida, the way half the retirees in the country do, and no one would have thought anything about it. Sotheby's would have auctioned off the collection with the name of the collector discreetly withheld."

"If he was watched so closely, how did he manage the blackmail?"

"I don't think he was watched *that* closely. Still, it's remarkable that he accomplished the blackmail so well. Though from what Grace has told us, George was extremely clever about it."

"The car phone. The office buildings."

Rider nodded. "He may have had Betty do the pickups of money while he made the calls."

"Wasn't George afraid that Van Doorn would tell their control about the blackmail? Surely he must have known he'd be the prime suspect."

"It was the one weak spot in George's plan. We'll never know how he rationalized that particular risk. Maybe he relied on the fact that if they investigated him, they'd find meticulous records of every dime he had raised, every dime he had sent on, no cache of stocks or bonds, no diamonds, no gold, nothing obviously valuable. George would have claimed innocence, and he might even have gotten away with it."

"Why didn't George's boss—uh, control—pull him in when Beeman arrived?"

"They still needed to get information out. Van Doorn was still working, and he was only one source. I believe there were others. Except for having to tape his programs at home instead of at the office, George was still doing a big part of the job he'd been given to do."

The pills they'd given me were taking effect. I could barely keep my eyes open.

Rider said, "We've got men searching the Whitney house for anything related to your wife. When we get the broadcast stuff decoded, even though Peter wouldn't tell you his source, we should be able to figure out who's been selling information."

"Who told you he didn't tell me—oh. Grace."

"Had her ears open every minute, that girl. Even with a gun to her head."

"Formidable." I sighed, half asleep. The world was turning double on me.

"Right," Rider was grinning at me from both his two heads. "You go ahead and drift off. Everything's in good hands."

They found Agatha's body while I was still in the hospital. She was in the Whitney house, under some empty wine racks that had been placed there to hide the existence of the shallow grave and the badly patched concrete. I asked them to have the body cremated and also I asked them to send somebody to talk to her folks down in Florida. I didn't want to do it myself. At that particular moment, I didn't want to do anything myself. I was still pretty heavily into painkillers, which was probably a good thing.

"The bullet in her body did not match the others," Rider told me through my drug-induced calm. "It looks like wrecking the car in the mountains was misdirection, Jason. We believe George killed your wife. Then he or Betty drove the car into the mountains, while the other one of them followed in the van. They left the main highway and went off onto the little-traveled gravel road which has that really ghastly drop-off; then they pushed the car over. They did it purely and simply because they wanted attention focused up there, not down here in the neighborhood. The baby was in the car because your wife was headed for the doctor's just before they killed her. They left the baby in the car so everyone would assume your wife had been in the car also. They knew you would never believe she had gone away and left the baby at home. It worked, of course. You assumed, everyone else assumed, that she had been in that car."

"Nellie said she was going to the pediatrician. Nellie saw her go into the garage."

"They caught her in the garage just as she was preparing to leave. Later, they moved the body into their house and buried it."

"Jerry used to sleep," I said. "Everyone commented on it. How much he slept. What a good baby he was." I stared out the window, waiting for the pain to go away. It came in waves, washing over me, but they gave me pills and it went away. "He probably was asleep when it happened."

I couldn't lie to myself that they hadn't known the baby was there, that they were incapable of killing him. Betty, maybe not; but George was. That was the worst of it. Remembering all the times I'd done favors for George. Remembering all the times I'd talked to George, laughed with George.

Rider didn't say anything.

"Why?" I asked him.

"Why? To raise money to pay for information. Simple espionage."

"It seems complicated to me. All that risk, just to steal some money." I sounded bitter, even to myself. Agatha died, just so they could steal some money.

Rider shook his head at me, his mouth set in a grim line. "Oh, Jason, if you only knew. Budgets. We've all got 'em. Somewhere in Czechoslovakia or East Germany or Russia right now there's some spymaster wondering what other gimmick he can come up with to stretch his budget. If he's like us, he keeps getting it cut and then the powers that be judge his effectiveness as though he still has all the money he ever had."

"Peter Van Doorn said something like that once. He said no matter what you gave people, they were never satisfied."

Rider clenched his mouth even tighter. "He told you the truth."

My leg healed, at least sufficiently to be put into a walking cast. I went home, where Mark and Eugenia Lowe fought each other for the privilege of looking after me, both of them annoying me thoroughly. Them and the ghost. In the hospital, I'd thought the ghost would be gone. Agatha had been found. Her ashes had been sent to her folks. They'd had a service and spread them on the farm where she had grown up. The only other place she'd loved was this one, and I couldn't see putting her ashes in the back yard. It was too near the place she had died. The farm where she had grown up was better.

The ghost should have gone away, wherever beloved ghosts finally go, but it hadn't. I could smell White Linen in every room I entered. I could hear Agatha's voice murmuring, but I was unable to make out the words. Sometimes I heard Jerry's laughter as well, that infant chuckle I had almost forgotten. I crutched around the place, trying to escape them, but they followed me wherever I went.

I almost stopped eating. When I looked in the mirror, I began to see the lean and angry man inside. I caught Mark looking at me out of the corners of his eyes, whispering about me to Eugenia. I thought of closing the shop, going away, but I had nowhere to go and an obligation to Jacob.

Sometimes in the evenings I sat in the bay window of the big showroom, looking at the Whitney house, staring at it, hating it. If I'd been able to move more easily, I might have set fire to it. I desperately wanted it gone, it and everything in it.

Grace came over a few times, bringing flowers, bringing food. She never stayed long. I guess I never asked her to. Mark took to staying late in the evenings, keeping an eye on me. I didn't care enough to tell him not to.

And the ghost stayed right with me, day and night. I began to be as angry at the ghost as I was at myself.

And then one evening I saw a shadow across the street. I was sitting in the bay window, staring out, and I saw someone walking, just the shadow. In a moment he came into the light from the streetlamp, and I saw it was an elderly man who lives in the house on the corner.

I'd thought it might be Stimson.

Mark came in behind me and said, "What?"

"I saw someone out there," I told him, "and I thought it was Stimson."

"I doubt he'd be openly walking down the street, Jason."

"I know," I said. "But I'll bet he's still watching the house next door." It had come to me, all at once. I was certain of it, cursing at myself for not having realized it before.

"You think Stimson's still around?"

"Somebody's been around. Somebody took that little tape recorder out of George's house. Somebody bugged my phone. Somebody tried to kill me with a bomb. I'd be around if I were him. I'd be listening. Watching. Doing damage control. His whole operation is in shambles. He doesn't know what Peter Van Doorn may have told me. If it was you, wouldn't you stick around? Watching me? Figuring out what to do next?"

I reached for my leg with both hands, swinging the heavy cast off the hassock onto the floor. Mark offered me his hand, and I heaved myself erect. "If whoever's watching or listening thought there was something over there that might give us information—"

"If he thought there was something over there, he'd break his neck going after it before we did."

"Let's give him something to go after," I said.

It was midafternoon of the following day when we left my front door on our way to the Whitney house. Grace was with us, and she went first to remove the seal from the door. Behind her, Mark helped me along on my crutches, propping me up as I went up the four steps that led to the Whitney front door. Once inside, I began to talk casually about each piece of furniture, its value, its history. I clumped laboriously up the stairs, leading them into Betty's room, still talking.

In Mark's opinion, and Hodgson's, if the Whitney house was bugged, the transmitter would be voice activated, very well hidden. No bug had been spotted when the house was searched, but weeks had gone by since then. There had been plenty of time and opportunity since to wire the whole house for sound. I was gambling that it had been.

I sat on the bed, talking to the ceiling, to the walls. "You see this highboy. I didn't look at it closely the last time I was over. Highboys of this kind sometimes had a small drawer set in at the back of one of the larger ones. You have to remove the larger drawer. Mark, will you pull these out?"

"I don't see anything," Grace remarked.

"You'll have to kneel down. If there *is* a hidden drawer, you'll see the small brass handles at the back of the drawer opening. Usually behind the top drawer, though occasionally behind the bottom one."

"Well, I'll be damned," Mark said, making drawer-pulling noises. "There it is!" And he reached in and pulled one out. We had no more expected to find a real hidden drawer than we had expected Stimson to be waiting for us. I shook my head at them warningly and went on with my well-rehearsed lines.

"It increases the value of the piece," I pontificated, hoping I wasn't overdoing it. "Pull it out, Mark. Let's see what condition it's in."

"There's a book in here," Grace said, her voice full of real astonishment. We hadn't expected to find either a drawer or a book, but there *was* a book there: leather-covered, loose-leaf, about five by seven. Grace fished it out and handed it to me while she went on talking. "A notebook. Look at this! It seems to be in code of some kind. It certainly doesn't make sense."

"Put it back," I directed in a peremptory tone, as I pocketed our find. "The FBI man will want to see that. We probably shouldn't even have touched it."

"Rider's not coming back to town until tomorrow," Grace objected. "Do you want me to call Hodgson?"

"No, no," I said testily. "Let's just let it alone until Rider comes back and then tell him about it. He's more likely to know if it means anything."

Then we went out into the hall while I continued my analysis of the furniture.

Grace asked, "So you think whoever sells this stuff will get a good price?"

"Oh, yes," I said. "Perhaps better at a private sale than at an auction. Who does it belong to?"

"The lieutenant says if the FBI doesn't seize it, the IRS will, and if they don't, the city will. One way or the other, it'll be sold. He just wanted to have a good idea of what was here."

It sounded like a lame excuse to me, but it was the best

we'd been able to come up with. "I've got the list I did previously," I said. "I'll give you a copy for your lieutenant."

We left the house. Grace lingered behind to apply a new seal to the door but soon caught up. We went back to the shop and climbed the flight of stairs to my place. I couldn't wait to get the book open.

"My Lord," Mark said over my shoulder. "Dates, places, names: every piece of furniture with the price and where they got it."

"Provenance," I agreed. "They knew the provenance made the pieces more salable. Look at all the different places they bought them. And they used a different name each time."

"No wonder I couldn't find out where they got the stuff." He made a disgusted face.

"Now what?" Grace asked, practical as always.

"Now we put this little gem away and wonder if anyone was listening. And we wait for it to get dark." I tried a not-very-successful smile. "And when it gets dark, we all go in through the doggie door."

It took both of them to get me through the doggie door and silently up the stairs. We waited in the dark. Grace had put a chair in the closet for me and made a space where she could stand behind me. She wanted to keep an eye on me this time, I was sure. Mark was in the office across the hall. Hodgson was in the bathroom with Al. None of us made a sound.

"Too damned many people." Hodgson had cursed when I'd proposed the plan.

"I'm going to be there or no one is," I'd told him. "And I need Grace and Mark to get me there. Besides, if it weren't for them—for me—you'd be a long way from solving this thing."

"All right, all right." Fuming, considering, telling Al to come inside, Joe to stay outside. Next door, Eugenia was waiting to turn off all the lights in my house except for those in my back bedroom. Those she'd leave on, indicating that I was there, reading perhaps, separated from this place by the whole bulk of my own building.

"Shh," breathed Grace in a leaf-fall voice.

I'd heard it at the same time: the sound of someone coming up the stairs. I hadn't heard the door open. Perhaps this visitor had come in the way we had.

A flashlight beam flicked across the carpet, darted around the room, across the closet door, which was open only an inch. Light shone on the highboy. The flash was laid on a chair, the chair dragged over the carpet, making a ragged sound. Then there were gloved hands on the drawer, pulling it out.

All at once beams of light from three sides: from Grace, from Mark, from Hodgson.

Squinting at us was the crouched figure I'd anticipated, the white hair, the trimmed white beard, the hand fumbling in his coat.

"Don't," said Hodgson. "Don't even think of reaching for it. All right, Al."

Al was bigger and bulkier than the crouching man. Al pulled him up, his hands behind him. Hodgson found the gun and took it away, carefully. Mark turned on the lights.

"Mr. Stimson, I presume," Hodgson said with a fierce grin.

"No," I said. "Not Stimson." The crouched figure had brushed his hair back, when he knelt down, and I'd seen his ear. It was one I'd seen before, both in the flesh and in one of the pictures Rider had shown me. Propped on my crutches, I reached forward to jerk away the beard and the hair. The beard didn't come loose. It and the moustache had been expertly glued on, hair by hair, so well done that they defied detection. The wig came off, though, and the glasses fell with them.

"My God," Grace said with an almost hysterical yelp. "Renard!"

Al and Joe took Renard/Stimson away. He did not say a word. The rest of us went back to my house, and I made coffee for us all while we conducted the autopsy. I did not confess how foolish I felt for not having recognized Renard's car the evening my garage blew up. It was the same one I had followed at the police station when I recovered the desk box. I had seen it then under streetlights and should have recognized it. I kept my chagrin to myself and poured coffee.

"Short of putting a man in the FBI office itself, the next best thing would certainly be to have one on the police force." Hodgson put down his coffee cup and buttoned his coat. "I have no doubt the gun he was carrying is the gun that killed Jollaby and the Whitneys."

"I wondered why he never did anything about the case," Grace said. "He didn't want to, did he? If he could have put it off on Jason, he'd have thought that was great."

"You'll be able to post-mortem this one for years," Hodgson said. "Renard may tell us something, but we may never know why other things happened. The best we can do are close guesses. In a lot of cases, that's all you ever have."

"Do you know how he got on the police force?" Mark asked.

"They probably faked records for him to show he'd been on the force in some other city, Detroit or Chicago or L.A. If we checked the files in that city, there might be other papers giving a false background. It doesn't cost much to plant false records in a few personnel files, give someone a little history."

"All that ferocity," I said. "All that bigotry. That wild story he let get around about his wife's suicide. He was playacting. And when he came here, when he harassed Mark, he was just trying to find out if we knew anything. And why did he steal the desk box?"

Mark said, "Because he saw the reference books and knew it was valuable. Maybe he wanted to find out just how valuable. That's when he started on the trail of what George had been doing, right then."

Hodgson shrugged. "We may never know how much of him

is real or why he did the things he did. You have to admit he's some actor."

I had to admit it. He had been some actor. When they had taken him away, he had gone wordlessly, no bluster, no questions, just one look at me as though he would like to have slit my throat.

Hodgson buttoned his coat. "I think we've spent enough late nights on this one. Thank you for the notebook from the Whitney house, Jason. I know you're interested in the stuff over there, so I'll return it or a copy as soon as I can. Can I drop anyone?"

Mark shook his head. "I have my car."

Grace said, "Me too. I'm taking Eugenia home. Will you be all right, Jason?"

"Fine," I nodded. "Fine." That wasn't the right word, but it would do. Actually, I felt empty.

They went down the stairs and out, leaving me alone. I walked slowly around the apartment on my crutches, thumping past each room. In the living room I turned the thermostat down. In the kitchen, I made hot chocolate, very slowly, then sat down and drank it sip by sip, peering out the window into the darkness. All my urgencies seemed to have gone away. It was enough just to sit there, watching the night. When I was finished, I washed the cup and put it away.

I clumped my way to the head of the stairs and turned out the downstairs lights and the porch lights, my hand resting on the slanting wire that held the new chandelier in place. It hung there like a prismatic waterfall, intercepting the light from the recessed fixture above and throwing it into every corner of the hall, one of a long succession of chandeliers for sale that had hung here since Jacob bought the building twenty years before. The crystal pendants chimed quietly, then rang again as a small warm wind swept from somewhere, gusting up the stairs and across the balcony where I stood. The door to the front bedroom swung open.

The phone rang. I found myself still standing there staring

at the bedroom door, not thinking of anything. The crutches caught on the carpet, and I cursed mildly at them as I limped to the phone in Mark's office.

"Jason?" Someone distressed.

"Yes?"

"It's Emmy Montoya, Jason."

"Emmy. What is it? Has something happened to Jerry?"

"We're at the hospital, Jason. The doctor's here. Jerry isn't breathing right. The doctor needs permission to operate. . . ."

For a moment I couldn't speak. "Put him on," I said.

An officious voice came on at the other end, telling me to get there quickly, sign papers, or the boy would die.

"No," I said.

Silence at the other end.

"He's had eight years of bedsores and pain and no thoughts. Enough is enough, doctor," I said. "He doesn't need any more. No. If Jerry dies, it's because it's time."

He started to argue with me and then stopped. I guess he was thinking, because in a moment he said, "I'm sorry, Mr. Lynx. You'll have to come over and put that on record."

Emilia was on the phone again, terribly upset.

"Shhh," I said. "Shhh, Emilia. It's all right. We knew it might happen this way." I felt the sigh start at my ankles and come all the way up. I couldn't tell if it was pain or relief. "Where are you, Em?"

She told me the name of the hospital. "Are you coming over?"

"I still can't drive, Em. I'm on crutches. I'll come as soon as I can."

I hung up the phone and went back into the hall and through the open doorway into Agatha's room. The south window was open, only a crack. Perhaps the cleaning people had left it open to air out the room.

All I could smell was snow. Her scent was gone.

"Agatha?" I said.

There was no answer. The empty silence hummed with a

vacancy I hadn't heard before. There was no one in the apartment but me.

When I called Grace and told her I needed to get over to the hospital, she asked what had happened and I told her. She didn't say she was sorry. She just said it was sad, that she'd come over right away to pick me up. There was affection and kindness in her voice. Something in me warmed to it, needing it.

I went to wash my face and change clothes so I could go to the hospital and say no without looking disheveled or unsure of myself. Agatha would have expected that much. After all that had happened, it seemed strange that looking dignified while I let our son die was the only thing left I could do to show I loved her. To show I loved both of them.

A. J. Orde, who previously worked as an investigator for a private employment agency, is now devoted to the raising of Minor Breeds livestock at the family ranch near Taos, New Mexico.